P9-DSY-452

# A CHILD OUT OF ALCATRAZ

ORANGE COUNTY LIBRARY

# A CHILD OUT OF ALCATRAZ

BY

*Tara Ison*

FABER and FABER
BOSTON · LONDON

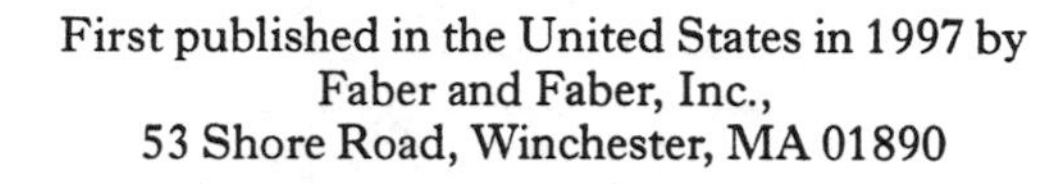

First published in the United States in 1997 by
Faber and Faber, Inc.,
53 Shore Road, Winchester, MA 01890

Copyright © 1997 by Tara Ison
All rights reserved under International and Pan-American
Copyright Conventions, including the right of reproduction
in whole or in part in any form.

Library of Congress Cataloging-in-Publication Data

Ison, Tara.
A child out of Alcatraz : a novel / Tara Ison.
p cm.
ISBN 0-571-19910-0
I. Title.
PS3559.S66C48 1997
813′.54—dc20 96-43420
CIP

The Swimming Lesson, © 1965, 1993 by Mary Oliver.
From *No Voyage and Other Poems* (Houghton Mifflin).

This is a work of fiction. Names, characters, places,
and incidents are imaginary or used fictitiously. Any
resemblance to actual events or to persons
living or dead is entirely coincidental.

Jacket design by
Ha Nguyen

Printed in the United States of America

*To my mother and father,*
*who always read every word.*

*Acknowledgments*

Thank you to the many friends whose support, patience, and affection helped keep it going, especially Tina Gauthier and Cyndi Menegaz for their page-by-page insight and enthusiasm; Teddy Howard and Bob Striegel for the ferocity of their approval; Elizabeth Pincus for the inspiring example; Jill Halper, Mike Pankratz and Thom Daniels, Michel Horvat, Jennifer Davidson and Tara Sandler, Ellen Svaco, Leslye Kasoff and Barbara DeLucia, Mike Myers, Erika Korda, and Duane Capizzi for the much-needed encouragement; and Michelle and David Bader for their loving sanctuary. There aren't thanks enough for Beverlee Ison and Bill Ison, who gave it all.

Also, a very grateful thank you and much appreciation to my agent Wendy Weil and my editor Dan Weaver for their soothing guidance and exhilarating faith.

## The Swimming Lesson

Feeling the icy kick, the endless waves
Reaching around my life, I moved my arms
And coughed, and in the end saw land.

Somebody, I suppose,
Remembering the medieval maxim,
Had tossed me in,
Had wanted me to learn to swim,

Not knowing that none of us, who ever came back
From that long lonely fall and frenzied rising,
Ever learned anything at all
About swimming, but only
How to put off, one by one,
Dreams and pity, love and grace,—
How to survive in any place.

—Mary Oliver

# Alcatraz, 1951

## *Olivia*

If I go in the kitchen, I'll be given a task. Nothing with knives, or forks, or tools with sharp edges and prongs—no, one with training wheels: shelling peas, or opening a cardboard box. Maybe something with a wooden spoon. My mother is there, standing guard in the kitchen, fervently beating and slicing foods into dinner. Daddy comes home from his "shift" at 6:05, tired, his hip hurting, and she needs half an hour before then to clean up the kitchen and herself; she will take the pins from her snails of hair, set out the dishes and woven place mats, and get ready the instruments for his martini, the things she keeps hidden. That's my favorite part: the bottle of clear gin, kept chilled and away in the Icy Heart refrigerator; the glass-and-chrome shaker glinting at me like the lighthouse; the wire strainer curled like a piggy tail; and the jar of fat green olives, each stuffed with its pretty red slice of pimento.

I love the martinis. I like the olives because they sound like my name, but I don't like how they taste, salty and bitter. Daddy lets me suck out the pimento, then puts the olive on his finger like a puppet head. By the third martini, the third olive, I can sit on his lap for an entire puppet show while he fluffs my hair back with his other hand. He gazes at my mother when he's ready for dinner, or touches her earlobe and says her name—Vivian?—warm and deep as a bowl of

Grandma's pudding, usually, but sometimes, when dinner is late and he's extra hungry and tired, it sounds more like he's biting her name in half. *Viv*ian!? He likes us all to eat at 6:45, because that is the rule.

But it's still too early for the martinis, although I hear my mother hurrying, setting things down too hard and quick. Stella never helps her in the afternoons; she prances off with her friends in the City after school, far across the dangerous Bay. Once she came in to dinner an hour late, breathless and full of City smells, saying the fog had slowed down the ferry. But it wasn't very foggy that night, the moon was sharp. My parents said very little at the table, waiting for the other to handle it. Daddy tells us what the rules are and says they are important, but handling us is my mother's job. Now that Jerry and Stell are older she thinks Daddy should handle us more, but that night he only studied the meat on his plate, chewing it, struggling to cut its tough fibers, and told her everything was delicious; she gave up and served him more vegetables, and no one said anything. Daddy likes it when we're all quiet, anyway.

So Stell still comes in late, despite the rule, with or without fog. She gets teased a lot by the boys, even the older ones—they walk by our cottage howling *Stella!*, something from a movie—but she likes it. It makes Daddy angry and he glares at my mother, but still no one says anything. Jerry might roll his eyes and snort, but Stell just giggles and says too bad those boys aren't as cute as Marlon Brando.

Jerry gets the run of everything; by the time he was nine and I was four, he swore he had the key or could pick the lock of any gate or cell door on the island. It's the smart kind of boast, because I'm never allowed to witness this and so I can't ever prove him wrong—this is what really counts, a lot more than whether or not he actually does what he says. So I listen to his stories and watch him sneak off with his friends to the forbidden cliff leading to the tiny beach, or the long zigzag road Up Top to the cellhouse, or the coves on either side of the ferry dock. All of this is against the rules, but the boys do it anyway. They go to fish, or play Guard and Con, games with shoving and pieces of broken glass. Once Jerry showed me what he said was an old grenade from the war that he found washed up on the beach; he threw it at me and I screamed and screamed, but it was just a rotten old potato. It split open on the ground, stinking, and he chased me with it, smushing it in my hair. I had to run inside to my mother; she picked the potato out and promised to talk to Daddy. But nothing happened to Jerry. Next time I will run further away from him if I have to, even to where I'm not supposed to go; I can play only on the footpaths that are calling distance from our cottage, and the big cement rectangle the grown-ups call the parade ground although there's never a parade.

But I could stray off my path, by accident. I could say I got lost; it wouldn't be my fault then, not really. Anyone can get lost, and that isn't really breaking a rule. I could meet Daddy on his way home from work, way up on the footpath, and have him sooner. He might swing me up on his shoulders and let me wear his cap with the gold braid.

I escape by crawling on my belly across the living-room floor, below my mother's view over the kitchen counter where she's chopping something up. The front door is never locked; it opens quietly, but groans as I close it behind me. I sense her head snapping up to attention, to look, and hear her call, questioningly, "Olivia?", too late, after I'm gone.

It's quiet; the parade ground's swings and bicycles are empty and still. Most of us have already been called home for washing up, for dinner. The first evening fog from the sea is just starting its thick roll across our island, and I think of Grandma coaxing a layer of dough over her pies, trapping in the fruit. The foghorn howls at us sometimes a dozen times a day, but we don't hear it anymore—like the seagulls shrieking *squawk squawk* or the wink of the lighthouse at night in my bedroom window, it's more noticeable when it *isn't* there than when it is. Sometimes I wake up in the middle of the night because I *don't* hear the howling and the silence is too loud and dark. The fog coats us before moving on across the dangerous Bay to the City, to blot out the bright-orange lights of windows reflecting the sun; at sunset it looks like hundreds of fires blazing in those tall City buildings.

I can play all I like on the parade ground, but to get to Daddy, to get far past the main road to the other side of the prison Up Top, I will need to squeeze through the hole in the fence and sneak past Mr. Lucey high in the Road Tower. The men in the prison Up Top are being punished for something, and it's Daddy's job to help take care of them. I'm not sure why men being punished get such a big house all to themselves, a house that looks like a castle and is bigger than all of ours, even the warden's. I like Warden Swope; he wears rimless eyeglasses like two little clear stop signs, but sometimes Daddy grumbles that he pits his men, the officers, against each other. But that sounds like two dogs fighting, *pitted* against each other, and all the fathers here are very nice, too nice for that. Warden Swope does have a dog, though, which we aren't allowed to have; once I heard my father ask my mother about his colt, and I thought he meant we were getting a pony. But my mother said No, Daddy means something else. Warden Swope and his wife have parties for us on holidays, and last Christmas they went caroling with us, the children, up by the prison. Afterward, in the stillness between the final note of "heav-en-ly peace . . ." and a foghorn, we heard the men inside yelling out "Merry Christmas" to us. It's the closest I've ever been to Up Top. Daddy brought home the set of place mats a prisoner made for us as a gift, woven with bright colored threads. We use them all the time, but I think they are too pretty to eat on.

But they're bad, those men, that's why they are convicts and have been sent here to our island, up to the Big House. This is what Jerry and his friends call it, and while it *is* a big house, I'm not sure why they make it sound like the only one. Across the Bay I can see other Big Houses in the City, with orange fire in their windows, but the bad men are only sent here to be punished. Sometimes, when they don't know I'm listening, I hear Daddy tell my mother that it's Hell up there. I don't know what rules those men have broken to be so bad. I know what *I* do to be bad; I tell a lie, or get too dirty, or too loud, and I'm sent to my room. But I almost never do these things, and mostly even when I do the grown-ups don't notice, they don't see it in me. I don't know what came first—if I was always a good girl, born that way, and so they started calling me that, or if they told me that's what I am and so now I have to be. Sometimes I think that if I'm too dirty, or too loud, they might send *me* up there, to the Big House. But deep down I know anyway that these are little-girl bad things, things that make no ripple, a pebble kicked from the dock into the sea. Grown-up men have to do bigger things to be convicts; their badness is larger and in shadows, hard to picture. I asked my mother once what they really did to be bad and she didn't answer; later I heard Daddy tell her to tell me they didn't eat their brussels sprouts. But she's never offered me this. She might be waiting for Daddy to handle it, but I think she knows that I know not eating your vegetables is only a get-sent-to-your-room kind of bad thing. A little-girl broken rule, not important enough to make me a convict.

I skip across the cement rectangle, past the apartments that face our cottage, through the fence, and begin the climb up the main road, the one you can see the Golden Gate Bridge from. The Road Tower ahead marks as far as I'm allowed to go; Mr. Lucey sees me and waves, friendly, from a hundred feet in the air. His daughter Alice and I used to hopscotch together, but now she's seven, a year ahead of me, and goes to the City on the ferry every day for school. Somehow this puts more between us than just the Bay; I am now, to her, only worth ignoring. Mr. Lucey himself turns away from me—he gazes out at the Bridge, his gun propped in his arms like a baby.

I leave the main road and crawl through the grasses and rocks, sneezing at the fluffy parts of seagull feathers; they whirl around like there's been a pillow fight. I skirt around the big walled square that Daddy calls the Recreation Yard, which is usually blocked from our sight, way Up Top. The water tower must give a good view, and there are no fathers there. Even so, even if someone sees me, hears me, I suddenly don't care. Let them see me breaking a rule and doing something bad, a bigger kind of bad. Let them see me. I think for the first time that if I *am* sent to the Big House, I'll have Daddy with me all day, not just my mother guarding me inside our cottage. I hurry on, sneezing, my knees getting scraped.

A familiar hum comes from the other side of the big wall, a sound like my brother and his friends playing softball on the parade ground when I'm in my room. There's the crack of bat against ball and the hum swells; I look up to see a ball sail over the cement wall and land with a dull bounce ahead of me on the path, exciting me.

These balls—*convict* balls!—are important; Jerry and his friends hunt them in the forbidden pockets of shrubbery up here, and trade them like baseball cards. Sometimes fathers bring them home for the boys; they compare the newness, the burn of the bat. The more worn from convict play, the more handled, the more sweat-smeared, the better. Now I can have one, something to bargain with. I don't know what I will bargain *for*, but just having one will be a kind of power.

I run ahead for the ball, reaching—It's *my* ball, this one's *mine*!—but stop short, because it's lying near the feet of a man. Not a father, but a Bad Man being punished. I've seen them before, unloading big boxes down at the dock, or when they deliver clumsy, brown-paper packages of laundry to our mothers. But never this close. This bad man wears coveralls and thick gloves and carries a pair of big scissors that cuts branches. He reaches down for the ball, then looks up at me, startled. He only has one eyebrow, a thick caterpillar of hair stuck above his eyes. We look at each other. He leans over, picks up the ball, and holds it out to me, smiling, making the caterpillar wiggle. I look at the ball in his outstretched hand, tempted. But this is breaking a rule; I'm not supposed to be here, I'm not supposed to have this, and now I'm scared. How will I explain the ball? Only the boys have them. I'll have to keep it hidden away, a dirty secret, and its only value is in its display.

I shake my head and back up carefully, away from him, around him, so I don't touch anything bad even by accident. The caterpillar dips in the middle when he frowns. He curls up his arm then and flings the ball back over the cement wall, staggering a little like part of him went with it. From over the wall the hum rises again, welcoming. The man turns away from me; his branches are waiting. I don't want to be bad any more, I only want to see Daddy. I want my olive puppet show, and my juniper-berry kiss.

No one sees me. The wooden rungs on the water tower are splintery, and it's getting cold. I look down into the Recreation Yard; it looks a little like our parade ground, that's all, except for the walls and barbed wire. And they're there, all the other bad men, the convicts, maybe a hundred of them. Some are playing softball, but most are strolling in pairs like older girls, or sitting huddled on concrete steps. They don't scream and chase each other like we do on our parade ground; I can't even hear their voices, only the faint wordless sounds from the softball game, athletic and male. And Daddy is there, yes, arms folded, in his coat with the brass buttons that poke me in the face when he hugs me. He stands straight, still, watching—this is what he does, then, this is a "shift," which always sounded like more movement to me. In the chilly quiet, clinging to the rungs, I am watching, too. I am having a shift. When he leaves to come home, I can run into him on the zigzag path, and he'll know I didn't do anything bad, that I only got lost.

As I watch, waiting and shivering a little, one of the bad men goes up to Daddy, to ask him something, I think; can he go to the bathroom, or get a drink of water. But there's a yell and a flash of something metal, and suddenly my father is holding a long stick he grabbed from nowhere, a stick that arcs through the air over the man's head, and just as my father's stick smashes down on the man's face the first foghorn of the evening howls out, startling me so I almost lose my grip. The man puts his hand up to shield his face, but my father strikes him again, one more time, then one more pounding time; there's a red pulpy spray before the man drops down fully onto his hands and knees, in the howling, fading echo of the horn. His arms and legs crumple and spread like a wad of paper. Other prisoners carefully turn back to their games, their quiet talk. Two men I recognize from Dr. Yocum's office, where I get vaccinated, hurry across the yard to the man. My father turns away and looks up to signal to Mr. Lucey in the Road Tower, then he adjusts his cap with the gold braid and glances at his watch for the time.

The coldness finally hits me; it is freezing, and I am numb. I run home with the spreading fog, breathing in bowls of it, choking, although it is nothing, really, but thick icy air.

Mommy looks up from the warm kitchen when I throw open our front door. The table is set with the pretty convict place mats; the room smells like potatoes, like cooking vegetables, like warmth.

"Olivia, didn't you hear me calling? Have you seen Stella? Where's your brother?" She still has blonde snails pinned against her ears, and is gently shaking a bowl of emerald Jell-O to see if it's chilled hard, anxious about the time.

"Look, sweetheart, it's getting late, I have a big-girl thing for you to do, OK? Come on, Daddy'll be home soon. What's wrong with you? Close the door, did you run all the way from the playground just to help me? What a good girl you are . . ."

In the kitchen she hands me a wooden hammer with dull metal prongs jutting out of one end, and a slab of red meat, hemmed with waxy fat. She lays the meat on a wooden board, hits it hard with the hammer several times, then gives the hammer to me.

"We're having chuck steak, and this makes it all soft and chewy, OK, sweetheart? Can you do that? Watch your fingers, now. That's my girl. You do the meat, I still have to . . . oh, dear . . ." Her voice trails off as one hand fusses with a pin curl, the other fumbling to return the Jell-O to the refrigerator, to set out the martini shaker and the jar of olives. They stare at me like little green eyes, rubbery with brine, each pimento a slice of red pulp. They make ugly puppets, these olives. I am too old for puppet shows. When Mommy leaves the kitchen I will hide them far back in the refrigerator, behind the Jell-O.

The board is already damp with thin, ruby juice. I bring the hammer down onto the meat and the prongs sink into the flesh; it shudders, it takes it, listening to me, and I hit harder. This pounding is somehow satisfying, something solid and full of power; it is how I thought owning one of the convict balls would feel. I hit harder, gasping out swallowed fog with each blow. Flecks of juice fly up and bead my hair. I hit the meat with force, cleanly, beating it tender.

# Isla de los Alcatraces

## *The Prison*

California is the edge of the continent, as they say, the last place to go, where people collect and cling and remain for fear of falling off. Like sheep in a Hardy novel, herded flush to the edge of a coastal cliff by zealous dogs; the sheep, pressed on, begin dropping off one by one or in woolly pairs to crash and split on the rocks below, then are rinsed away by the sea. The dogs, looking down, drip saliva from their grins and we suspect them of malicious intent. You have to clutch at California, and hold on when it tilts; it is far too easy to lose your grip and slip off this edge of the world, far from the madding crowd, especially when herded.

But there is a place to land, seemingly safe, an ostensible toehold: a small, rocky peak in the shape of a footprint, which juts up in the San Francisco Bay one and a half miles from the northern tip of the city of San Francisco. It is the last firm foothold before the Golden Gate's sweep to sea, having obstinately withstood centuries of chewing currents and chiseling men. It is a buoy of sinking mountain, a rising pancake of land, a sandstone life preserver; if you are indeed huddled at the edge of the continent, and your grip slips, you could, before washing out to sea, grab a final hold here.

This little island's first recorded name was given not by the people settled in the area for thousands of years—people who collected birds' eggs from its crags and shellfish from its coves—but by its recorded discoverer, Spanish explorer Juan Manuel de Ayala, commander of the first European vessel to sail into the arms of the Golden Gate, into the Bay, in 1775. He noted a tiny crude island, without harbor, fresh water, or shelter, covered with birds and creamy with their dung, and so named it, either for the pelicans, *alcaraz,* or the cormorants, *alcatraceo,* both of which shared the island in thick numbers as home: *Isla de los Alcatraces*. The Bay area was to be explored and settled and argued over by more discoverers—Mexican, Spanish, English, Russian, American—and dozens of later misspellings and mistranslations on maps and charts finally narrowed down the name of the island to one word: Alcatraz.

The 1848 gold rush inspired the United States to seize and claim California as its cherished own; the barren little rock in the Bay was declared the perfect site for fortification and defense of San Francisco and its harbor from invaders. The first deliberate shapings of Alcatraz began—blasting the island's slopes into leveled mesas for barracks and cisterns and 150 cast-iron cannons—to transform the twelve-acre rock suitably for its first official function: the U.S. Army Post of Alcatraz Island, or Fort Alcatraz. A lighthouse was built, vital for the safety of swelling marine traffic; a siege-proof brick Citadel went up at the island's peak. Topsoil was brought in for gardens, for by 1860 officers were bringing their wives and children to live in pretty little Victorian houses on the most heavily fortified site in California, hoping to ease the isolation of life on a desolate rock in the middle of the busiest harbor on the Pacific Coast. Merchant ships and U.S. military vessels sailed back and forth, but no foreign invaders came.

The Civil War freshened the pretense of the fort, but when Confederate rebels, or even European allies of the Confederacy failed to invade the West Coast, the rocky little symbol of national defense became for the first time a place of detention and punishment. Union Army deserters or officers refusing to swear a loyalty oath to the Union government, Confederate sympathizers celebrating Jefferson Davis, men suspected of any treasonous activity—including Native Americans refusing to accept the violently encroaching United States of America, or anyone reveling in the death of President Lincoln—were put to work at hard labor on Alcatraz. Prisoners peered past the island's rocky edges, at the icy green Bay water whipped up by wind and legendary currents, and stayed put. By 1907 Alcatraz was officially the United States Military Prison, Pacific Branch; from 1909 to 1912 a three-story concrete cellhouse of bullying and gritty design was constructed by prisoner labor, atop the first level of the old Citadel.

The 1906 earthquake had brought the first civilian prisoners to be warehoused at Alcatraz, even before the new cellhouse was built, when city jails were declared temporarily unsafe due to fire; prisoners returned to the mainland with dark stories of life on the Rock. Rumors of harsh ball-and-chain treatment, of prisoners brutalized and kept in damp Spanish dungeons, made for a growing humanitarian discomfort for the citizens of San Francisco. The theory of penology was changing; imprisonment should not merely be a punishing end in itself, but a means for rehabilitation. In response to grumbling, the Army renamed the prison a "Disciplinary Barracks," offered vocational training, and planted more daisies and geraniums.

But worldwide peace made for a lack of military prisoners, and the celebratory 1920s made Alcatraz' function seem uncomfortably quaint; screeching gangster cars and tommy guns and urban massacres outshone the crime of badmouthing the government in public. By 1933 the Army was sick of its crumbling investment, tired of the criticism and the cost; Alcatraz was up for grabs just when J. Edgar Hoover needed a colorful weapon of his own to win back a public disillusioned by the Depression and inflicted Temperance, enthralled with Little Caesar and Dillinger. The Government handed over the little island to the FBI and the Bureau of Prisons the same year it ended Prohibition, the same year Franklin Roosevelt was inaugurated and Hitler, newly Chancellor of Germany, began building concentration camps. La Isla de los Alcatraces was again reinvented, and, with a quick makeover, began a new trumpeted career in July 1934 as the United States Federal Penitentiary, Alcatraz.

# Education

## *Vivian*

Vivian Goodman received an automobile for her eighteenth birthday: a brand-new 1933 Chrysler Plymouth roadster, sleek and glistening as a peeled pear, rich with the salty smell of leather. The value of the gift was not lost on her; her father, Harry, had sworn to Vivian's mother Sylvia, who felt freedom granted without responsibility imposed was pointless, if not downright dangerous, that Vivian would well be made to appreciate all that went along with ownership of such a vehicle. Their daughter was, after all, an adult now, and starting college, and the automobile would launch her meaningfully, literally, on the road to her destiny. Harry and Sylvia had found their own destiny in an automobile, a 1908 brand-new black Model T Ford—only the seventeenth one sold in the country, and Sylvia's wedding present, as Harry had informed her parents—in which they'd left Wisconsin and driven west to California, Sylvia's tatted-lace wedding veil fluttering behind them, to begin their life together. Now Harry was proud to give his own daughter both a sense of destiny, and such an expensive, profoundly American, and forward-thinking gift in which to seek it. Sylvia, who liked imbuing her daughter with a sense of purpose as well, agreed, but only after Harry swore Vivian's last summer at home would be spent learning the workings of the Plymouth to such a degree that if, en route, the car were to fall apart in a harsh Midwestern windstorm, she would have the capability to reassemble it from scratch, by herself. So Vivian, always a good student, began her adult education with thick books on the theory of the internal combustion engine; she curled up in the sunny bay window of their little Brentwood house, studying avidly and eating oranges. Amelia Earhart had made her solo transatlantic flight only last year, and Vivian now pictured herself speeding across the dusty country with a long silk aviator scarf fluttering behind her, disdainful of disbelievers, her cheeks smeared becomingly, authoritatively, with engine grease. I'm going to cut my hair, she thought, really, I'm really going to do it. Symbols were not lost on her, either.

Vivian's fourth-grade school report, dutifully brought home to Sylvia and Harry, had borne a penciled note in the margin: "Vivian is a lovely little girl, but often interrupts to ask questions or make statements. She must realize the importance of listening to others, and must learn more respect for authority." The next day Sylvia telephoned in sick to her seamstress job at the Goldwyn studio lot, and drove the family's gleaming Model T to Vivian's school, where the teacher informed her that Vivian was too loud and assertive and should be taught to engage more pleasantly with others in order to learn the social graces she would need as she grew older. Sylvia replied that this advice was not necessary, and furthermore, she was taking Vivian out of school early that day to attend a political rally. Harry closed his clothing shop at noon, and joined his wife and child to cheer on the Progressive Party's presidential candidate, Robert La Follette. Coolidge won, to the Republican slogan of "I like silence and success better than socialism and sovietism;" Harry and Sylvia explained to Vivian that silence was, yes, a virtue, but only when one truly had nothing to say, for historically it was a means of control imposed on a People to keep them down—to give up one's voice was to give up one's personhood, and she should never be afraid to speak up. Did she understand? Vivian nodded, and later gave a report of the rally and election to her class, including her parents' comments on pogroms, the ACLU, and labor politics; her teachers stopped making helpful suggestions to Sylvia and Harry, and instead eyed them suspiciously when they picked Vivian up at school; classmates, and their parents, began steering clear.

But her English compositions were displayed on the school walls with gold stars; her math tests received thick red-penciled scores in the nineties; she always had the right answer, first—and these things were prized by her parents, were what, she felt, mattered. If they didn't make a viable social currency, something she could cash in for friends, oh, well, those girls were all so silly, anyway; she'd much rather read at recess or visit her father's shop after school, instead of that squealing and skipping around chalk-marked squares on the playground. For her tenth birthday, Sylvia and Harry proudly bought her a deluxe edition of the *World Book Encyclopedia*, and Ford Motor Company stock in her own name. On weekends the three of them all went to the beach and soaked in the sun; Vivian swam for hours in the warm, salty waves, happy as if she'd been born in water.

What is meant by the social graces became more clear to Vivian herself at thirteen, with the advent of the first school dance. The boys at school mostly ignored her, but boys on the street, ones that didn't know her, had been giving her second looks for a while now, so she must be pretty, pretty enough, at least. She waited, and hovered near conversations among other girls at lunchtime, picking up bits of information, until it seemed to her that all the pairings had been made; the girls, noticing her, giggled loudly and walked away with shrugs. She made up her mind then to ask Howard Allen. he outscored her in math, was short, and had scaly hands. But maybe that made him shy, and anyway, she hadn't heard his name mentioned. She approached him at lunch, where he sat studying on the other side of the cafeteria, and suggested they attend the dance together, making it sound, she hoped, like a school assignment it was important to score well on; they could help each other out. He looked up, blinking a little, and informed her the *girl* doesn't ask the *guy*, didn't she know that? And he didn't need her help, thank you, he was going with his sister—by *choice*, not 'cause he had to, because why would any fellow want to go with *Vivian*, her family were pinko Jews anyway, and she was such a stuck-up smartypants, always barking out answers, a know-it-all! He couldn't stand girls who thought they were so smart. Nobody could. Stunned, she watched him hurry away from her, swinging his scaly hands.

So there *was* a problem, then—and the problem was *her*. But how could she be bad, when her parents thought she was so wonderful? Were they wrong, or was Howard Allen wrong? How could there be a different, changing rule for this one, same thing that was her? And there was no point in questioning the rule, now that she'd so obviously broken it. The cafeteria girls were watching. For the first time she didn't feel smart, not at all; she felt lip-bitingly and bitterly stupid. But no, her parents couldn't be wrong about her; she'd understand the rules better when she was grown-up, that's all. She went home and announced she was going to be a Doctor, or maybe an Engineer, something important and socially relevant, and studied away the whole night of the dance. Harry and Sylvia told her with tears how proud they were, and decided to make their by now third traded-up Model T last another year, so as to put aside more of their earnings for Vivian's college education.

In 1929 Harry and Sylvia sold the Model T for cash and liquidated the family's precious stock portfolio, vowing never to invest another cent, or buy another car, from that anti-Semitic bastard Henry Ford. They debated what to do with their money—reinvest, buy a bigger business, a bigger house?—nervous about gambling with their daughter's destiny. A few days later the U.S. Stock Exchange collapsed, sparing them; they tucked their cash away in mattresses and pastry canisters, and prepared to ride out the storm. Harry kept his little store open, refusing to put his aging clerk out of work; Sylvia got a full-time job at the Warner Brothers Studio as Head Seamstress, and for two years the family lived on backyard oranges and apricots and Sylvia's flour-thickened stews, tucking away their pennies along with their dollar bills.

Vivian wanted to attend the new nearby Westwood campus of the University of California and live at home to keep expenses down. Her parents had dreamed of Radcliffe, but regretted not being able to send her in style—and, well, an east-coast school might have a quota on Jews, anyway. They reached a financial, sentimental, and geographic compromise: the University of Wisconsin, at Madison. Harry and Sylvia spent the bulk of their remaining money on Vivian's creamy Chrysler Plymouth; she cut her long blonde hair to earlobe length and packed a trunk full of fashionable clothing made by Sylvia from scraps of costumes worn by Warner Brothers stars. She kissed her parents and climbed in the car, pulled on leather driving gloves, and allowed herself a flashy revving of the engine. Sylvia and Harry, weeping with pride, waved goodbye, elated their true investment, their daughter, had brought them such riches. Vivian drove off, happy and grown-up, determined that the rules now would all start to make sense.

The first time Arthur Thornton finished a bite of food, wiped his mouth with a paper napkin, and laid his hand palm up on the table, expecting her to place her own in his, Vivian's heart leaped up high and snagged in her throat, so that she tasted her own blood, briefly, before it plunged back down. Queasy at the salt, she slipped her hand in Arthur's just as casually, as if boys had been reaching for her hand since birth, and finished her chocolate malt. His hands were beautiful, smooth-skinned and warm, not scaly at all.

Madison, Wisconsin was green and lush and brought out the wave in her hair. The weather disoriented her, and it took a few shivery months of skipping out to class without a sweater before she realized that sunshine in the window did not necessarily mean warmth. She moved into a dormitory ("Girls: no alcohol, pets, or men allowed in rooms!") that faced Lake Mendota, the first body of water she'd seen that wasn't an ocean, wasn't bitter with salt. A reputation had preceded her; word that she'd arrived by automobile *alone*, driving *herself* cross-country, from *California*, had filtered through the dorm and the greeting girls filled in her blanks with the idea she was daring, adventurous, a New Woman. Vivian silently blessed her parents with bestowing upon her a value far exceeding that of the car itself; she was instantly popular for her mobility, but even more so for her Golden Girl semblance, the imagined scent of the sea in her hair.

What she did have to earn were academic credentials; the work was hard, and no one was granting any credits for illusion in the classroom. Her professors were intimidating—rumpled, flanneled men in their forties with tobacco shreds in their folds, and crisp, tweedy women in their fifties with off-tinted face powder—all of whom grew irritated when she tried to dissemble her good grasp of anything. Vivian, having spent her high-school years quiescently, in an uneasy submission to the threat of a hazy rule and her own fear of seeming too obvious, loud, smart, realized with relief that her parents had been right all along; how she used to be, once was, was just fine, was *good*. She began raising her hand with the answer more, choosing more challenging themes, arguing aloud with classmates and questioning her professors, and finally, in her second year, received praise and high marks, approval, all the more precious now for having been hard earned. She declared Engineering her major, and increased her course load; other girls, on their way out to their dinner and soda-fountain dates, to their weddings, loudly bemoaned their own inability to be as studious and dedicated as she. Yes, she would be a Jane Addams, a Frances Perkins, a Marie Curie; she would be a Professor, a Scientist, an Engineer, go on to a higher degree, teach, write books, lecture, build things. Have a life's work. She felt a burst of energy, and then sudden fatigue all at the same time.

During Vivian's third year her dorm mates planned to crash a dance for the University of Chicago; she casually offered transportation, which gave rise to the assumption that the whole trip had been her idea, and therefore her responsibility. Sylvia made and sent her a formal, a floor-length, plunging satin thing Vivian thought looked like a gown Claudette Colbert might wear to lounge naughtily on a divan. It made her self-conscious, but she was determined to take credit for this daring plan; when she met up with the other girls in organdy frills and they shrieked at her sophistication, she felt better. The six of them going—three girls, three boys—piled into the Plymouth; Vivian noticed one of the boys nudge another and raise an eyebrow in her direction, and thought to herself, again, that Sylvia had known what she was doing. She was still used to making a negative impression on boys; the nudging, the raised eyebrow, fluttered in her stomach, made the satin stick to her flushing skin.

They drove to Illinois, tipping flasks into their mouths between flashes of oncoming headlights; at the ritzy Drake Hotel they tumbled out, feeling reckless, amused with themselves for this plot, and slipped into the ballroom. Vivian danced with a boy from her Intermed. Chem. class; they were just beginning a tipsy debate on what exactly "radio-activity" was, when there was a tap on Carl's shoulder and she was handed over, with a wink from Carl, to a very tall, good-looking boy. The song changed to "Begin the Beguine," and she felt the boy's hand press the satin against her back.

"Hope I didn't cut in on anything serious?"

"Oh, no . . . we were celebrating. Those French scientists won the Nobel Prize. Radioactive elemental something."

"He's not your steady guy?" A deep voice that vibrated against her chest, like the huge instruments in orchestras, the bassoon or the double bass, the cello.

"Oh, Carl? No . . . not so steady." She felt herself breathe alcohol on him, and dropped her face downward slightly so he wouldn't think her a lush.

"You're all crashing, aren't you?"

"Mm-hm. From Madison."

"Ah. Snuck across state lines. I could turn you in."

"Will you?"

"I don't think so. We'll see." He smiled. "I do take bribes."

"Ah, corrupt. What's your major?"

"Pre-law. My last year. I'm going, I'm planning to go, to law school."

"Not another corrupt politician?"

"Nah, not *politics.* Law enforcement, later, maybe. I hate politicians, those crumbs."

"Even Roosevelt?"

"Don't tell me you think *he's* not corrupt."

"Saint Franklin?"

"Oh." She felt his grip on her loosen; she lost her balance slightly, realizing how she'd been leaning her weight against him.

"It's just that . . ." She paused, not wanting to stumble again. "Well, at least he's trying to make changes, help the people that can't—"

"Yeah, sure, it's rough now, and a handout's OK in a pinch, but you can't carry people."

"No, of course not—"

"Drags the whole country down. I mean, look, he's no commie stooge or anything, I'm not like a lot of folks around thinking that. But he's no saint."

"Well, it's my parents who think that, to be honest." His hand firmed against her back again; she felt steadier, relieved. "And I don't necessarily agree with everything my *parents* think," she added.

He smiled again. "Good. I like a girl who has her own mind."

"As opposed to one on loan?"

"Think you're pretty quick, huh? That's good. I like that."

"And even the *saints* could be corrupt, right? Which one was it . . . Saint Somebody . . . he liked to burn heretics, I think. No one's all good or all bad. Have you taken any Psych? We were assigned the *Future of an Illusion,* and—"

"I like the way you dance," he said. "You're good."

"Thank you." She paused. "Not that I'm keen on Freud, actually—"

"No, but look, there *is* a right and a wrong. They're, uh . . ." He paused. "*Absolute* concepts."

"In theory, but—"

"See, that's the problem with psychology, it tries to explain everything away."

"Not explain away, just explain. A three-year-old's influenced by factors he can't control, so it helps to look at—"

"So that three-year-old grows up a killer, and it's all 'cause Mom and Dad messed up?" He shook his head. "I'm telling you, it's the science of excuses. I didn't even *have* a mom and dad, I turned out OK."

A pause. "I'm sorry. What happ—"

"It's those foreign intellectuals, muckrakers, sob sisters, they eat that psychology stuff up."

"Well, what about circumstances? Say this three-year-old's a good kid, but he grows up and can't get a job. He steals the proverbial loaf of bread to feed his own kids, gets caught, and, I don't know, sent off to that new place out in San Francisco, the island? Shouldn't we—"

"Hey, *I'd* want to know how hard he tried to get a job. Guy can't take care of his wife and kids, I blame *him,* I don't go crying to Saint Franklin."

"I can't believe you think—" She stopped when she saw he was grinning at her. Oh, I sound like an idiot, some freshman coed, and he's trying to rile me, that's all. She smiled back.

He squeezed her hand. "I'm just saying there's right and wrong and it's that simple most of the time. Psychoanalysis for crooks and spoiled rich kids, *waa waa waa,* come on! Folks know what they're doing when they break the rules, when they mess up big. 'Why I Turned to a Life of Crime,' yeah, cry me a river. You know, Hoover's got the right idea with that prison. Round up the bad eggs, lock 'em up on the Rock." He grinned at her again.

"Yes, well . . . I guess I don't know that much about it."

"I'm sorry, I didn't mean to cut you off before. Go on, you wanted to make your point?" His hand slid down her satiny back; she closed her eyes a moment, feeling lulled.

"No, that's all right. You're right, I sometimes get a little, oh, argumentative."

"That just shows a lot of spirit. I'm Arthur. Thornton."

"Vivian Goodman."

"So how's this, maybe I can drive you back home later? If you're not a minor."

"Oh, I drove everyone."

"You've got a car? Your own car?"

"Well . . ." She felt awkward, wanting to affirm herself indulged, maybe, but not spoiled. "See, I drove out here from California."

"Alone?"

"Yes."

He stopped dancing a moment. "Your parents let you drive all the way out here by yourself? That wasn't very responsible of them, Vivian."

"No, I suppose it was responsible of *me*."

"Not with what's going on these days. Don't you read the papers? Geez, anything could've happened to you, a girl driving alone. I'm telling you, that's dangerous. I wouldn't let *my* little girl just drive off like that!"

She felt suddenly that maybe this was true; didn't her parents *care*? Hadn't they worried? But, no; she thought about the summer with her father spent lying under the car, sweating, with a wrench, and her mother's insistence on collect telephone calls twice a day; the maps they all poured over after dinner, discussing how every one square inch equals five hundred square miles; this route, or that highway; the hotels she'd stayed in, large ones in little towns or small ones in big towns, sweeping triumphantly into the lobby after ten hours on the road and the hot bubble baths before going to bed; the Midwestern wind on her bare neck, the fluttering scarf and Amelia Earhart. No, she and her parents both deserved a defense. But she was suddenly tired from the long night, anyway, and his voice, this Arthur Thornton's voice, was richly authoritative, and she liked the feel of his arm, and she'd already sensed that how he touched her was affected by what she presented him with.

"Maybe you're right. Maybe it was a dumb thing to do."

"I wouldn't let you go."

"No?" She couldn't think of what else to say, of anything else to say.

"No. Not ever." And she liked that, too. He brushed her naked earlobe with a finger, and she decided just not to think about it anymore, maybe all the thinking was making her tired.

She liked his name, Art, or Arthur, faintly chivalrous, king-like. And the way he said her name, *Vivian,* he always added it into sentences where she wouldn't expect to find it, so their conversations seemed personal and specific, although afterward she often couldn't recall what was said, could only remember the shape of his mouth, not the words. But his voice was so solid, it thickened everything he said, like when Sylvia added egg yolk or blood to her sauces. When he told her she was beautiful she felt shocked, but then it seemed the most important and substantial thing in the world; she recalled his saying that for weeks, the flavor of every letter. She thought of her women professors, their stiff tweed and their thin hair twisted in little buns, and felt sorry for them.

She didn't tell her parents about him, not after the first time the telephone rang in her dorm ("Had to track you down, Vivian, but lucky for me there aren't many Goodmans around"), nor after the first time he drove up to see her, in a car loaned from a pal in his boardinghouse, to go have burgers and see a movie. They sat in a diner and talked about *Modern Times,* and when he took her hand and she felt that blood beat in her throat she knew she had to telephone her parents, soon, because she hadn't expected any of this and they'd know what to do. They always knew what was best.

But she didn't telephone them; something told her they wouldn't understand, they wouldn't prize this for her, not like math quizzes with thick red As to go up on the icebox, not like her plans for a life's work. She told herself this was independence, finally, a natural growing away from them, she didn't have to tell her parents everything, did she? They'd always wanted her to be independent; well, that meant from them, too, didn't it? To make her own decisions? Decide for herself what was important, what she wanted? How else could she prove her independence? And easier to prove it this way, with Arthur's help; easier to build something, a life, with someone else than all on her own.

They went swimming in Lake Mendota on a surprisingly warm spring day, with a picnic of egg sandwiches and bottles of beer—she discovered Arthur liked to drink, more than she did, really—and wiggled their toes together underwater in the silt. She surprised him with her love of the water, and swam out alone to the middle of the lake, liking his protective warnings not to go out too far all alone, not to stay long in the cold water, not to tire herself. She dove underwater, still unused to its freshness, its chill, its lack of salt; the ocean always seemed to buoy her up, but here it was easy to dive down deep, into thick, dark silence. Even today's bright spring sun barely filtered down. She thought about how she loved swimming alone, how you *did* have to be careful, though, responsible, with no one there if something were to happen. No one to see you, or hear you; even if you make it up to the surface, it might be too late to be saved. She took in a mouthful of clear, icy water, tasting it, but swallowed too soon; she choked a little, drawing more water into her throat, her lungs. She tried rising up, then, swooshing faster to the sun, panicked at all that water pressing over her, freezing her, out here alone. She broke the surface, sputtering with adrenaline, desperate to breathe, and screamed for Arthur to save her; he'd been watching for her from shore and dove in immediately, helping her to swim back, buoying her up. She drooped onshore still choking and coughing fluid, and laughed at herself, at her silly panic, feeling drained and exhausted; he wiped the water from her chilled face and hair and asked her to marry him.

She telephoned her parents from the justice of the peace in Madison, while Art paced back and forth and synchronized his watch to the City Hall campanile, and told them she was getting married in twenty minutes. Sylvia burst into tears and handed the phone to Harry, who asked Vivian if she was sure, truly sure, this was what she wanted and what about school? Sylvia took the phone back and said Vivian *knew*, didn't she, that she didn't have to marry this young man just to go to bed with him? Didn't Vivian *know* that? Vivian, embarrassed, told her mother it had nothing to do with that, surprised at her pleasure in telling her mother she was wrong, while remembering how the smell of Arthur's skin shifted at his hairline. She tried to explain that this was . . . different, it was an answer to everything, it solved everything. Sylvia said she didn't realize Vivian's life was such a problem that it needed to be *solved* by anything, and Vivian replied No, I just mean that I'm ready for a real life now, Mother. Sylvia begged her to take more time to think. Vivian said she was tired of thinking, as Art looked at her and pantomimed the passing of time on his watch. She promised her parents it would all be wonderful, and she'd call them soon. Harry said they knew she would, and after all, she could always go back to finish school, right? Once she and this young man were settled? They loved her very much; she was, always had been, such a good girl.

"Hey, what did your folks say?" They were driving, Arthur was driving Vivian's Plymouth, back to the dorm to pick up her trunk. They had decided to live cheaply in Art's Chicago boardinghouse until he finished out the school term.

"They'll get used to it." She curled up next to him, thinking how odd it felt not to be driving. Arthur was a good driver, better than she was, actually, more focused. "I said we'd make it out over the summer, after you graduate."

"If we have enough money."

"They'd send us some."

"I don't want to start off borrowing from my in-laws, Vivian."

"You're absolutely right."

"And I'll be working this summer. You know that. Two jobs. I don't have enough to take care of you and pay the first term of law school yet."

"I know."

"When I was a kid . . . I mean, everyone always thought summer was great, you know, for vacations. I always worked. I had to."

"Well, now we'll work together. We'll build something together."

"Yeah, but *you're* never gonna have to work, *really* work. I promise you that."

"I wouldn't mind."

He kissed her hand. "That's what killed my mother, working too hard. Doing a man's job. And my cousin who raised me, Essie, I told you about her?" Vivian nodded. "Jesus, she'd work a twelve-hour day herself, never complain, you know, a lot of spirit, then at night she'd stay up to read to me. Worked her fingers to the bone looking after me, so *I'd* get ahead, and I never got the chance to make life easy for her. I swore to myself . . . and she was smart, too, like you." He kissed her hand again. "There was one story she liked, about this farm boy, he works real hard but nothing ever happens to him, so he decides to go off to war, to *do* something with his life, right? He wants to *be* something. This kid, I think his name's Claude—"

"Sounds like *One of Ours*."

"What?"

"The story, *One of Ours*. A Willa Cather novel. She won

the Pulitzer for it, maybe ten years ago. I don't know why, really, it wasn't one of her best. At least *I* didn't think—"

"You want to finish the story?"

"What?" she said, taken aback.

"Go ahead!"

"Oh, Artie, I only—"

"Go ahead, you think you know it. Go ahead. Tell it!"

"I didn't mean that. Really. I'm sorry. I don't know it, c'mon, what were you saying?"

He said nothing, just looked ahead, driving.

"I always do that, it's a terrible habit. Cutting people off. I'm sorry, sweetheart."

He nodded, accepting it, still looking ahead.

"It might not even be *One of Ours*. I could be wrong." She reached over and took his hand again. "Arthur?"

"Hey, are you hungry? Why don't we stop for a bite?" He pulled off the main road, into the gravel path of a small cafeteria.

"Okay. Sure."

He leaned over before getting out of the car, ran his hand down the back of her hair, and kissed her. She put her hand on the nape of his neck to hold his mouth to her a moment longer.

"Honey . . . I'm sorry I sort of snapped at you. . . ." He touched her earlobe.

"That's all right. . . ."

"No, it isn't."

"It's been a long day. We just—"

"So, let's start over." He kissed her again. "Mrs. Arthur Thornton."

Vivian blinked, smiled. "That doesn't sound like it's mine, yet. I'll have to get used to it."

"You sure will. I feel bad, though, you know . . . I can't even get you a ring," he said softly.

"Oh, I don't care about that. I don't even like jewelry."

"A girl oughta have a wedding ring, though. I promise you, Mrs. Arthur Thornton, you'll have a ring, as soon as I can."

"It doesn't matter, Arthur. It's just a symbol."

He kissed her again and they decided to skip dinner to go straight to her dorm. Arthur insisted that only his great need to be with her excused the breaking of the dorm rule, and only this one time. But it was, after all, the middle of the day and they thought no one would be there; and anyway, even if Vivian were caught, it wouldn't make any difference now.

# Uncle Sam's Devil's Island

## *The Prison*

Thus the quality of rotten eggs in a general basket would be improved by picking out the most putrid ones for wrapping.

ANTHONY TURANO,
"America's Torture Chamber,"
*The American Mercury*, September 1938

The island as a place of exile is an ancient and pervasive theme: the Romans dumped their unwanted onto the Greek isles; England populated Australia with excess convicts; the Russians used the island of Solovetskiye, hiding criminals in a nook of the White Sea; even Napoleon was sent off to stew on St. Helena. The Count of Monte Cristo began his true education in life as an inmate of the foreboding Ile d'If. America itself took in hordes of "indentured servants" offered cheap from European courts and prisons, the New World being a place that, although not technically an island, was considered a wilderness safely across a wide sea. The Italian *isola,* for island, has given us the word "isolate." As a place of quarantine for the infected, the diseased, the leper or lunatic, an island is the obvious choice; the flip side is the island as Escape to Paradise from a harsh Society—the self-exiled man who goes off by choice to live idyllically alone on a deserted isle is glowing with health, ruggedly isolationist and free of spirit, not trapped at all. Fictional young lovers cast away on tropical sands learn desire, and hardy shipwrecked families learn self-reliance, all while developing golden suntans and a love of fresh fruit and seafood. The island child left behind when the native tribe is whisked off to civilization grows up a Rousseauean child of Nature, free of malice or guile, befriended by wild dogs. *Lord of the Flies*, where the child's true instinct when left to flourish in isolation is savage, not pure of heart, is more the exception in the genre, but it is an elastic theme—the island may either imbue its inhabitants with its spirit, or the occupant's inherent nature can determine the character of the island.

Almost a year before Alcatraz opened for business as a Federal Penitentiary in 1934, the *Literary Digest* published an article called "America's Devil's Island and Some Others," reminding the reader of ongoing international experiments in isolation and punishment, such as France's "Devil's Island" in Guiana, Italy's prison off the northern coast of Sicily on the island of Lipari, Spain's Villa Cisneros in Africa, and England's colony on the Andaman Islands in the Bay of Bengal. The author concluded that such medieval and ominous-sounding comparisons with the American endeavor were unjustified; Alcatraz, with its brand-new, state-of-the-art modifications and scientific advancements in penal theory would be wholly different, as it was "thoroughly modern, with steam heat, running water, and recreation facilities." *Newsweek* also pointed out that on Alcatraz, "being a part of California, the climate is 'wonderful' . . . there is a library, motion picture theatre, and bowling alley. The place is at it's best in Spring, when flowers turn the island into a riot of color."

The *San Francisco Examiner* described the new prison of "startling contrasts and extremes . . . a prison with all the facilities demanded by the most liberal penal reformer and, at the same time, a prison with incredible possibilities of conversion into a hell hole." Whether an Alcatraz prisoner found his time served in a "soft spot" or a "hell hole" was going to "depend entirely on the Government and the man it selects as warden"—implying, inadvertently or not, that a prisoner's conduct might well be irrelevant to how he is treated, when weighed against the inclinations of his keeper.

James A. Johnston was second choice for keeper of Alcatraz; the attorney general had at first felt the reform-oriented Johnston was perhaps too humanitarian for the job. Johnston accepted the responsibility of the post, and spent the next eight months overseeing Alcatraz' transition from nineteenth-century soft iron to twentieth-century tool-proof steel.

For inmates, the rule would be Rules. No commissary, no inmate council, no convict trusties. One inmate to a cell, confined for fourteen or fifteen hours a day, or a full twenty-three hours for troublemakers in Solitary who did not work in the industry shops. The food was reputed the best of the entire prison system; eat all you want at mealtimes—a replete con is a relaxed con—but food left earns a skipped meal, or time in Solitary. Life was a regimented routine, from the wake-up bell at 6:00 A.M., followed by bells to line up, return to cells, leave cells for work, return to cells, leave cells for meals; a Pavlovian pattern of existence, drilled in, unwavering. One exercise period per week, on Sundays, which could be spent instead at chapel. No movies. A march to the basement once a week for a shower, a *hot* shower; steam keeps an inmate soft, we don't want a man hardened to cold water, inured to the shock of a swim in the Bay. One visitor a month, blood relative or wife only, after an inmate has served his first three months without incident; the inmate may then submit a written request to the Warden for approval, who will send a confirmation letter to the visitor with the chosen date—the visitor must then bring the letter to show the ferry pilot. All mail not only censored, but retyped and a carbon copy only released to the inmate. No news of the outside world. Most of all, infamous of all, was the rule of silence, the straightjacket on speech—a request to pass the salt at mealtimes, fine, but otherwise no communication between convicts, between convict and guard. The first federal prisoners at Alcatraz were thirty-two felons left over from the Army, soon to be joined by trainloads of the nation's incorrigibles, including Al Capone. The two things to eventually snap Capone's mind were advancing syphilis and the rule of silence; he wore a path back and forth to Solitary for punishment of weeks at a time after attempting to talk guards and other inmates into lackeying for him, after boasting aloud of his former life, unable to accept being muted into anonymity, into just another con, AZ #85.

No convict would be sentenced directly to Alcatraz by a federal court, or paroled from Alcatraz itself, in order to avoid a convict's release into the Bay Area community and access to reporters, press, and public opinion. Johnston himself would have no say in which Federal prisoners would come to serve their time on the Rock; fellow wardens throughout the country were invited to select from their own prison populations the problem convicts, the chronic escapers, the big shots, the troublemakers. Alcatraz was to hold the worst of these rotten eggs, but the men and their crimes would belie what seemed the most stringent and consistent of criteria; while most were indeed the vicious and the violent—murderers, rapists, kidnappers—other men were to wind up on the Rock, through bureaucratic shuffling, for possession of marijuana, the theft of little more than pennies, or sodomy. Or merely the label of being incorrigible, a nuisance, which, when given by someone in power, is quite enough.

A news conference was held in August 1934, and the press was invited to inspect the new island prison—the last invitation to be extended for thirteen years—to hear Warden Johnston announce: "Mr. Attorney General, Alcatraz is ready." Cummings congratulated Johnston on his efforts, and added "We are looking forward to great things from Alcatraz."

In 1936 Joseph Bowers was serving a twenty-five-year sentence on the Rock for robbing a small-town grocery store of about $17. He had already attempted escape by slashing his jugular with a piece of broken eyeglass; his throat sealed shut, he was sent to work the incinerator on the west side of the island, throwing garbage down a sixty-foot chute to the sea. The morning of April 27, Bowers turned from the waves of heat and toward the gleaming, new Golden Gate Bridge, and began to scale the twelve-foot wire fence. The Road Tower guard, Officer Chandler, shouted an unheeded warning, followed by several shots in the air. Bowers reached the top and swung his heavy body over to the side of freedom; Officer Chandler fired at Bowers's legs, as he later reported; at least one bullet pierced a lung. Bowers's body dropped the sixty feet to crash on the sea-dampened concrete embankment below. Citizens of San Francisco perhaps heard shots, but nothing more, and that in itself was not unusual; guards often engaged in target practice around the grounds, and the sound of gunfire carries—to the mainland, to traffic on the bridges, into the prison cells.

The second inmate to die on the island did so more quietly; Edward Wutke slit his throat with the thin, tiny blade from a pencil sharpener and successfully bled to death. Rufe Persful didn't go so far in the summer of 1937; he only chopped off the fingers of his left hand with an ax, either genuinely crazy or that desperate to be seen so, which is essentially the same thing. The *New York Times* reported that Alcatraz investigators called the act an "exhibitionist fit," and according to

Warden Johnston "there had been many cases of convict exhibitionism throughout the country and that they resulted from the typical yearnings of imprisoned men to nourish their ego with attention." Director of Federal Prisons James V. Bennett said Persful was "a psychopathic case, and was such long before he came to Alcatraz. It is probably the seat of all his troubles which landed him here." Evidently it had no bearing on his being sent to Alcatraz in the first place.

The City didn't hear the escape siren's debut until December of 1937. Buddies Theodore Cole and Ralph Roe were working in the mat shop, collectively serving 149 years for various bank robberies, kidnappings, and escape attempts, including a cellmate murder by Cole at a previous institution. They sawed through iron bars, smashed a window, and climbed out; a guard returning to the mat shop noticed the hole and the absence. The siren was sounded. For the first time, housewives on the island and in the City fearfully slammed shut their doors against roaming Alcatraz felons; Coast Guard cutters on alert filtered their way around the Bay in the fog; FBI agents joined with San Francisco police to comb Fisherman's Wharf—all while the locked-up convicts celebrated that two of their own had bested Uncle Sam.

Warden Johnston at first insisted there was no escape, then, conceding the escape, that there was no danger in it, as there was no possible chance of success. The fog was too thick that day; the current unusually swift; the water especially cold, all the more so to men used to soaking up that steam heat. Of course they drowned. A massive search found no bodies or clues. Roe and Cole were officially listed as "missing," and the housewives eventually unlocked their doors, everyone mumbling in still-lingering protest at their levied vulnerability.

There was no siren sounded on May 23, 1938 when Officer Royal Cline had his skull crushed by a hammer blow from Thomas Limmerick, helped by James "Tex" Lucas, and Rufus "Whitey" Franklin, all doing time for bank robberies and kidnappings. The three inmates escaped the wood shop building, crawled along a catwalk, and attacked the Model Tower with hammers and pieces of metal pipe, not realizing the window glass was shatterproof. Inside, Officer Harold Stites opened fire, hitting Franklin in the arm and Limmerick in the head. Franklin flew back from the impact into strings of barbed wire, and later had to be cut free. Lucas surrendered. Officer Cline and Limmerick died; Franklin and Lucas were given additional life sentences for first-degree murder.

By 1938, despite a virtual blackout of information to the public, Anthony M. Turano wrote in the *American Mercury*:

> [It is] obvious the plan was richer in moral indignation than sociological wisdom. . . . It is true that, except for an occasional beating administered by guards, the punishments are not directly corporeal, but clumsily psychological. . . .
>
> The prison rule that is really supposed to inculcate a lasting respect for the majesty of the law is the one of condemning every inmate to almost perpetual silence.
>
> Their summary execution would reflect more humanity and official dignity than the maintenance of a costly suite of torture chambers.

The French had since abandoned their own Devil's Island, but the American endeavor was in its infancy, and a "lasting respect for the majesty of the law," it was hoped, would take only a little time to grow to maturity.

# Just Married

## *Vivian*

Marriage gave Vivian less to do than she'd thought. Arthur spent the summer working days as a law clerk and nights as a security guard at Marshall Field's; his in-between hours were reserved for sleep and some food. His two rooms at the boardinghouse included a small kitchenette, and Vivian exchanged her textbooks for cookbooks; Sylvia sent her long letters and complex recipes with five-dollar bills folded into the pages ("This calls for fresh peppermint, which I know is very dear, but it's not worth the bother if you substitute, so here's a little extra, don't tell your father!). Harry also sent letters, full of newspaper clippings about Hitler's Nuremberg laws and Roosevelt's Social Security Act, with his penciled commentary in the margins, and more five-dollar bills carefully stapled to the page bottoms ("Just put this aside for an emergency, your mother doesn't have to know!"). She spent her mornings reading in the hush of the University library, and her afternoons preparing Arthur's early evening meal in the solitude of their little suite, remembering yes on brussels sprouts, no on carrots. Finally feeling deadened by the stillness, she put aside a few of her parents' five-dollar bills for a good Philco radio. Singing along loudly to crack the silence, she measured and chopped and stirred with a chemist's precision, but nothing ever came out quite like Sylvia's. Arthur was usually too tired to notice, and told her, chewing, that everything was delicious; he was a lucky guy that she took such good care of him, and did he have clean socks for his night shift at the store? A short nap and he left her again, in bed with a book, feeling sulky and untalked-to and ungrateful. She appreciated how hard he worked; she knew it was for her, for their future, and decided it would be easier when he started law school—after all, he'd be home more, even if he spent his time studying. She tried knitting socks—dark-blue argyle, white diamonds—needles clicking to the radio, following Sylvia's written instructions, but Arthur's foot went right through the toe of the first finished one; he gave her a big, appreciative kiss anyway, and told her not to bother about things like socks, a store-bought pair was only fifteen cents. He woke her up one morning, excited, to tell her Marshall Field's had offered him a job as security manager of the store; a lot of responsibility, the money was excellent, it was steady, it was good training in management for all kinds of things. Confused, she made proud sounds while mentioning his plans for law school, but he brushed all that aside; he was a married man now, he wasn't going to throw away more years as a schoolboy. He was going to take good care of her, and in these times that meant a steady job with a good income. He'd be a fool, an irresponsible fool, to pass this up. Besides, even if he was in school all day, he'd still have to work at night. This way they'd have more time together, and isn't that what she'd been complaining about? She agreed, of course, and when she discovered she was pregnant a few months later they congratulated themselves on their foresight. Her early weeks of pregnancy she spent throwing up, disabled by fear and nausea, feeling guilty at being unable to make Arthur anything more than cold sandwiches, watching color fade from her housebound skin, and queasily listening to the radio describe how Amelia Earhart had disappeared forever into an ocean.

They moved to their own apartment and Vivian traded in cookbooks for baby and child-care books, feeling, as her pregnancy advanced, that she had a crucial exam coming in a few months' time and she had to cram hard in preparation. She gave birth successfully to a girl they named Stella, for Arthur's cousin Estelle. Arthur cried the first time he held the baby, and Vivian knew, in an etherized haze, that all of her hard work and study had produced an A. She babbled something to him, before going back to sleep, about being sure to tape the baby up on the icebox.

A year or so later Vivian's doctor congratulated her on being pregnant again; Vivian felt instead she was being told to take a failed course over in summer school. With Stella she'd made so many mistakes, she was sure—forgetting to sterilize bottles, not picking her up when she should or picking her up when she shouldn't, flipping her over at night like a pancake because she couldn't decide on face-up or face-down, Why can't the experts decide on that?, she'd wail to Arthur—that she started a list of What To Do Differently This Time the moment her body started to swell.

Arthur didn't understand her fears, her obsession; she was a wonderful mother, just trust her instincts, she wouldn't be so tired if she didn't worry so much, would she? But if I don't worry, who will? she found herself wanting to snap back; after all, Arthur had changed a diaper exactly three and a half times in eighteen months, and would probably give Stella a splintered chicken bone to suck on if she wanted it. He was wonderful with the baby when he was in the mood to be, which, if Vivian was lucky, was also when she needed him to be, but it was understood the child, the children, motherhood, were her job. So if I don't feed her, she doesn't eat; if I don't change her, she gets a rash—why do you act like these things are unimportant, then tell me motherhood is the most important job in the world? And if I let her cry too long you get upset, and I have to take care of you, too, coax you into a better mood. So isn't it my job to worry, she wanted to say; you worry about *your* job all the time, and I listen and listen even when I've been up all night, and frankly, sometimes I think your job is a hell of a lot easier, and mostly more trivial, than mine. Try not even being able to go to the *bathroom* alone because you can't leave Stell unattended. Try bending over to pick up a screaming little girl who needs to be changed and fed while an extra thirty pounds of baby is squeezing your insides flat, and your center of gravity is so thrown you can't even stand up properly, you can't have five minutes, *five minutes* during the day when you're not taking care of someone else, and oh, what am I saying, it *is* my job, after all. I'm just tired, acting spoiled, immature, he's right, it'll get easier. He works hard, too. So she said nothing, but wondered, sometimes, what she was doing there, when she couldn't even remember the first thing Arthur ever said to her, or the smell of the nape of his neck, the look in his eyes she loved. How did she ever get here? She couldn't quite retrace in her mind the steps of the journey, literally, how did she get from home to Wisconsin to Arthur to babies? And why couldn't she remember, for didn't she, after all, drive herself?

But Jerry, named for an old childhood buddy of Arthur's, was an easy baby, and Vivian calmed down a little; she was, she realized, all too familiar with the routine of it by now to be frightened anymore. Stella considered her baby brother some kind of family pet rather than the human doll Vivian had assumed would interest her, which quelled her secret hope the little girl would be naturally inclined to help take care of her brother. Vivian took them to the park and watched them spill apple juice and sand on each other, watched them romp and fall down and romp again, and knew that something was missing, in her; that those instincts

Arthur always complimented her on simply did not exist, not in the manner he assumed. She loved the children, of course, but, but . . . there was a flaw in her, like color blindness, or a body's inability to process sugar. She watched the other mothers marveling at the wonder of a new world through their children's eyes, and couldn't escape the fact that seeing the world constantly through a child's eyes simply bored her to death. Or worse, that her own world, through her own eyes, was leadenly, inescapably, dull. Landlocked.

She loved Arthur too, of course, and she knew he loved her, but it seemed he loved her most when she gave up little pieces of herself, to him—pieces she didn't quite get to taste first from her own plate before handing him a forkful and going by his judgment of their taste. Such little things to give up, really, ways of doing things, insignificant choices, preferences, opinions, but weren't those all the little pieces that made her, her? Didn't he notice the little holes left, or is that how he liked her, made porous by love? And every time she handed a piece over, smiling, wanting to please him, she wondered if she had a limited supply of herself and what would she do the day she ran out? But she watched him love her all the more, and so felt safe and a little relief at being herself lighter, and a little fear. Small attentions, too, and the tiny sticks of support and encouragement that went to him, propped him up, oh, she shouldn't miss those at all. Maybe her parents had spoiled her, giving her too much of that, too much ego. She found herself phrasing what she already knew as questions—Is that a full moon? Oh, who's in that movie again?—asking things instead of stating them, letting him have the pleasures of confirmation, letting him fix things. Maybe this was just a new way of loving, of how a grown-up loves her husband, selflessly, she thought, and I'm just not used to it yet, still not used to it.

She noticed how Arthur's writing was an odd, childish

mix of capital and lowercase letters; how he read only the headlines of newspaper articles before talking about them; how once, after he told her he liked it, she'd served him her muddled facsimile of Sylvia's meatloaf for five nights in a row for a joke and he never noticed or complained, and a dull appetite is sign of a dull mind, isn't that right, what Sylvia used to say? No, that's silly, really. She longed for her parents, she longed for an ocean, she longed for other people to talk to besides grown-up, serious Arthur and her squirming, infant children. But then Arthur would pick up Stella to kiss her good night, so sweetly, or rub Vivian's swollen feet in the same sure and unselfconscious way he used to take her hand across the table, and she'd tell herself to stop it, just stop it, she'd better grow up and stop squirming herself and appreciate how lucky she was. Time would solve this; she merely had to do her time until the children were a little older, and then she would return to what was hers, a sense of a life that didn't feel so parsed into pieces, a life they were building together. Maybe even go back to school. She let her hair grow long again; Arthur liked it that way.

When they heard about Pearl Harbor over the Philco radio, Vivian and Arthur took each other's hands, and, after the initial panic that the world was coming to an end and where would they go to hide if the Japs bombed Chicago, sat down to discuss what to do with their lives, their life. They decided, mutually and rationally, in the first actual conversation Vivian could remember in a long time, that Arthur would quit his job and enlist in the Pacific War; that Vivian and the children should return to live with Sylvia and Harry; and their own future must now selflessly take a back seat to the greater issues of their country. They put Stella and Jerry to bed early and made love, also for the first time in a long time, feeling solemn and purposeful. They sold their furniture, packed their bags and the children into Vivian's rusting Plymouth, and drove back to California, while Vivian struggled to pack away the thought clinging inside her head ever since the scratchy Philco broadcast over dinner, a shameful, immoral thought—Thank God there's going to be a war!

# The Trial

## *The Prison*

> Perhaps the best thing about Alcatraz is the cold silence that rests over the island. . . . This impenetrable wall that separates the prisoners on Alcatraz from the rest of the world is perhaps the hardest thing these men—considering their usual bent—have to bear.
>
> At Alcatraz they are buried in dark silence and completely deflated.
>
> *San Francisco Chronicle* editorial, 1936

> The whole psychology of Alcatraz seems bad . . . [it] builds up a sinister and vicious influence among the prisoners.
>
> ATTORNEY GENERAL MURPHY,
> to the *New York Times,* June 1939

Warden Johnston rescinded the "rule of silence" for inmates in 1937. Earlier leaks to the press of self-mutilations and insanity, of prisoners stabbing each other, or guards brutalizing prisoners, required some sort of accommodating gesture. Paroled inmate Verill Rapp had told the Associated Press that "three inmates of Alcatraz have become insane and a fourth is verging on madness because of inhumane treatment"; the story was picked up by papers across the nation. News of several inmate work strikes were reported in 1936 and 1937, their demands: 1) pay for their industrial work, as at other federal institutions; 2) a lift on the ban of outside world news and newspapers; and 3) commissary privileges for candy bars and cigarettes. Strike leaders were chained for a time in the damp basement cells, and the general population put on bread and water.

Warden Johnston waited for peace to be restored, letting enough time go by to emphasize that he was running Alcatraz, that the rescission of the rule of silence was simply a generous gesture on his part, not a yielding to pressure. No commissary, no newspapers. He told the *New York Times* in May 1937:

> We get the supercriminal, or at least, those with superego, and our job is to defeat that ego. . . .
>
> We have brought all of them to the realization that they are not as big as they thought they were.

Five men held in Solitary for their participation in a strike sawed through the cellfront bars, broke a cellhouse window, spread the bars, and slipped down to the small beach on the island's west side just before dawn on January 13, 1939. A guard, mysteriously absent or unaware during the actual escape, finally spotted the empty cells and set off the alarm. The five escapees were found half-naked on the foggy beach attempting to tie a driftwood raft together with their clothing, bruised and cut from the rocks, all of them trapped between armed guards in boats and armed guards on the cliff behind them. Two dove in the water and were shot, one being killed, while the others shivered and surrendered; they were given longer sentences and slapped back in Solitary. San Franciscans were outraged at the ease of the escape, and how far, it seemed, the inmates had gotten, how close to themselves. The Bureau of Prisons held the inquest, like a doctor performing his own exploratory surgery. Where were the armed guards inside the prison's gun galleries? Sleeping? How could the men saw through steel tool-proof bars? The explanation was simple; in 1933 only half the cellhouse bars had been replaced with that lauded tool-proof steel—the bars on Segregation cells in Cellblock A had not been refurbished since the Army days; they were flat, of soft iron. This would be looked into; meanwhile, Solitary for the surviving escapees this time meant two years chained in the basement cells, beneath Cellblock A.

After their release back into the general population and a return to work, one of the accomplices, Henri Young, killed another, Rufus McCain, in a stairway of the industry shops. His case became the "Trial of Alcatraz," for Young's attorney put the prison itself on trial for the brutality and inhumanity inflicted upon Young, driving him to murder. Direct testimony was heard from Alcatraz inmates for the first time, a litany of abuses, and Warden Johnston himself was called on to defend his creation publicly, a man renowned for humanitarian reform. A judge declared the basement cells where Young had been held, the "Spanish Dungeons" referred to by the press, to be unconstitutional. As a result, Young received another three years for involuntary manslaughter, instead of the gas chamber for murder; the informal sentence on the prison itself was negligible, or, actually, advantageous: an allocation of funds was made to refurbish Cellblock D, separated by a concrete wall from the rest of the cellhouse, for Solitary Confinement. Problem solved. D Block cells were larger than those of B and C Blocks, and the upper tiers had a nice view of the Golden Gate Bridge, but inmates here would be confined twenty-three hours a day. Six special cells on the ground level—six pitch-black and empty boxes with solid doors, five with a toilet, one with a drainage hole—were thereafter called the Hole, or Isolation, or their more clinical euphemism, the Treatment Unit

After civic indignation over the prison horrors died down, the moral cynicism returned: all those men testifying about how awful it is in there are criminals, after all; of course they'd say anything; what's a little perjury next to kidnapping and robbery and murder? Maybe those men are getting just what they deserve; nobody made them break the law in the first place. And, of course, the war came, and citizens had far more important things to worry about; let the scrim of fog roll back in and screen the island from our sight.

# Duty

## *Vivian*

In 1942 the country sang "Be Careful, It's My Heart" and listened on the radio as Joe Louis knocked out Buddy Baer to retain his world heavyweight crown; sugar, coffee, and gasoline rationing began, soon to be followed by shoes, meat, cheeses, and canned goods; Congress decided to draft boys over eighteen and the U. S. Supreme Court decided Nevada divorces were good enough for them; the city of Los Angeles went to see *Mrs. Miniver* at the Pantages, and Vivian Thornton went dancing at the Coconut Grove. She and several co-workers had just ended their eight-hour shift at Douglas Aircraft, and refused, although it was midnight, to trade in their energized senses for a good night's sleep. Instead, the women shook their hair free of its nets, the men ran washcloths over their stubbled faces, and they all piled into Vivian's Plymouth for a cruise downtown to the Ambassador. The Los Angeles seen at age eighteen and the Los Angeles lived at twenty-seven were two different cities, Vivian found; it had exploded while she was away, and rippled past wherever she reached, like chasing a vision, revealing something new and full of flavor just ahead. And it felt like such a long, long time since there'd been anything new, any color or live music or salt, at all.

Arthur had immediately taken to Vivian's parents, calling them Mom and Dad, embracing Sylvia and deferring to

Harry, thanking them for turning out such a wonderful girl, reiterating his promise that taking care of his wife and their children was the most important job in his life. He told Vivian, privately, that he felt he found the family he'd never had; Essie had tried to be both mother and father, but in the end was just Essie. And he understood Vivian better now, too, he said, seeing the home in which she'd grown up, her good fortune. Their children would have this, the stability, the love and the home, the plenty.

Sylvia and Harry liked their son-in-law for the qualities they found admirable—his seriousness, his sense of duty—but both wished he could have been simply, say, a next-door neighbor, or distant cousin they could invite now and then to supper, rather than the man their daughter had married. They couldn't quite get over their own disappointment, the sense that Vivian had liquidated her assets too soon. But they insisted on having Stell and Jerry sleep in their room, so Vivian and Arthur could have some privacy for the short time left before Arthur went off to war, which to Vivian was a sign of sanction. En route to the bathroom one night she heard the four of them in the kitchen—Sylvia reading to the kids, Harry making root beer floats for all of them—and felt, finally, that she was grown-up, that she'd passed childhood on to her children, exactly the way life was supposed to go. And how funny, she thought, to feel that only now, back with Mom and Dad, how I never really felt adult when I was busy with the kids all day on my own.

The last Saturday Arthur was home, Harry and Sylvia took the children to see *Bambi* at the Fox Theatre in Westwood Village three times in a row, so their daughter could be alone with her husband. Arthur took Vivian out to a last lunch, and presented her with a little velvet box containing a tiny circle of rose gold.

"I promised you, didn't I?"

"Oh, Arthur . . . it's beautiful. So simple. It's perfect."

"I know you don't go for flashy stuff."

"You're so thoughtful . . . it's exactly what I would have chosen."

"I just thought, you know . . . a girl gets married, the world oughta know." He grinned, sheepish, and put it on her ring finger. "Especially if I'm not gonna be around."

She shook her head, wiped away the perfect tears at the corners of her eyes, and kissed him across the table. They finished their lunch, then, and found themselves with nothing left to do, nothing left to talk about, and so joined the rest of the family at the theatre for the third showing, in time to see Bambi's mother shot by hunters. They both cried a little until Stella, dulled to the death by its repetition, impatiently pointed out it was only a movie, which made the grown-ups chuckle. After the newsreel showing staged film of fighting men, they all went for ice cream. A little embarrassed at Arthur's tears, Vivian murmured something to her father about Arthur's maturity and innate strength of character—He's a rock, Dad, really; Harry, annoyed with her for leaving school to marry a man she felt she had to apologize for, tersely replied that a man who didn't cry now and then didn't deserve to have his daughter for a wife, for who could live with a rock?

Arthur had enlisted in the Marines—better a Marine private than a Navy petty officer!—and left for basic training looking like the newsreel husbands, handsome and serious. Vivian, crying on the platform with dozens of other wives, squeezed Stella's and Jerry's hands so tightly they wailed, and pulled away from her to kiss their father again. She wasn't sure what to do now, and so took the children to see *Bambi* for the fourth time in order to keep crying; no one in the theatre minded, a woman crying alone with her children was becoming an increasingly familiar sight. The newsreel had changed, now showing staged film of women taking on jobs in defense plants, doing their share for the war effort, joining up to "Do the Job He Left Behind!" Her ring finger wasn't used to the wedding band yet, and she began a habit of pressing on it with her left thumb so it gapped, as if to give the finger some breathing room.

She received letters from him, censored to paper lace, that she carried with her to show people until they fluttered away bit by bit and she regretted not saving them properly in scrapbooks. His handwriting, when that was all she had of him, was endearing, not annoying; the letters were the first he'd ever written to her, and she felt, as during their courtship conversation, that what he wrote to her was unlike anything ever written to anyone else, truer and more personal. She felt tugs of love so strong it distracted her from realizing how little she missed him. She wrote long letters back, struggling as over term papers to choose the perfect word, full of details about the children and their schoolwork and how their Victory Garden was doing, that they'd planted brussels sprouts especially for him, for when he came home. She didn't mention Sylvia and Harry taking the children to demonstrate against the internment camps for Japanese Americans, or that she was collecting catalogs from the University of California, or anything about what she was doing with her time, other than the brief mention of getting a part-time job at an aircraft plant in Santa Monica; she knew he didn't want her to work, but after all, their personal desires had to take a back seat to the greater issues of the country and her duty now was to be selfless.

President Roosevelt came to appreciate the strength of German military aircraft; in 1938 he announced to his Cabinet the need for an American air force of at least 10,000 planes, and a desired production quota of 20,000 a year. As with motion pictures thirty years earlier, southern California found itself the leader of a booming industry; by the time of Pearl Harbor, a third of Los Angeles factory workers were manufacturing airplanes. At the war's peak California was producing more than a third of the nation's 40,000 planes a year.

Eleven million women were in the national labor force when the war started; four years later the number had jumped to almost nineteen million and counting, as seven and a half million women got jobs, often under the guise of patriotic duty, but, just as often, for economic necessity—the men were gone, prices were high, and kids had to be fed. By the time Rosie the Riveter appeared on the cover of the *Saturday Evening Post* in 1943, Vivian had been promoted twice at Douglas Aircraft and was supervising almost a hundred and fifty of those nineteen million women, still telling herself that the swelling pride she felt was only in doing a good job for her country. Just how the men must feel, off at war, without the danger, of course, no, hardly the same at all. Not nearly as important, but still. It was fun, to be honest, a little like college again, except that most of the women had husbands away fighting and children at home. Stell and Jerry were looked after by their grandparents and Vivian didn't, at first, realize how lucky she was; when stories began to circulate about children being locked in cars for safekeeping during the day, or tied to a yard fence while desperate mothers went to work at the Job He Left Behind, she was appalled. The parking lot at Douglas Aircraft became crowded with children left to play while their mothers punched in for their patriotic duty; Vivian, after her first promotion, convinced her supervisor to let the women turn an empty storeroom into a playroom, making up projected figures of increased output by less-nervous mothers, and sick leave made unnecessary. The women took turns, every half hour, keeping an eye on the children, and began granting to Vivian certain other responsibilities and authorities on behalf of them all. Even the male workers, the few remaining at the plant, followed her orders; some were more resentful than others at being told what to do by a woman—especially a woman in coveralls—but the supervisor was pleased as Vivian's projections came true, and the men were outnumbered, anyway. Vivian was promoted again, with little ill will from anyone—the awareness of Duty, the larger purpose in which they were all engaged, won out over resentment, and the common bond gave way finally to a sense of fun. They all shared letters, the men and the women, teased, gossiped, flirted, went to movies before or after hours, went dancing. And beach parties in the mornings, on weekends, the ocean Vivian had missed so much; the water seemed warmer than she'd remembered, and soon her skin soaked in enough sun and sea to glow again. She could also, once more, boast offers of transportation; the Plymouth still ran, thanks to Harry's care, and was again packed with people and taken out for nights on the town. The nightclubs were crowded, the women outnumbering the men, here, too, but always there were soldiers on leave or coming out of stateside hospitals who needed to dance, even with a proudly married woman fussing with her rose gold wedding band. She always asked where they were stationed, if they knew her husband Arthur, Corporal Thornton? No, they didn't, placing their hands more respectfully on her back, but this Arthur was sure one hell of a lucky guy, with a gal like her to come home to.

In the summer of 1944 Arthur's battalion was sent to the Marianas, an island cluster including Saipan, Guam, and Tinian, in the mid-Pacific Ocean, south of Japan. The first goal was taking Saipan, in what was meant to be a three-day battle; American officials were still underestimating Japanese tenacity. Japan had held the islands, an important stepping-stone to the Philippines, for over twenty-five years, and despite, or because of, the war's tilt in America's favor, was not about to hand them over.

Corporal Arthur Thornton climbed onto the Saipan beach next to his battalion buddy Frank Farrell, to the not-so-far-off sound of invisible Japanese gunners firing from beyond the dunes. Arthur and Frank were a team since Basic in 1941; soon after meeting they'd slapped each other hard on the back, showed pictures of wife and girlfriend to the other's appreciative whistle, and called each other Buddy, sensing the other would be, for the lifetime they hoped would come, My Old Army Buddy, that dear-bought bond, a relationship closer than marriage, sibling, or parent. Frank's gal Darlene lived in Phoenix, and had just sent him a sifting of sand in an envelope, to remind him of home. The buddies, by now on active duty in the Pacific for a year and a half, chuckled over women's ignorance of war; they were sick of sand and swore to each other that once home they'd take Vivian and Darlene dancing, but never, ever, to the beach.

The sand had yielded Frank's most precious treasure, however; earlier, during their first true battle and before their stomachs were hardened to living on greenish roots and watching men die, their superior officer, Second Lieutenant Bradley Pierson, was blasted apart in front of them on the beach at Guadalcanal. Frank, vomiting into the sand, was first to crawl forward; he dragged the body back, discovering Pierson's beloved Colt .45, brought from home, buried beneath him. He slipped it into his trousers, and later shared the discovery with Art; they swore themselves to secrecy, making a pact of its ultimate ownership. Their mutual appreciation of the weapon—an unarticulated respect for it as a symbol of both lost innocence, and of manhood finally achieved—cemented the friendship forever.

A lull in the blasting and Arthur stumbled slightly, sheepishly; Frank ran ahead, grinning, yelling back that if Arthur got that promotion he'd be goddamned, fighting like an old lady, and if they both walked off this goddamn island, Arthur owed him a hell of a lot more than one beer, when the dunes lit up again and half of Frank's head was blown away, just as he was dropping to the damp sand. Against a direct order from his sergeant, Arthur threw himself forward to grab hold of Frank's body and drag him back; Arthur was hit in the side, a graupel of bullets shattering his hip. Not even a goddamn goodbye.

Arthur exited the war to spend August and September in a Marine hospital with pins in his hip and tubes in his veins. He received an honorable discharge and a Purple Heart, but what meant most to him—gave him the most pride, and the most despair—was having disobeyed the order to try to help his buddy. This time, at least he'd tried. Also the Colt .45, nicked by a Japanese bullet, which he'd taken, weeping, from Frank's things and kept for himself, swearing he wasn't ever going to cry again. No, nor give anyone else up, let anybody leave him; he'd lost too many people already.

The three-day battle for Saipan eventually lasted over a month, resulting in 3,400 American and 27,000 Japanese casualties. In the end Saipan was taken, and U.S. troops would turn next to Guam.

Vivian arrived home late from Douglas one day after an unexpected meeting with her supervisor, breathless with news for her parents to hang on the icebox; she found a telegram already taped there, waiting for her—Arthur was wounded, but all right, and would be coming home in September. She said nothing to her parents about the meeting or what her supervisor had discussed with her, but only how thrilled she was, how lucky, and told Stella and Jerry their father was coming home. Jerry, at four, barely remembered Arthur in the flesh but was in love with his photograph, his handsome father in uniform. Stella insisted on having a new dress, not something made by Grandma. Douglas was beginning the slow layoff of women workers as the war wound down; the women were sincerely thanked and told they could go home now, back to their normal lives, to real life. Vivian put away the University of California catalogs, and used her final paycheck to buy new clothes for herself and the children to wear the day of the homecoming, the day of return to their normal lives. When Arthur exited the train at Union Station, honorable and proud, with a soon-to-fade limp, she burst into tears and couldn't stop crying, finally pulling away from his embrace to let him hug his children.

They spent the holidays quietly, relearning normal life with a tiny Christmas tree and Sylvia's glowing menorah, listening to the war wrap up on the radio; Arthur went daily to the VA hospital for physical therapy and came home to practice his exercises with Vivian's help. He was told not to rush his recovery, and didn't; it was soothing to be a wounded soldier at home, with his children loving him and Vivian reading to him at night, with Sylvia's wonderful food and Harry's respectful listening to stories of war. He allowed himself this brief retreat to childhood, well earned and never had, knowing it was just a respite. Vivian went about with cheery smiles, focusing completely on getting Arthur well, feeling bloated and sick inside and trying to tell herself it was merely the rich meals Sylvia made in ongoing celebration. She realized she was pregnant in April, the day it was announced Roosevelt had died of a cerebral hemorrhage; again, she couldn't stop crying. But Sylvia and Harry were crying, too—hanging black cloth over mirrors and arguing whether or not Roosevelt had really sold out the Jews—while Arthur tried telling everyone it was time, he'd sold out the whole country long ago; the nation was entering a new era and needed new leadership. Vivian excused herself to go throw up, and thought longingly of a medicine to take; perhaps an ancient remedy was growing in Sylvia's Victory Garden, dried herbs, something violently purgative, to rid her of this. Then she thought of Sylvia's bright knitting needles, right there in that basket, stabbed into balls of yarn. But she'd heard the stories, about blood and punctured, screaming women; she couldn't do it. She was too far gone anyway, almost four months. Her wedding band was even feeling tighter, closing in on her finger; she thought she should probably take it off now, while she could, before it got stuck. And she'd have to explain that to Arthur; he'd certainly spot its absence, the white, unsunned skin ring it would leave on her finger. No, she had no choice; she told Arthur the happy news.

It thrilled him, galvanized him; a new baby, an increase in his family, one more person added to his life, and all his. He decided he was whole again, ready for full, normal life—ashamed, really, for lying around like a bum, better damn well get out there and find a job before the country was flooded with returning men looking for work. An ad at the post office caught his eye; a government job, good salary, benefits, needing skilled and dedicated men, willing to train. He took the civil service exam and passed with high marks, then took the train to San Francisco for an interview, without giving Vivian any real details—no point in getting her hopes up. They grabbed him fast, a fine, college-educated man, with army service and actual experience, of a kind, in security. If they noticed the slight limp, the catch in his wounded hip, they said nothing: this is a fine man, a soldier ready to die in service to the country. Many of their best men had gone to war, and they were understaffed. He telephoned Vivian and informed her of the good news: he was gainfully employed, at $2,040 a year, provisionally upon completion of a training service by the Bureau of Prisons, as a correctional officer at the U.S. Federal Penitentiary, Alcatraz, California.

She threw up again, sold the Plymouth and bought a Chrysler Windsor station wagon, packed up the children, kissed her parents goodbye, and followed him north to live on a rocky and unswimmable island without beaches at the entrance to the San Francisco Bay. Arthur sailed through his training and with his first paycheck bought Vivian a brand-new Icy Heart refrigerator and a Hotpoint range; they ordered furniture and home accessories delivered by ferry across the Bay from San Francisco department stores for their new home, their first real home. Soon the bombs fell on Hiroshima and Nagasaki, and for all intents and purposes the war was over. A month later their third child, Olivia, was born. Arthur, feeling his family safe and secure and fortressed, congratulated himself again on his foresight, proud of getting, finally, what he'd always wanted, to where he'd always wanted to be.

# Man of the House

## *Arthur*

A black horse looks shinier than a white one. Even when it's an imaginary horse; ten-year-old Artie Thornton and his buddy Jerry, despite an agreement to trade off, always started out with an argument over who got to be the Robber, the Outlaw, the Indian, even the Pirate, which didn't really require a horse at all, even an imagined one. It didn't matter; the Bad Guy had more fun, and his horse was cleverer, swifter, sleek. And although rules dictated Death at the hands of the Good Guy, the Bad Guy got a more spectacular end: blood spurting, and gurglings, and last-minute clutchings at gun or bow and arrow to take out one more Good Guy, one more You're Comin' with Me, Pal, BANG, on the way out. Yeah, Bad Guys rode the shiny black horses; white horses were for princes in sappy fairy tales girls read, yeah, real *fairies,* those guys!

They played mostly at Jerry's house, which faced a big dirt lot yielding wonderful pieces of greenish broken glass and scrap metal, or at Artie's house when Essie was at work. She didn't allow them to play their favorite games, at all; at one time she accepted that her jurisdiction ended at the front door and what they did on the streets, well, boys will be boys, but since that cop brought Artie home she'd gotten a lot stricter. It wasn't a big deal, really; Artie and Jerry had gone into town, a Jerry Good Cop chasing an Artie Robber. The

Jerry Cop, bored with an uninspiring pursuit, had threatened the Artie Robber that unless he really did something—not holding up a pretend train or robbing a fake bank—he was giving up the chase and going home. Artie bit his lip, but in honorable outlaw fashion seized two apples from an outdoor stand and took off. Jerry pursued as promised, but both boys were overtaken by a real officer of the peace. Jerry, appleless, was released with a warning, and scampered off across the dirt lot toward home—no hard feelings, they had traded off fairly. Artie was marched to his front door, and Essie. She promised the police officer the boy would be appropriately punished; the officer, noting her stern face and frayed but boiled-clean apron, believed her. As soon as he left, Essie slapped Artie hard across the face, which hurt a lot more than being riddled with fake gunfire, and escorted him straight back to the fruit stand. There Artie apologized for his thievery and made good the cost of the apples, with his own pennies painstakingly earned cleaning out chicken guts at the local poultry farm. Not a spectacular end at all.

Essie had taken Arthur to live with her in 1915, when he was just over a year old. That autumn harvest his mother Claire had tied the little boy to a nearby tree to keep him safe, and joined her husband Horst in the fields; one of their two farm hands was down with measles, and they could only afford the rental of a steam-powered threshing machine for two days. Horst and the other farm hand steadied the belts attached to the pulleys of the thresher, which relentlessly spun its axle; Claire began feeding in armloads of wheat, as row after row of curved metal rods pulled the stalks in, to be whirled and shook and separated from the grain. She glanced back, briefly, to check on Arthur, and the sleeve of her calico dress caught on one of the pointed rods; the men didn't hear her first screams over the steam engine's churn. Horst finally spotted her kicking feet and raced over, screaming himself; Claire was being slashed apart, the curving rods like a giant tiger's claws, and Horst, reaching in to pull her out, was caught across the neck and back; his spine was severed just as his throat was ripped open. He died instantly, but Claire had to bleed a while longer, her blood dripping into the thresher to mix with the harvested grain. Little Arthur, his throat hoarse from crying, was eventually untied and handed over to the care of a spinster cousin, related through some undetermined lineage. Estelle couldn't take on the farm as well; it was sold for not much, and the money, in accordance with Claire and Horst's instructions, was set aside for the boy's keep and education. Essie took the boy to live with her on the outer edge of Chicago. She hired out as a maid, and arranged with her employers to bring the child with her every day; she was a hard and cheerful worker, and they were willing to oblige.

When Arthur started school she got up at 4:30 to set breakfast out for him before her five-mile walk to work. He awoke later in the still-dark morning to find cooling oatmeal or a rare egg left for him on the table, with a clean and starched shirt for the day. He ate and dressed himself, then met up with his buddy Jerry for the walk to school. Afternoons Artie went to the rich house on the shaded street where Essie would be preparing a fried chicken dinner for her employers, who didn't begrudge her scraps for her own table. While Essie cooked and cleaned she helped Arthur with his homework, checking answers she knew were right or wrong thanks to her own fifth-grade education. He told her how smart she was, as smart as his teachers; she'd grin, and hug him, and say too bad her looks weren't as smart as her head, she'd have gone a lot farther. But Arthur thought she was beautiful, anyway—weren't horses beautiful? By the time he was nine, however, his education exceeded hers and she stopped helping him with math and spelling and history; instead, she read aloud at night, from precious books given or loaned by her employers. Arthur spent less time on homework now, anyway, for he felt it was time he worked after school to contribute to the household; donated scrap meat was shameful, it was only right they should buy their own when they could—even if he brought home only the dried bacon end, or a fatty piece of shank, which Essie would insist he eat himself, a growing boy, really, she'd been snacking all day, why, she was getting fat! He pressured her to make soups and stews, then, for dinner, and dropped the meat in the pot when she wasn't looking. Early mornings he fed and watered the sheep and pigs in his neighbor's small pens, then delivered papers and ran errands for small grocers on the outskirts of town; after school and weekends he chopped at cords of wood and did gardening for young widows and aging parents, all of whom had lost their men in World War I and needed a boy about the place now and then. It left little time for running around with Jerry, but he had a responsibility; after all, he was the man of the house.

After his humiliating slap from Essie, whom he loved, he burst into tears and bitterly whined that she couldn't treat the man of the house like that. She grinned again and told him when he stopped crying, when he was *really* a man, he could be king of the castle and tell her what to do; until then, he wasn't going to shame her and he wasn't going to ruin his own future. She knew right from wrong and would beat it into his head if she had to. He waited glumly to be old enough to be really a man, but just after his sixteenth birthday Essie died of a tumor that killed her quickly, eating through her empty stomach in just a few weeks. He buried her next to his parents, now finally the man of the house, but with no home.

By 1929 Chicago was famous for its urban gangs of racketeers and extortionists, its "Shotgun Man" serial killer and child cannibal, its Saint Valentine's Day Massacre and Public

Enemies. The Crash and the dive into the Depression made for increased opportunity, and more business; the mythic mobsters needed a vacation now and then, or a getaway, and drove across state lines in their shiny black cars to wooded Wisconsin resorts in Rhinelander, Eagle River, or the Wisconsin Dells. The summer before starting at the University of Chicago, Arthur and his buddy Jerry lucked into jobs at a lodge near the Dells, thanks to the influence of Essie's old employers, who remembered the clean and well-mannered little boy favorably. They knew they were lucky; it was the peak of season, work was hard to get, and even small tips would go a long way toward Arthur's first year of college; Jerry was just going along for the ride, but both of them had high hopes for spotting a hiding-out gangster, maybe a famous one. Dillinger's there, huh? Nah, he's in jail. I think. Maybe Capone'll make it up. You're dreamin', he wouldn't waste his time in some joint out here! Anyway, they just nabbed him, something about taxes. Nah, we'll maybe see Nelson, or Pretty Boy Floyd. Floyd! Ah, you don't know nothing! He's in Ohio. Or Oklahoma, I think. You hear about that Kelly guy? Machine Gun Kelly? Yeah, I saw his picture. I want a hat like that, pretty slick, huh? Hey, what about the Barker Gang? Yeah, maybe . . .

The reality was twelve-hour days on kitchen duty, in the laundry—Geez, Artie, this is for girls!—cleaning up and carrying bags for tourists from Milwaukee and Madison and St. Paul who'd saved all year for this trip to the wilderness and had little to spare for tips to two able-bodied boys who were getting a free stay in the place, anyway. They snuck out to the dark river at night with bottles of near beer filched from the kitchen, having tried and failed to lure the few girls working as maids and waitresses to join them. No luck there; the girls weren't having any. Jerry and Artie dismissed them as stupid backwoods gash, anyway, their bleached hair and sweaty cotton dresses; Jerry liked the Garbo type, mysterious, and Artie wanted a serious, smart girl, like Essie, yeah, but better looking for sure, she was horsey as hell, but a good gal. No, a girl like Norma Shearer, maybe, who'd be working in a dive like this to save her money for the future, to build a home and have a family, not just to blow it on crummy jewelry. A girl worth taking care of, treating well.

The thrill they were waiting for did come at the summer's end, when the resort owner, Mr. Wallace, called the staff together to tell them he'd gotten a phone call, a *mysterious* phone call, from a fellow who sounded pretty big, *very* big, in fact, coming sometime soon, looking for some peace and quiet. You get that, everyone, peace and quiet for this fellow and his pals! Everyone got excited, speculating, and took turns sneaking out at night to wait for the car, which, of course, would arrive in the dead of night, with Mr. Big probably seated in the back, maybe even behind a curtain, drinking real champagne from France. Artie and Jerry hid out every night, far down the road from the resort, and were rewarded by the sight of a long, black roadster zooming through the woods, sleeker than any car they'd seen, obviously not your regular tourist's car belonging to some family from Madison or St. Paul. It cruised past, raising dust, and the boys ran into the road after it, hoping the license plate would help determine the owner. They got to arguing again over whether or not Pretty Boy Floyd would drive all the way over from Ohio just to hide out at this crummy place, and failed to see the second roadster coming up the dark, unlit road; the driver honked as it made the turn, and Jerry shoved Artie out of the way just in time, but was himself struck. He bounced up and smashed into the car's front window, shattering the glass, and the car screeched backward, throwing Jerry free from the dashboard. His body sailed forward and landed on the ground; one leg was crushed under the car's tires as the car spun around with a squeal and took off, back down the road, still honking the horn. Another screech as the first car spun a circle and headed back, too, at the sounds of trouble; more dust flew into Arthur's face, where he still staggered alone at the side of the road, and coated the dead body trickling out its blood on the ground. A man's fat hand threw a wad of bills out the window as both cars drove off, shiny and dark as the river at night, as black horses gleaming in the sun.

# Patriotism

## *The Prison*

San Francisco's first air-raid alert was the night of December 9, 1941; much of the city remained stubbornly aglow, however, especially the gleaming prison in the dark Bay, flashing lights like a diamond on black velvet. Alcatraz' strategic position as front porch to the City was again a concern to military officials, who chastised Warden Johnston for his lack of compliance. Johnston cited prison security—they couldn't tell him how to run his prison—but eventually gave in, and the island inked itself out for subsequent drills in readiness against Japanese attack. The job of air-raid warden was created to make sure the lights went off; if bombs were coming, he would alert and direct officers and their families to the air-raid shelter in the basement of 64 Building, the largest residential complex, built to guard the dock in the days of the "Disciplinary Barracks." No air-raid preparations were made for convicts; they could squirm under their bunks, and scream all they liked. The basement segregation cells were now out of use, otherwise especially nervous inmates might have acted up in order to spend the war down there, tucked away in the safety of the building's bowels.

For the first time, however, the convicts were allowed news of the outside world; Johnston saw to it the peaks and valleys of the war were posted to encourage a vicarious patriotism, and a spirit of sharing and sacrifice. Several officers had left to fight in the war, and many inmates wanted to enlist, fevered for freedom or fighting; Johnston considered it, especially for men shortly due for release or with naval experience, but the Bureau of Prisons rejected the idea. Other inmates nurtured the hope of Japanese invasion; surely San Francisco was a desirable chess piece, and, as officially deemed antisocial Americans, the inmates would be liberated to join the fight against the United States. But not even the arrival of a few U-boat Nazis, seized by the Coast Guard off the coast of Florida, stirred vengeful patriotism or traitorous anarchy; the men weren't kept that well informed, and the Japanese were an enemy right next door, not some foreign Huns rampaging in countries far off in Europe. The Nazis only stayed a little while, anyway.

Alcatraz' real war effort was its industry; its manufacturing shops won government contracts to produce uniforms, brushes, and rubber goods, to repair harbor buoys and cargo nets. Inmates working in industry shops would at last receive time for good behavior, and wages ranging from four cents to twelve cents an hour, depending on the four grades of service. Johnston instituted payment "to stimulate, encourage, and reward industrious and cooperative inmates," and workers had to sign a contract which allowed a percentage of their earnings to be sent home to their dependents.

The most impressive of feats was the massive laundry—an odd and expensive undertaking considering the island had not one drop of its own water—which serviced inmates, island employees, federal agencies, and Army and Navy posts for the entire Bay area. Roughly one-fourth of the prison population were employed, processing over 150,000 pounds of laundry each month. There was an instance here of prisoners fighting for their country; in March of 1942 several inmates patriotically attacked a fellow worker who suggested a laundry slowdown.

A job description for Laundry Assistant Foreman read:

> Inmates are rewarded for good work by promotion, good reports to the classification committee, and a verbal "pat on the back."
>
> This latter is very effective and can often change a prisoner's entire outlook on life.

But Alcatraz was still Alcatraz, and a pat on the back is not freedom. John Bayless, doing twenty-five years for bank robbery, jumped into the Bay while on garbage duty in September 1941. The water was colder than he'd expected; he turned around after a few feet and swam back, to wait onshore for guards to come and get him.

In April 1943, Harold Brest, James Boarman, Fred Hunter, and Floyd Hamilton, together serving seventy-five years plus life for bank and postal robberies and kidnapping, took three guards hostage in an industries shop, tied them up, broke a window, and made their way to the water. The alarm sounded, and the men were fired on in the Bay. Boarman was hit in the head; Brest, holding him up, let go to climb into the officers' launch, and Boarman's body disappeared in the water. Hunter was found freezing and deflated in a cave at the water's edge. Hamilton, once Public Enemy Number 1, and a hanger-on to Clyde Barrow and Bonnie Parker, was assumed drowned and declared dead along with Boarman. He was found two days later; he had clung just underwater to a small cluster of rocks—Little Alcatraz—off the northwestern tip of the island, and finally crawled back onshore and into the broken window of the industries shop for shelter and warmth and sleep.

Four months later "Ted" Huron Walters strolled away from the overstaffed and under-guarded prison laundry, climbed a fence, and dropped down thirty feet onto shoreline rocks. Hurt and frightened, he tied cans around his waist for buoyancy, and dipped a toe in the water; too damn cold. He waited patiently for alerted officers to climb down the cliff and take him home, back to the steam heat and neighborhood of the cellhouse.

Even before the war's official end, Alcatraz' patriotism was spent; the mat shop and glove shop and brush shop slowed to medium hum, the laundry and tailor shops slowly emptied of uniforms. Even the escape attempt of John Giles was a quiet, domestic affair, involving merely the personal and intimate act of a change of clothing; Giles had served eight of his twenty-five years for postal robbery as a dock worker while gradually secreting away, piece by piece, an entire army uniform. On July 31, 1945, he put on the uniform and strolled onto the army launch on its way from Fort Mason to Angel Island; the Associate Warden sped to Angel Island on a prison launch and was waiting to greet Giles on his arrival. Giles was quietly escorted to the Hole, where he would hear nothing, less than a week later, of the atomic bombs and the war's end. It would have made little difference to him, anyway.

The war was over and peace returned to the rhythm of bells, inmate counts, line-ups, marches out, all in smooth rotation, everyone going about their measured time. Officials relaxed; existence was justified—existence of their own function, and that of the concrete buildings and steel bars and catwalks and barbed wire. It was harder to find a justification, a reason to continue, for those being rotated, the human cogs. For inmates, the rhythm was a closed circle, not a crescendo; it built up to nothing, but tightened in on itself, winding tighter, building only tension.

# Mutiny

ALCATRAZ TEENS CLUB is our newest island must-do! Meetings for islanders 13–19 will be once a week, dues 25 cents! Come on, Boys and Girls, have a hand in planning fun activities and events!

CARD PLAYERS don't forget: Alcatraz Pinochle Club is switching to Thursdays in the Social Hall! 7 P.M.

WELCOME to the newest Alcatraz family member: Olivia Claire Thornton, born September 7! Olivia belongs to our recently arrived Officer Arthur Thornton and his lovely wife Vivian, who already have Stella, 7, and Jerry, 5. Congratulations!

*The Pelican,*
Alcatraz newsletter, October 1945

## *Vivian*

She was getting her body back, finally, she thought. Eight months it's been, since Olivia was born. It had taken longer this time to feel her body was hers again, private, that bones and skin and organs were back in place serving and supporting her, not the child she was carrying. That she was herself, not a vehicle, not a filling-up shell. Her waist was almost as slim as before, her cello curve that Art loved, sleeping with his hand tucked in its curl above her hip. Her stomach was taut again, almost taut, just fine, it's good enough. The gray suit, I think, the Lily Ann, the one I haven't worn since last fall. The smart one.

They'd arrived on Alcatraz while Vivian was barely five months pregnant and still able to wear the loosest of her regular clothes, thank heavens, as she had few things ready. After Jerry was born she'd packed the maternity wear that carried her through the first two pregnancies—those tent blouses with Peter Pan collars, those frilly, flowered dresses that turned her into an enormous, pregnant, baby doll—and given them away before leaving Chicago, sure they would never again be needed. Her mother had raced to stitch warm smocks together for her, but the first weeks on Alcatraz she made do with her Brentwood wardrobe: tailored, elegant, linen dresses and thin wool suits with clean, adult lines. She shivered in their drafty apartment overlooking the dock, feeling uncomfortable and queasy in the fishy island air.

Arthur was mostly gone those same weeks for his correctional officer training; he was learning boxing, jujitsu, wrestling, the use of firearms and gas; he learned the workings of Alcatraz, the layout of the cellhouse, the metal detectors, and the six guard towers; rules and regulations dealing with contraband, how to handle locks and keys, how to shake down cells. He came home late at night after the children were asleep to share it all with her, invigorated by the daily challenges. No, she didn't have to worry about him around all those dangerous cons; guards on the cellhouse floor aren't even armed, see, so we can't have weapons taken away and used against us. Safer that way. That's what the gun galleries are for, us watching them from big cages up against the walls, out of reach—now, in there we get tear gas, a .30-caliber rifle, and a .45 revolver, just like on tower duty, except tower guards get a Thompson submachine gun, too. Oh, and a gas billy, see, that's a club with tear gas inside. Warden Johnston, a helluva guy, really knows what he's doing, really takes an interest in his men, guards and cons alike. You know he interviews every one of those cons personally, learns their whole history, everything about what makes a con tick. Did Vivian ever hear about "color psychology"? Johnston had the cells painted in different colors, see, like green at the bottom, then grey to about six feet, then white; he's always experimenting, it lessens the monotony, easier on the eye, makes the cells look larger. Humane. Hey, I got a look at Robert Stroud, remember that con who had all the canaries at Leavenworth? Supposed to be brilliant guy, wrote a couple of books about bird care. Still psycho, though. He says the public demanded his release, they were gonna let him go, yeah, sure, until the war. Now he says he's a prisoner of war . . . the guy killed two men! One of 'em was a guard somewhere! Anyway, he's in Solitary for life. The other fellows here, the guards, they're good joes, men doing a helluva tough job. Did I tell you we have one guard to every three cons here? Most places it's one to ten. And Johnston handpicked most of these guys, all specially trained, if it weren't for the war I might never have even got this job. Important work, it's damned prestigious, that's what they all tell me. Jesus, we're lucky. Hey, there's sort of a party for us, a welcome to the Rock. Next Friday, at the Officer's Club. Did I tell you, there's even a bowling alley there! You'll be up for it, won't you honey? How're you feeling tonight? How's this, let me get you a glass of water, and another blanket, you just lie there and relax . . .

The other officers' wives had thought her very sophisticated, at that first gathering welcoming her and Art. She'd worn her gray suit, her blond hair loose with a slight prewar Veronica Lake dip, and the other officers had appraised her stealthily from their groupings at the bar. The wives gathered around her like a fence, appraising openly and with approval, knowing her advancing pregnancy would soon maternalize, de-sex her, and warmly declared her terribly smart. She thought over what she'd been saying before realizing they meant her appearance. Since then she'd taken pains to live up to this idea, this new way of being smart, difficult to maintain during a nauseating pregnancy wrapped in homemade flannel smocks. It was important to be smart, still, it was worth working at. Arthur was so proud of her. And it was much easier after she'd had the baby, after they'd moved to one of the little cottages on the parade ground that faced more sun. Her pumps were not smart: old, low-heeled, pregnancy-sensible. She needed new shoes.

Today she would buy new ones, smart ones. Today she would go shopping in the City. She liked this island life, being surrounded by water, no swimming, though, unfortunately, but it was time for a bigger piece of land under her, even for a small space of time. The ferry came and went across the Bay, taking convicts with court dates and school-age children supervised by working or shopping mothers to the mainland, but Vivian had not made that ferry trip since coming home from Saint Francis Memorial with Olivia last autumn; infected stitches and an entire winter's drear had kept her home with the baby, watching the infant wriggle become a crawl, the gassy smiles turn to chuckles. Dr. Yocum came down from the prison to check on her and the baby, and other wives had visited from time to time, friendly, full of advice and hints about living on the island, charming stories about watermelon parties on the dock and formal dances in the Social Hall. And clubs to join, our own post office over in 64 Building, the little island store. Just a regular neighborhood, like any other. But no one here, really, to talk to; even dear Mary Beth, Officer Shotz's wife, always coming over to help out, but well, she's practically Sylvia's age. So Vivian talked to Olivia mostly, singing her silly songs, narrating life: Well, let's go in the kitchen now, sweetheart, and start

Daddy's dinner . . . so, here we are diapering you . . . look, Olivia, seagulls, what sound do they make? *Squawk, squawk, squawk. . . .* Maybe they should try to buy one of those television sets, she saw an article about them in the paper. Appliances here are tricky, though, something about the power plant generating the wrong electrical currents. Why, Mary Beth blew her toaster out! Arthur tried explaining it to me, all about AC to DC, I suppose I wasn't really paying attention. But a television would almost be like having other people in the house, at least the sight and sound of them. So quiet out here on the island, silent much of the time. No cars or traffic, no urban flow of noise. Silent except for the seagulls, or children on the parade ground in the late afternoon, or sometimes the sound of gunfire from officers on target practice. Once in a while the drifting sounds from the City, from people laughing or dancing at the yacht clubs.

Well, today was the big day, she'd planned it for weeks— Art was off for an eight-hour shift on Tower duty; dear Mary Beth, who worked mornings as a stenographer at a real-estate office in the City, would pick up Jerry from kindergarten and Stella coming from second grade, and entertain them at Playland in Aquatic Park until 3:00. Vivian was to meet them at Fort Mason at 3:30. for the ferry home, all of them together going home after their loud, busy Day in the City.

She dressed Olivia first, in the bright yellow jumpsuit knit by Sylvia with her bright needles, so that Olivia would be smart, too, and settled her in the fancy new stroller Art had bought, which so far had only rolled back and forth across the parade ground. Then she dressed herself for this day, her day in the City to buy shoes and whatever else, thanks to a generous wad from Art tucked in her purse. A City day to spend craning her neck at tall buildings, watching other smart women stride nattily across pavement in clicking high heels and little hats, maybe eat a hot dog from a corner stand, maybe chat with salesgirls, ride a cable car.

First a pair of silk step-ins, not new but pristine, unstained by any embarrassing smears. She washed her underwear herself in the bathroom sink, scrubbing the sometime maroon stains, waiting till Art had gone to work, never leaving them in the basket to go up to the prison laundry; Arthur had intimated soon after they'd arrived that this would be indelicate, convicts handling her underthings. Oh, that reminds me, I have to save that brown paper from yesterday's laundry delivery, Jerry wants it for a kite.

A brassiere that finally fit, now that her breasts were back to normal, free of fluid, ornamental. She'd hated using the breast pump, feeling like a cow at milking time, but it relieved the pressure on her swollen breasts, hastened the end of those creamy leaks on good linen blouses. She often thought it must be easier to nurse, that somehow this artificial milking was contrary to something. At Saint Francis during her twenty-minute shift with Olivia, she'd held the baby, this baby she hadn't wanted and thought of stabbing away, who'd gone from a grain of sand inside her to this pearl, and felt a swelling of emotion that caught her by surprise, a happiness and relief to have her; at that moment she felt her breasts swell, too, as if reaching, wanting to link her to this child. Olivia. Arthur had wanted to call the baby Frank if it were a boy, for his Old Army Buddy, but it was a girl, and Vivian's turn; she chose Olivia, for no one, just liking the sound of it. The nun-nurse left the room; Vivian tugged open the neckline of her nightgown, eyes on the door, and cuddled the baby against her left breast, her heart. Her nipple grazed Olivia's right cheek; the baby turned instinctively, her little lips mouthing the air like a guppy, searching. Vivian glanced around furtively, sweating, feeling this was an inappropriate act, and guided her nipple to the baby's mouth. Olivia clamped down on it with an unbabylike force that made her gasp, and began to suck. Vivian felt the milk leaving her, drawn out in a tugging, lulling wave, feeding this baby who rested a tiny hand on the side of her breast as if holding on. She felt an ache in her breast and an ache between her legs deeper than the twinge of stitches. The intensity shook her. She closed her eyes, smelling the sweetness of the baby's warm head, her own fresh sweat, the smell of her own warm milk spilling gently from the corners of Olivia's mouth, and felt the waves flow between her and her child. The nurse came in, with a nurse's bustling crispness, bearing sterile gauze and alcohol, and caught her.

"Now, Mrs. Thornton, you don't want to do that, dear. That'll throw the whole feeding schedule off, won't it? Best to keep her on a steady schedule, *that's* what'll keep her from colic, you know. Formula's special made for that. You've had two others, haven't you?"

And pulled the baby gently away from Vivian's breast, wiping off her foamy lips with a piece of gauze, mumbling about germs and the overused, hanging breasts of native women in *National Geographic,* about good sterile rubber nipples. She removed the baby to the nursery, glancing back at Vivian with faint disapproval, leaving her feeling guilty, selfish, and vaguely dirty.

No, of course the nurse was right; her breasts went neatly and without stretch marks into her best, pre-baby brassiere, and Olivia was a healthy baby, following the formula, chubby like the cherubs on boxes of laundry detergent. The magazines were clear on this; don't let having a baby ruin your figure, take away your attractiveness, there's no excuse for that; keep yourself tight and trim. Brassiere fastened, strapped on, followed by garter belt and nylons, smooth, unrun and innovative nylons, she hated them, really, sticking to her legs like leeches. Half-slip, silk blouse, the slim skirt to the suit—still a little tight, but for the day, this day, she'll manage. Suit jacket: wide shoulders, tiny, nipped waist, a diagonal slash of buttons across the chest, soft gray wool. There, tight and trim. She looked in the mirror, appraising; thirty-one years old, married almost ten years, three children, but still good. Still smart. The blond hair, too long for fashion now (but Art loves it like this), went up in a twist; small pearl earrings, small hat, small gloves. Extra diapers? Yes, and an extra bottle of formula, better take another sweater for her, too, and the wonderful new book by Dr. Spock, tucked away in the large talcum-and-vomit bag of baby things, that stored in back of the stroller. She tied the matching yellow bonnet on Olivia's head while the baby chuckled at her and grabbed a finger in her mouth, gnawing with her two teeth, her little sharp porcelain chips. Good for the baby, too, to get out, see something of the City. Socks for Arthur, don't forget. Vivian maneuvered the stroller to the door, its new wheels still stiff, tucked keys in purse, purse under her arm, and, humming, left the house.

It was Thursday, May 2, 1946, a little after 9:00 A.M.

## *THE BATTLE*

Just past 1:30 in the afternoon Bernard Coy, doing time for a Kentucky bank robbery, was enjoying the relative freedom of a prison housekeeping job: passing a mop over the satiny floor of Broadway, the central aisle between B and C Blocks. On this day, Thursday, May 2, 1946, Coy mopped as usual, his chambray prison clothing a little looser on him than in weeks past, glancing often up at the gun gallery above his head that ran the north lateral length of the cellhouse; from here Officer Dean Burch observed A, B, and C Blocks, moving from time to time on precise schedule through the heavy door leading to the gun gallery of D Block. Officer Burch was the only armed officer in the cellhouse, out of reach of convicts, but he served another crucial function: keeper of Key 107, which opened the steel door leading from the main cellhouse to the Recreation Yard and industry shops. He had already lowered the key on a cord down to the cellhouse guard, Officer William Miller, who unlocked the steel door and sent inmates on their way for afternoon work details. Officer Miller had then returned to his desk beneath the gun gallery in Times Square, the space at the end of Broadway near the snitchbox to the dining hall—but without sending the key back up on its cord to the unreachable heights and safety of the gun gallery. Today he slipped it, unseen, into his pants pocket. Inexplicably, without thinking, perhaps with the most casual thought of returning it later up to Officer Burch. Later, he never had time to explain the why of it properly, this breach of policy. For now he went back to work at his desk, paying little attention to Coy.

Marvin Hubbard had filed a writ of habeas corpus on March 15, claiming that during his arrest in Chattanooga—for kidnapping a cop, stealing his guns, and driving the car across state lines—the FBI had beaten his confession out of him. There was medical evidence from a Chattanooga hospital to support this. He was due for a hearing in four days, on Monday, May 6, 1946; today he lingered on kitchen duty in the dining hall. Hidden against his body was a carving knife.

Coy watched as Officer Burch in the gun gallery left to check on a disturbance in D Block, then signaled Hubbard through the glass window of the dining-hall door; Hubbard knocked on the door, and Officer Miller allowed him to enter the cellhouse, closing the dining-hall door behind him. The officer prepared to search Hubbard when Coy attacked him from behind, pinning his arms; Hubbard threw punches until Officer Miller was unconscious. Coy used the officer's key ring to open empty cell 403 in C Block, then locked him in the cell. Hubbard put on the officer's coat and cap, and took up his place at the desk while Coy opened other cells in C and B Blocks, releasing Clarence Carnes, Miran Thompson, and Joe Cretzer, all of whom took up posts as lookouts. Cretzer and another Alcatraz inmate, Sam Shockley, had already tried escape in 1941; they'd joined two other men working in the mat shop, attacked and tied up three guards, then worked over an hour to cut through the window bars. Cretzer was well known by then as a violent man—his long record of violence had increased exponentially from crime to crime—yet they were all peacefully persuaded out of the attempt by one of their overpowered hostages, Officer Paul Madigan, later Warden. They untied the officers and were placed without struggle in Solitary. Five more years here would make a difference.

Coy stripped down and greased up his bony body with kitchen lard, a body he had systematically starved over several months' time. Hubbard hoisted him up the twelve feet to the caged gun gallery; Coy climbed to its curved, barred top, spread the bars with a homemade bar spreader made from brass toilet fittings, and painfully, painstakingly, squeezed himself through. Officer Burch returned to the gun gallery from his duties in D Block; Coy dropped down on him from above the door. They fought. Coy finally managed to choke Officer Burch with his necktie, leaving him unconscious, and tied him up with the cord used to lower Key 107 down to the cellhouse officer. He dropped Officer Burch's revolver down to Hubbard along with ammunition, and entered the D Block gun gallery carrying Officer Burch's rifle. He pointed the rifle at unarmed Officer Thomas Corwin patrolling the floor, and ordered him to open the door from D Block to the main cellhouse; on entering, Officer Corwin was grabbed by Thompson and Cretzer, and locked in cell 403 with Officer Miller. Officer Miller, regaining consciousness, told Officer Corwin that Key 107, the key to outside, was in his pants pocket; they hid the key down the cell toilet.

Other inmates began yelling, wanting to be released. Coy opened cell doors in D Block, releasing other inmates; Sam Shockley—"Crazy" Sam, I.Q. in the mid-sixties, a hearer of voices, a witness to hallucinations—came barreling out, overexcited, followed more cautiously by others. Most, including Robert Stroud in his second-tier cell, stayed put, wary of getting involved.

Coy and Cretzer's first goal was releasing a friend, Whitey Franklin, locked in the Hole for smashing Officer Cline's skull with a hammer in the 1938 attempt. Thus their first failure was the realization that no key in their possession would open the barred inner door to the cell, and attempting to do so electronically would set off an alarm in the Armory. Whitey wasn't worth the risk. They apologized to him, and moved on to their next goal: pick off the Tower guards, obtain their weapons, get over the wall in the Recreation Yard, down to the dock, and seize a boat, seize their freedom.

They had the rifle, the revolver, the carving knife, a few clubs, and the key ring from Officer Miller. They gathered at the locked door to the Recreation Yard, one lock away from freedom. No key on Officer Miller's ring would open the door. There was no key on the cord still restraining Officer Burch in the gun gallery. There was no key. They decided that Officer Miller must have it; Coy, Cretzer, and the others dragged him from cell 403 and demanded the key. Officer Miller insisted it had been returned to Officer Burch in the gun gallery. Infuriated, the inmates kicked and beat Officer

Miller until he was again unconscious, and dumped him back in the cell. Cretzer, the tension building, began screaming in frustration that Frisco was as far away as ever.

They increased their hostages; one by one, steward Robert Bristow, Officer Ernest Lageson, and Officer Joseph Burdette from the kitchen entered the cellhouse on routine business, were captured, and placed in cell 402 with Officers Corwin and Miller while the inmates continued searching cell 403 for the key.

Officer Edward Stucker sent several inmates from the basement clothing room up the Recreation Yard stairs to return to the cellhouse; they came back down, announcing there appeared to be no guard in the cellhouse to let them in. Officer Stucker checked for himself, was spotted by Cretzer, and hurried back down to the basement; locking himself in with the inmates, he telephoned the Armory guard, Officer Fish, explaining only that there was a racial disturbance in the cellhouse so as not to alert the suspicious inmates he'd trapped himself with.

Officers Weinhold, Simpson, Sundstrom, and Baker were dispatched to check on the trouble; they entered the cellhouse and one by one were taken hostage. Weinhold was placed in cell 403 with the others; Simpson, Sundstrom, and Baker were put in cell 402. Officer Fish in the Armory, hearing nothing back from his men, sent out a call to all posts. No reports of trouble. Still uncomfortable with the situation, he telephoned Associate Warden Edward Miller, who was below the Dock Tower on inspection, talking to the Dock Tower guard, Officer Jim Comerford.

Coy finally thought to check the toilet of cell 403, and found the missing Key 107. Brief elation, followed by despair; the lock on the door to the Recreation Yard was so mangled by their earlier attempts to force it open with wrong keys that the right key was useless. Furious, Coy broke through a window in the kitchen and fired at Officer Elmus Besk in the Hill Tower, hitting him in the leg. He shot next at Officer Irving Levinson in the Road Tower, who dropped to the ground, pretending to be hit. Officer Barker on the yard wall dropped to the ground when he heard the shots at Levinson; Coy, firing at him as well, believed him struck down. Inmates in the Recreation Yard scattered, ducking at the sound of gunfire, not knowing if they were targets, not knowing anything.

Coy and Cretzer fired through another window at Officer Comerford on the Dock Tower, who ducked from the shots. Associate Warden Miller hurried up to the cellhouse; he informed Officer Fish in the Armory to contact Warden Johnston, and, armed with a gas billy, entered the cellhouse alone. Inside he moved cautiously down Broadway, seeing nothing amiss. The inmates were quiet. Coy, dressed in an officer's uniform, appeared from the end of C Block, hiding his rifle behind him. Associate Warden Miller turned, recognized Coy, and raced for the exit as Coy opened fire; he accidentally set off the gas billy in his hand, which exploded in his face just as he arrived at the door to Administration, screaming for Officer Phillips on the other side to let him in.

Associate Warden Miller, face burnt, reported to Warden Johnston, that yes, there was in fact serious trouble in the cellhouse. The siren was sounded. It was 3:20 in the afternoon.

The inmates knew it was over. Cretzer began screaming at Coy again, screaming that their only chance now was ridding themselves of the hostages that could name them. Cretzer took the .45 automatic and approached cell 403; he pointed the gun at Officers Weinhold, Corwin, Miller, Lageson, Bristow, and Burdett and began to fire.

## *Vivian*

Two-thirty P.M. Union Square on a sunny afternoon is lovely; Vivian sat on a bench, idly watching passersby, feeding the pigeons, feeding the baby, drawing out the last moments of her day before the return to Fort Mason. What a gorgeous city this is, so vertical and jagged, exciting. Los Angeles so flat in comparison; oh, I have to come in to the City more. Olivia had been sweet, cooing on cue at salesgirls who'd eyed her apprehensively while Vivian fingered stockings and slips, then winning them over into wistful gurglings of their own. A good baby, cooperating with diaper changes in the ladies' lounge at Macy's, waiting to spit up until Vivian had a spare diaper over the shoulder of her gray suit, yes, she might have come into the City long before this! Even *Baby and Child Care* said so, her brand-new copy of it already tip-folded and heavily underlined, it's good to get a baby out. Finally, an expert I trust, that grandfatherly smile, sheer common sense! She tugged back Olivia's bonnet a little, letting the rare sun fall on her baby face. A beautiful May day; thank God it didn't rain today. The City felt festive, as if the war ended just yesterday, not almost a year ago. Women looked around at the men on the streets, many still in uniform, still dazed at having them back, giving them big, proud smiles whether they be the age of son, brother, father, or lover.

Thank God Art wasn't really hurt, she thought, checking through her shopping bags. Dark-blue argyle socks, he likes those. Yes, he came home with both legs, I'm grateful, so lucky! He's so happy here, loves his work, so full of purpose. Talks about Warden Johnston with such respect, sort of the father he never had, maybe, now that we don't see Dad very often. She examined again her day's other purchases: the new dress for Stella, who was starting to sniff at her grandmother's creations; a toy truck for Jerry, who really wanted a toy gun but wasn't allowed to have one on the island. He won't be happy, probably yell, but what can I do? Lunch at the drugstore counter, to compensate for the money spent elsewhere, most of the money Art had given her, but he won't mind, he's so generous. To compensate mostly for the money spent on herself, really, on the soft gray suede pumps on her feet. Oh, I know, impractical and silly, dangerous, actually, getting around on the island and its rough paths, the other wives wear flats mostly, but still. I'll have them forever, they go with the suit, I'll wear them when we come into the City, when Mary Beth watches the kids now that Olivia's not such an infant, and Art and I come in for dinner sometimes. Top of the Mark, maybe, for cocktails first, or the St. Francis Hotel, then Ernie's. Art in a suit, not a uniform, maybe Mom will make me something in black, a little black velvet cocktail dress . . . Olivia squirmed with her bottle, wanting the solid food she'd been working on the last few weeks. Vivian kissed the top of her head.

"Okay, sweetheart, we're going home soon. Just finish this for now, you already ate your carrots . . . we'll give you something more when we get home, big-girl food . . ." The dialogue with babies, explaining, soothing, reasoning, as Olivia babbled back.

Twenty of three. Vivian stood up, still holding the baby, considering. Easier to put the bags in the stroller and carry her, I think. The new shoes weren't that comfortable, the heels a little spiky, higher than she was used to. Should she slip her old ones back on? . . . No, I'll just walk a block or two, get out of the crowd, then find a taxi.

She headed up Powell, gazing in the windows at Saks, settling the baby better in her arms, gripping the handle of the stroller. Should've gotten the blue dress for Stell, the one with lace, so pretty with her hair . . . Stell's dark curls, looking like Art as a little boy in the photos she'd seen, but so pretty, even at eight, girlish, flirtatious with her father. Jerry, too, like Art, a little pudgy Arthur, a blustering little boy playing soldier. Only Olivia is blond, hope it'll stay that way, looking a little like me. I'm the only one in the house like me, sometimes, I think. The street was getting steeper. Better cut across, grab a taxi at Sutter. Or maybe I should grab the cable car, yes, I haven't done that yet. The Powell–Hyde line, Art said it would take me straight down Hyde, to Aquatic Park, right near Fort Mason . . . he was right, that I shouldn't take the car, probably would've just gotten lost . . .

She crossed the street, jaywalking (Arthur would have a fit!), tugging the stroller after her, struggling a little for balance. The right heel of her pump caught on something, No, it's *stuck*. Stuck in the cable-car track. Vivian leaned over, trying to wriggle free; the heel was wedged tight. No free hand, can't put the baby down right in the middle of the street, the stroller's full of stuff . . . She tugged desperately, as the Powell–Hyde cable car, heading south, chugged over the crest of a hill and down toward her. She let go of the stroller to free a hand and it rattled off down the street at a diagonal, hitting the curb and overturning. She panicked, clutching the baby—those things can *stop,* can't they, cable cars have *brakes!*—trying to kick herself free, straining her ankle.

"Let go of the shoe!" She heard yelled at her from somewhere, a woman's voice, but in her confusion kept kicking away. Olivia began to squeal.

"Hey, lady, let go of the shoe, I said!" The woman yelling at her upset her more. "Just let go of the fucking shoe!"

Vivian felt Olivia grabbed from her; she groped to hold on to the yellow jumpsuit, even then, at the back of her head, shocked by the language, as the woman pulled the baby away from her and raced away. Arms empty, Vivian watched her go, run off with her baby, as the cable car bearing down on her bellowed a warning. She tugged her hurting foot from the shoe and jumped clear as the cable car swept past, heavy, bumping along, unmoved. She staggered to the curb, narrowly missing an oncoming, honking Packard, and sat down, stunned and shaking.

"What the hell is wrong with you?" Vivian looked up; the woman was standing there, holding a screaming Olivia, soothing her. "I mean, Christ, splattered by a cable car! You want to get killed, fine, but you have a baby here! Are you crazy, or just stupid? I can't believe—"

"Excuse me, what? Do you mind? Talking to me like that . . . !" Vivian stood up and grabbed the baby back in her own arms. "How dare you? Really, how *dare* you speak to me like that! I don't know who you think you are, I don't even *know* you!" She heard her own shrieking voice, shrill and ringing. Calm down, you're making a scene, she thought, but it distracted her from the fear. "I'm perfectly fine, I don't need your help, or your insults! Just leave me alone!" She shoved the woman violently away from her with a free hand, feeling a surge of power. "Go away, I didn't ask for your help! How *dare* you!? I've *never* been so . . . so . . . I don't even know you!" She ran out of things to yell, and so waved her free arm again at the other woman, wildly, like waving away a swarm of bees, waving away the shaking.

"All right, stop screaming at me! I'm sorry!" The other woman backed up, shrugging. "You're on your own! Good luck navigating the sidewalk! Christ . . ." She left, shaking her head, merging with the crowd of uninterested passersby.

Vivian stopped to gasp in some air, hiccupped like Olivia, and looked back toward the street in time to see the remains of her imprisoned gray pump flattened by a passing taxi. She dropped down on the curb, then, hiccupped once more, and began to cry. Loud crying, embarrassing, babylike. She cried into the baby's head, deflated, spirit razed.

"Oh, come on, stop crying." The woman, that vulgar

woman, was back. "Don't do that, you're scaring her more, come on. Is it a her? Look, stop crying, it's OK, really. Please . . ." The woman retrieved the errant stroller, straightened the packages, and brought everything back to where Vivian was sitting and sobbing, her feet in the gutter, sticking to old paper coffee cups and cigarette butts. "Your foot's getting wet. And your other shoe's getting dirty, not that you had a pair anymore, anyway. The mate's ruined."

"Everything's ruined."

"What?"

"Everything! This whole day . . . such a wonderful day, a good day, and now I'm just going home, and . . . everything's ruined!"

"It's just a shoe!"

"It could've been the baby!"

"But it's not." The woman sat down next to her. "All right? You're OK, she's OK, so everything's fine, right?" She patted Vivian's shaking back. "Hey, think of it, you'll probably wind up in Herb Caen. 'Loony Lady in Shoe Distress' or something, but otherwise—"

"I'm not loony!" Vivian snapped.

"No, of course not." Pat, pat, pat.

Oh, how embarrassing, being seen like this. She's trying to be kind, I'm sure. "I'm sorry, you're very nice to help, really," said Vivian. "I'm sorry I was so . . . impolite."

"That's all right."

"I don't usually do this . . ."

"You don't usually scream at people you don't know, or you don't usually throw yourself in front of a cable car?" The woman, a girl, really, with long auburn hair in a loose braid, smiled.

Vivian tried to smile back, feeling irritated again. "Yes. Both. Either."

"You must be a tourist. No self-respecting San Franciscan would try to kill herself that way. Even a loony one. Try the bridge next time. The Bay'll get you."

"Thank you, I'll remember that." Vivian suddenly wanted to get away from her, from this inflicted intimacy. She's a stranger, after all, and yes, I'm glad she was here, but really, this is getting too personal. Unsettling. And I don't like her. "Well, thank you again!" She dug a shoe box from the stroller and found her old pumps, put them on.

"You always carry a spare pair?"

"No, I have to go now. Thank you, really." She stood up, still unsteady. "It's getting late, I have to go."

"Right. You want to get a cup of coffee or something? Calm down a little?"

"I'm calm."

"No, you're not."

"Don't tell me what I am!" Calm down, she's young, that's all, lacking social graces, probably doesn't realize how rude she is, treating me like a child. "I have to go, that's all. I'm perfectly fine. Thank you for your help." She gave the girl a bright, impersonal smile and headed up the sidewalk, away from her, with her baby and stroller. The girl, wearing blue jeans, Vivian realized (on the street!) caught up with her.

"I didn't mean to offend you. I'm sorry. I was just . . . scared, you know? Just like you." The girl looked at her, sincere, serious.

Vivian nodded briefly, averting her eyes. "I don't like . . . I'm not a child, really. I'm just fine."

"I know." They looked at each other a moment. "But . . . I still feel an incredibly maternal urge to get you some hot coffee."

Vivian smiled, despite herself, and thought for some reason of Sylvia. Always giving me tea when I was little, when I got hurt, making me feel grown-up. Warm.

"Maybe even a Danish?"

Vivian laughed, and reluctantly met her look. She's friendly, that's all. Sweet of her, really, being so concerned.

"My treat. Earn me a Girl Scout merit badge. All right?" the girl asked, smiling.

"Yes, all right. That might be nice."

The coffee shop in the bustling Marina was crowded: salesgirls leaving work early, a few other mothers with children, some tussling teenagers. Still sailors everywhere, edgy with peace. One walked by with his girl, looking for seats; they both glanced back at Anna and Vivian, the girl wanting their seats, the sailor just wanting a look.

". . . almost exactly a year ago, then. Right, I was five months pregnant with Olivia when we arrived."

"Did you have her on the island?"

"Oh, no. Saint Francis Memorial." Vivian drank her coffee, bit an arc in her cookie.

"Yeow, nuns. You're Catholic?"

"No, Jewish actually. Nominally Jewish."

"That's too important now to be just 'nominal.'"

"I suppose you're right."

"Did you have family in Europe?"

"Oh, no. They all came over long ago, turn of the century, before then, even. We're very lucky, escaping it all."

"Are you following Nuremburg?"

"Well, yes, certainly. Maybe not as closely as I should be, really, but we get the paper and . . ." She felt insufficient. "You see, it's easy to feel a little insulated, living on the island. Isolated."

"I know."

"And during the war Arthur was in the Pacific, so I was more absorbed in that, following that side of things. I'm not as up on it all as I should be, as I used to be. World events. The Nazis."

"Mmm . . . most've those bastards'll probably end up in some cushy jail with French cooking and eiderdown quilts, free gall-bladder surgery. Can I give her this?" Anna held up a piece of cookie soaked in milk.

"Uh, yes, sure. She's been on solids a while. Well, the baby kind of solids. Smushed up vegetables, the Gerber food. *That's* made life easy, those little jars."

Anna, holding Olivia on her lap, watched her munch happily on the soggy cookie. "She looks like you."

"That's funny, I was just thinking that, before . . ." Vivian drank more coffee. "This is good. When I was pregnant I constantly craved sugar, and we could hardly ever get it."

"What's really funny is your living on Alcatraz."

"I know, 'living in a prison' it sounds like. It's really lovely, though, the view of everything . . ."

"No, that's not what's funny."

"What, then?"

"Oh, well, just . . . isolated, I understand what you mean."

"Our first apartment wasn't very nice, in sort of a big dormitory building. You can see it from the pier. But we were lucky to get it at all, Arthur said. Housing's still hard to find. And after I had her, we were able to move into our cottage. There's a gorgeous view, it's like seeing the whole world just outside your window. Arthur says he feels we're all safer there than living in the City. You know, no traffic, no crime. No one even locks their front door. Just like a little neighborhood."

"Is your family here?"

"My parents moved up to Pacific Grove a few months ago, after Olivia was born. It's funny, after you have children, you start dating everything that way. The year Stell was born, when Jerry was two . . ."

"That's down near Monterey, right?"

"Mm-hm. They'd wanted to retire, they love the ocean . . . but they really came to be near us, I guess. Near their grandchildren. Art's family's gone, really. Just us."

"Don't you get bored?"

"What?" Vivian looked at her, blinking.

"Don't you get bored?"

"Oh, we're still settling in over there, so . . ."

"So, once you've settled in? . . ."

A beat. "Well, I love my husband. I love my children."

"Oh, I know. That's not the same thing."

"Yes, it is. Of course, why not?"

"You love your mother and father, but you don't stay with them forever. You go out on your own and find another life, more life."

"And I found my husband and children, then."

"Is that more life for you?"

"It's the life of a grown-up woman, yes. I'm not complaining about anything. I'm very lucky. I have nothing to complain about."

Anna was quiet, drinking her coffee. "It seems like I upset you a lot."

"No, it . . . it seems like you want to find something wrong with me."

"Oh, there's nothing wrong with you."

"Well, of course, I know—"

"I never meant to imply you were . . . oh, I'm sorry. Look, she's beautiful." Anna bounced Olivia on her knee, and the baby laughed, struggling to stand in Anna's lap, to use her chubby colt legs. "She's absolutely beautiful. You must be thrilled. Completely happy. Your husband sounds wonderful. I'm not criticizing you. Christ, *I* don't have all that."

"No, you don't."

"Now it sounds like you're criticizing me."

A beat. "What do you do? Do you work?" Vivian asked.

"I'm a secretary at Levi-Strauss."

"Really?" Vivian felt let down, somehow, imagining something else, something different.

"Really. What did you expect?"

"I don't know . . ." She paused. "Don't you get bored?"

Anna laughed. "Absolutely. All the time."

"Why aren't you there today?"

"I was. I left early. I got my period, I wasn't feeling well."

"Oh, uh huh . . ." Vivian glanced around, hoping the sailors weren't listening. "Is that what you wear to work?"

"My boss is very understanding." Laughing, again. "After we mutinied. The guys were coming to work in blue jeans, the company *makes* these things, for God's sake. So the rest of us got together and threatened to quit."

Vivian nodded, feeling prim in her suit, her gloves. "You're not married?"

"No." Anna smiled. "My boyfriend lives in Oakland. He's a journalist for the Trib."

"How old are you?"

"Thirty."

"Really?"

"Yes, really again. Why?"

"I thought you were younger. I'm thirty-one."

"Funny. I thought you were older."

Vivian's face fell a little. "Well . . . I am. Older than you."

"Read: more responsible."

"Maybe more responsibilities." She brushed crumbs from her gloves. "I used to work."

"Really? What did *you* do?"

"During the war. Defense plant in Santa Monica."

"Rosie the Riveting Queen."

"I liked it. My mother watched the kids, I made some good friends, you know, all of us in it together."

"Doing your share."

"Yes, but . . . even more than that, really. I got a promotion after I'd been there only a few months. Head lineman."

"I didn't mean to make fun, you know."

"That's all right. And then, well, I moved up to sort of assisting the head engineer. It involved more training, but . . . but it did mean something, really, helping support the effort. Contributing to something important." Vivian trailed off, feeling false. "I sound like a newsreel, don't I?"

"So what happened?"

"Why do you think something happened?"

"Go on, then, life was a newsreel? . . ."

"Well, yes, and then . . . well, the war was almost over. They started letting us go, of course, the women. The men were coming home, needing those jobs. And my supervisor called me in, the big boss, actually I thought it was either to fire me, or maybe make a pass . . ." She laughed, awkward, and cleared her throat. "Anyway, he offered to let me stay on. I could go to school at night, to UCLA, and finish my degree, you see, in engineering, and then they would move me up again, a real position. More money, maybe even an office. Well, I was shocked, I mean, *really* . . ." She laughed a little again, and took a sip of coffee.

"What did you do?"

"Nothing. Arthur came home. And then, of course, I got pregnant, so . . ."

"I'm sorry."

"Oh, no, that's awful! Don't be sorry for me. I was one of the lucky ones, having a husband come home to me."

"That's life in a newsreel again."

Vivian pushed her coffee cup away, exasperated. "Excuse

me, but, honestly, that's very rude. You can be very rude, you know that?"

"And impolite."

"And narrow minded. I *am* one of the lucky ones. Why do you make fun of it all?"

"Oh, I must be jealous."

Vivian stood up, and gathered her things. "I'm blessed with what I've got, that's the truth of it! You can't possibly appreciate it, obviously, because for God knows what reason you'd rather run around like an overage child in blue jeans who doesn't want to grow up, and act like a real person!" She fumbled in her purse for some change. "That's what's sad, really. I should feel sorry for *you*. I'm sure you think it's a lot easier to be argumentative, to just criticize everything—"

"I'll get it, I told you."

"No, thank you, I don't need you to buy me coffee! I have a husband who takes care of me, I don't have to work at some—" A mechanical wail, faint but piercing, interrupted her. Coffee-shop patrons glanced around, bewildered.

The girl turned to her sailor: "Honey, is that an air raid?"

"That's Alcatraz," Anna said to Vivian.

"How do you know?"

"You've never heard it?" Vivian shook her head no, and roughly took Olivia from Anna's arms. "That's the siren on Alcatraz. There's something going on over there. An escape, probably. You better go."

"Oh my God . . . I have to get my children—" Vivian grabbed at her packages.

"Here . . ." Anna scribbled on a napkin. "Look me up sometime, you can yell at me some more." She tucked the napkin in Vivian's purse. "I hope everything's all right."

"I have to get to Fort Mason . . ." Frantic, Vivian pushed

through the crowd to the door, calling back. "Thank you for the coffee! . . ."

"My pleasure."

*THE BATTLE*

Officer Weinhold, locked in cell 403 with Cretzer's automatic in his face, calmly advised the inmates, over the blaring siren, to give up. Cretzer replied if somebody was gonna get killed, Weinhold would be the first son of a bitch to die. Officer Weinhold replied he could only die once. As his friends raved and ranted, screaming at him to kill the bastards, don't leave any witnesses, Cretzer pointed the gun at Officer Weinhold and shot him twice, then fired at Miller, Corwin, and the other officers, his own little barrel of official fish. Next cell, and Cretzer shot at Officers Simpson, Sundstrom, and Baker. Two barrels of bloody human chum.

Cretzer instructed Carnes to enter the cells and make sure the officers were dead—if any were still alive, he was to cut their throats. Carnes, at nineteen the youngest inmate ever on the island, was in a state of shock; Coy had promised him there would be no killing. He entered the bloody cells, shaken: Officer Corwin's face had been blown away, the rest were badly injured and unconscious, or playing dead. Carnes exited and told Cretzer all nine officers were dead, praying Cretzer wouldn't check for himself and turn the gun on Carnes in a rage. Cretzer seemed satisfied. Carnes took Coy aside and asked if he could return to his cell, give it up. Coy agreed; Carnes went back to D Block and locked himself in. Shockley and Thompson followed suit. On the floor of cell 403, Officer Lageson surreptitiously drew a pencil from his pocket and managed to scrawl the names of the six inmates involved on the wall, circling the names Cretzer, Coy, and Hubbard.

## *Vivian*

"Vivian!" Mary Beth grabbed her by the arms, dragging her forward. "Where have you been? Oh dear Lord, it's awful. It's like a war, we can hear the gunshots—"

"What happened?"

"Some kind of revolt, they say. Maybe thirty of the convicts, they have machine guns! They've called out the Marines, the Coast Guard—"

"Where's Arthur? Where's Albert?" Mary Beth's husband was in his early sixties, a supervisor in the industry shops.

"I don't know! We don't know anything!"

Fort Mason was mobbed with wives and children, crying, jabbering frantically, repeating what little information there was, looking with squinting eyes toward the island. It seemed unchanged, undisturbed, save for the siren that continued to wail. Vivian found Stella and Jerry with the other children, a few dozen of them, ringed by wives and Red Cross workers with coffee. She handed Olivia to Mary Beth, and hugged them.

"Mommy, Jerry wants to go fight the cons and I told him he can't. He's too little, right?"

"Am not! I'm gonna blast 'em!"

"You're such a worm. Is Daddy gonna get shot?"

"No, no, of course not!"

"They won't let us back on the island," Mary Beth murmured to Vivian, handing her back the baby. "They say the convicts have taken over, they have enough ammunition for forty days!" Mary Beth was wringing her hands together; she stopped to pull her graying hair back in a tighter knot, sticking the pins in roughly, as if it would hold her together. "Albert wasn't feeling well this morning, I told him not to— "

"Ladies! Could I have your attention!" A man exited the office, waving his arms. "We have a copy of the telegram Warden Johnston sent to the *Chronicle*. I'd like to read it."

The wives surged forward, surrounding him.

"All right, now . . . 'Serious trouble. Convict has machine gun in cellhouse. Issued riot call. Placed armed guards at strategic locations. Most of our officers are imprisoned in cellhouse. Cannot tell extent of injuries suffered by our officers or amount of damage done. Will give you information later in the day when we get control. J. A. Johnston, Warden, Alcatraz'."

"Oh, dear Lord."

"What kind of injuries?"

"Who was hurt?"

Mothers went back to their children, hugging them again, desperately turning to each other.

"Mommy, I'm hungry."

"Where's Eunice and her kids?"

"Elise, do you have any extra diapers with you?"

"Barbara, can you hold the baby a sec?"

"I didn't bring anything warmer for Susie to wear!"

The officer tried to regain attention. "Now, ladies?! Ladies! The YMCA and the Red Cross have offered to put you all up for the night at a hotel, you and your children. We'll get you more information as soon as we have any, I promise. Don't you worry."

The children raced around at varying levels of awareness. Some peered wide-eyed toward home, absorbing their mothers' quiet fear; others began games of tag, hopscotch. The older ones, realizing they were to go to a hotel, a *hotel!* for the night, turned impatient, excited for the next step of the adventure.

"Arthur was on Tower duty. What about the Tower guards?"

"I don't know. We don't know."

"Who's still on the island? What about Carolyn, and her kids? Where's Suzanne?"

"They said any women and children on the island were barricaded inside the house, or the air-raid shelter." Mary Beth paused. "I'm ashamed to say it, but I'm glad we're not there. I . . . I just wish Albert were here."

They stood on the pier and looked out, across the Bay. The siren continued to scream for another hour.

## *THE BATTLE*

From the first sounds of gunfire heard on the Golden Gate and Bay Bridges, the first blast of the siren heard in North Beach and the Marina, people flocked to the piers, Fisherman's Wharf, the slopes of Russian Hill and Telegraph Hill, excited to watch. Marin reporters, adrenaline pumping, called Oakland reporters, called San Francisco reporters, everyone comparing, sharing, or covering up what they had. Senior editors knew to call Washington; if this was really good stuff, James Bennett, Federal Director of Prisons, would be contacted by the Warden and perhaps would know more than any local source.

Warden Johnston contacted the Navy, the Coast Guard, and the San Francisco police; the first boatloads of backup men headed across the Bay. Bennett, from Washington, directed men from San Quentin, McNeil, and Inglewood to head for the Rock. Thirty U.S. Marines arrived, past the sign on Angel Island erected for their homecoming a year ago: "Welcome Home—Well Done!" The one 150 or so inmates in the Recreation Yard were herded into a corner and guarded by sharpshooters standing atop the wall, to the beginning serenade of military planes roaring overhead and Coast Guard cutters circling the island.

Officers Stites, Mahan, and Oldham, and Lieutenant Bergen were ordered by Warden Johnston to enter the C Block gun gallery to rescue Officer Burch. It was assumed the rioters were holed up with their arsenal in D Block, but as the officers entered the D Block gun gallery, all was quiet. As they attempted to enter the steel door to C Block, shots rang out; the officers ducked, forced to fire blindly, holding their guns above their heads. Inmates trapped in their D Block cells were assaulted by bullets coming both from the gun gallery and from officers on catwalks hanging outside the prison walls, who opened fire directly into the cells; vulnerable, they hurried to barricade their cellfronts with mattresses, books, clothing, anything. In attempting to free Whitey Thompson, Coy and Cretzer had left open the solid doors to the barren isolation cells; these men were at the mercy of any well-aimed or lucky bullet.

The officers proceeded into the C Block gun gallery to rescue Officer Burch and were again fired on, by all sides; Officer Stites was shot and fell, and his body was dragged out with Officer Burch's.

Coy, Cretzer, and Hubbard sought refuge in the interior utility corridor running the length of back-to-back B and C Blocks with their rifle, revolver, and carving knife.

A full-scale attack on D Block was ordered.

## *Vivian*

The show was better at night; searchlights from patrol boats wove bright streaks across the dark Bay water; exploding grenades lit up the jagged, broken windows in the cellhouse; tracer bullets carved red lines across the sky and on impact blew out chunks of concrete, sending sparks flying to torch grasses around the prison and illuminate Alcatraz with dozens of tiny fires. The streets of Russian Hill, around the Presidio, in North Beach, were parade-packed with people inching along in cars. On the Embarcadero piers, at Coit Tower, in Pacific Heights, Aquatic Park, entrepreneurs peddled binoculars, hot drinks, and snacks to people wrapped in blankets, sitting on steps, watching the fireworks.

The Stewart Hotel on Geary left the wives and children without a view of any of it; they reluctantly gathered in the lobby, trying to warm up, many wishing they'd stayed at the waterfront.

"Well, no, Carolyn, I know we couldn't *see* anything from there, but I just *felt* better, that's all . . ."

"You're right, it was too cold for the children . . ."

"Excuse me, young man? Are you *sure* the warden knows where we are? He'll call with any information?"

"If all the prisoners are rounded up inside, I don't see why we can't go back . . ."

"Miss? I'm sorry, but would you please call Marine Hospital again? Just to be sure my husband isn't . . ."

"Maybe we should take the children to a movie? Take their minds off it?"

YMCA volunteers passed out clean diapers and baby formula; Stewart Hotel employees scrambled to find rooms in the already-full hotel, trying to be soothing, comforting, trying to be patient with the children running up and down hallways, taking over the lobby.

Vivian was put in a third-floor double room, now dormitory, with Jerry, Stella, and the baby, and two other women, one with two children of her own. Cots were brought in, and extra towels, and trays of food, pots of coffee.

"Mommy, I can't wear this to school again tomorrow."

"Stella, please don't bother me about that now. Maybe you can swap dresses with Kathleen."

"That's just as bad! And Kathleen smells funny."

"All right, you can wear this . . . look, I bought it for you today."

"I don't like it. It itches."

"You haven't even tried it on! Please, sweetheart. Look, this'll probably all be over with tomorrow, anyway."

"Unh-unh. They said the cons were gonna blow up the island." Stell began jumping on the bed.

"I know, how about a bubble bath? Joanie's next door, you can go ask her mom, and both of you can have a bubble bath, all right?" She remembered, faintly, how she used to love hotels, bubble baths in hotels.

She'd already given Jerry his new truck, hoping to quiet him down, but was outdone; well-meaning YMCA volunteers had handed out toy guns to the boys, those weapons they were always so hungry for, and Jerry now was tearing up and down the hallway with two other boys, reenacting the mutiny.

"I got you! You gotta play dead!"

"You're a hack, not a con, Thornton!"

"Nuh-unh, I'm a killer con! I already killed you and two other screws!"

Vivian took Olivia's dirty diapers to wash in the bathroom sink; the ammonia tang filled the room, the water scalded her hands. How am I going to sterilize her bottles? Maybe in the hotel kitchen . . . maybe I should call Mom and Dad, they'll hear about it, be so worried . . . Oh God, please, please, please . . .

"Vivian!" Mary Beth hurried in, carrying another tray of food. "Arthur's OK, Albert, too! The only Tower guards fired at were Jim Comerford, and Elmus, and Mr. Levinson. Some others are being held hostage, but Arthur's fine, he's guarding prisoners in the Rec Yard, and Albert's down at the glove shop."

Vivian sat on the edge of the bed, wet diapers staining her lap. "Oh . . . good . . ."

"Arthur sent you a message. They know we're all here, and we're just to stay put, where it's safe, until it's all over. He said to tell you. It might be a couple of days, but that's all."

Vivian nodded.

"I'm going to move in here, with you. Help you with the children."

"Thanks, Mary Beth."

"It'll be a little crowded, but . . . oh, dear Lord, I'm just so relieved . . ."

Vivian looked out the window, facing the Financial District lights. The City glittered at night. What a gorgeous view. Just like on Alcatraz, a view of the City from behind glass. A view of the whole world.

"Mary Beth?"

"Mmm?"

"Maybe I won't stay here tonight."

"What do you mean? Arthur wants you to stay here."

"I know, but you just said, it's so crowded. I'll go stay with a friend."

"Vivian? . . ." Vivian turned to look at her. "I don't understand, dear? What friend?"

"Just a friend. I'll come back tomorrow. If I take the baby, will you watch Jerry and Stella?"

"You mean you're leaving the children?"

"They're fine. They'll just play with their friends and go to bed. The Red Cross is driving them all to school tomorrow. They won't even know I'm gone. And I'll call you later, keep checking in." Not quite thinking what she was doing, Vivian gathered her things together, Olivia's things, and wrapped the baby up snug. "I'll call you later. Oh, Stella can have a bubble bath with Joanie. All right?"

"Well, all right, dear. I suppose . . . what should I . . ."

Vivian put her little hat on, checked her purse for a scrap of paper, picked up the baby, and left.

Macondray Lane was almost impossible to find. A taxi driver let her off at the top of Jones in Russian Hill, cursing at the traffic, refusing to get any closer—it was just a block or two that way, he said. The streets were crowded with people watching the battle down below, like theatergoers happy with their balcony seats. Macondray Lane, said one of them, helpfully, was just that way there, looks like an alley, lady.

Vivian headed down a tiny cobblestone path, surrounded by foliage, a place hidden from view from anywhere in the City. She would've walked right by it without seeing it, this bucolic little ledge of a street. At the very end was a small town house tucked under drooping vines, a dull pea green Victorian with windows facing the Bay. "A. SCOTT." She took a deep breath, and knocked.

Anna opened the door, a phone at one ear, and quickly motioned her in with a free hand; Vivian wasn't even sure she knew who it was.

". . . so, yeah . . . uh huh . . . yeah, she's just walking in the door, can you believe it? No, I'll tell her . . . so you're there till it's over? All right. Be careful . . ." Anna laughed at something said to her, then: "I will. I love you. Let me know. Bye." She hung up and turned to Vivian. "That was Robert. He's been circling the island in a *Tribune* boat. Plum assignment."

"Oh," said Vivian, not knowing what else to say.

"Your husband's fine. Thornton, right? Arthur? Robert checked it out, but I'm sure you know that by now, that he's all right?"

"Yes. Thank you." She looked around the room. The apartment was tiny, but warm: a small fireplace, books lining shelves—and an alcoved seat below a window overlooking Alcatraz, framed as perfectly as a picture postcard.

"I like being able to see it," said Anna, following Vivian's gaze out, curling into the window seat. "It was bound to happen, you know."

"What?"

"A mutiny." Anna smiled, and held her arms out for the baby, who was reaching for her with a wide smile. Vivian handed Olivia over and watched Anna bounce her on her lap. "I was going to head over to the Stewart to see you, but this is better. I'm glad you came. You're staying till it's over, right? You're staying with me?" They finally looked at each other and she smiled at Vivian as if it were just, had always been, that simple.

## *THE BATTLE*

By very late Thursday night officers had rescued the hostages from cells 403 and 402, one of them getting shot in the leg in the process. The hostages were rushed to Marine Hospital; Officer William Miller died later that night, his wife Josephine and two children by his side: Joan Marie, thirteen, and Billy, ten. Officer Stites had died almost immediately; he left his wife Betty and four children: Robert, fourteen, James, seventeen, and Herbert, nine, and an older, married daughter. The rest of the wives whose husbands were injured hurried to Marine Hospital; Officers Lageson, Weinhold, Simpson, and Corwin were in critical condition.

The pointless attack on D Block continued throughout the night, despite the inmates begging for it to stop: showers of glass, shards of burning metal from exploded grenades, random bullets. Water lines were ruptured and icy water flowed across cell floors, across huddled inmates, spilling down the three tiers like a fountain onto the cellhouse floor. At least the shattered windows were a benefit; they let in freezing drafts, but created ventilation for the clouds of tear gas and smoke filling up the cellblock. At one point Robert Stroud braved the battle to climb down and close the solid doors on the isolation cells, protecting the men locked inside. He also yelled out an offer to stand in the line of fire while officers searched D Block, to prove there were no guns. His offer was not accepted; the attack continued until Warden Johnston himself finally decided there were no rioters in D Block, as inmates had been screaming for hours.

By Friday morning the attack was redirected to C Block; Marines in full battle dress drilled holes in the roof and dropped grenades and fragmentation bombs into the utility corridor with string. By dawn on Saturday assault teams were marching down C Block, throwing open the doors to the utility corridor, and spraying the corridor with machine-gun fire. Early Saturday morning heavily armed officers entered the remains of the utility corridor and found the inmates' broken-up bodies tucked inside amid burst pipes, mucky water, and smashed concrete. Coy was still holding the rifle, still wearing the officer's uniform; Cretzer was clutching the automatic. They'd passed rigor mortis; both men were cold, limp. Hubbard was further back in the corridor; his body was still faintly warm, and he still held the kitchen knife.

Inmates held outside for two and a half days with no food in the freezing Recreation Yard were brought in, allowed warm showers, and fed. D Block inmates were allowed out of their cells as well; wounds were treated. It was announced that the battle was over. Cleanup began.

## *Vivian*

Some old dishtowels of Anna's made perfectly fine diapers, and Olivia drank regular milk from her scrubbed but not sterilized bottle with no ill effects whatsoever. That couldn't be said of Vivian, who woke up Friday morning terribly hungover from a jug of red wine she and Anna had shared. They'd curled up in Anna's bed with the baby between them, Vivian wrapped in an old oversized dress shirt of Robert's, the glow of Alcatraz in the window behind them, eating pizza Anna had coaxed a North Beach restaurateur into delivering.

"This is like being in college," Vivian gasped during a laughing fit, spilling wine on the white shirt.

"You did this in college?" Anna asked, pouring more wine. She was wearing a long white nightgown, her reddish hair unbraided.

"Um . . ." Vivian had to think a moment. "No, not really," which set her off again, laughing harder. "If I did, maybe I'd've stayed to graduate."

"Who cares about graduating? It's just a useless piece of paper."

"My parents cared. They were furious. No . . . disappointed."

"So why'd you quit? Get married?"

"I don't know . . . maybe I couldn't figure out any other way to disappoint them."

"Very rebellious of you."

"Yeah . . . the thing *not* to do. I was gonna be some big-time, famous, all-alone lady scientist with my hair in a bun."

"Is that a lady scientist rule, the bun?"

"I panicked in a lake. I froze. That's why I got married."

"Mm-hm. That's why people drown. When they panic. That idea, about just throwing scared kids into a swimming pool or something? Really fucked. I mean, it's natural for us to be in water, we all started life that way. Swimming's just remembering the water, but someone has to remind you. Your body'll keep you afloat if you relax."

"I used to love to swim. It's too cold here."

"Not if you're used to it. Here, look . . ." Anna pulled down an old scrapbook from a shelf and handed Vivian several stiff newspaper clippings.

Vivian looked at them, puzzled. "The 'San Francisco Mermaid'?"

"Read on."

"'Miss Scott conquered the turbulent waters and successfully swam the distance between Alcatraz Island and the San Francisco mainland' . . . wait, this is *you*? You *lived* on Alcatraz?"

"Long time ago. It wasn't a pen back then, though. Disciplinary Barracks. My Dad was an Army staff sergeant."

Vivian continued reading, stunned. "I thought swimming in the Bay was so dangerous. Arthur says that, it's the currents, right? That's why convicts don't try to escape."

"Yeah, try telling that to Arthur right now, that convicts don't try to escape." Anna poured more wine. "Why wouldn't they? What've they got to lose? That's the cruel thing about the place, really, they can see the whole world dangled in front of them, just across that mile and a half of water."

Vivian looked at the clippings again. "Was it really an 'easy swim'?"

"No. But I did it anyway."

"What . . . what made you do it?"

"I'm not sure . . ." Anna looked out, toward the island. "I don't really remember, you know, if it was my idea, or what. There was all the hype about dangerous criminals coming to the Rock, Uncle Sam's Devil's Island, you know . . . the Women's Clubs here really went nuts," Anna laughed. "I think they pictured hordes of gangster molls descending on San Francisco to help their men escape. Waiting at the dock with towels, or something. The government kept saying no, it's fine, no man can swim that Bay and live to tell about it. I mean, I'd been a swimmer forever, at school and clubs, you know, and . . . maybe I just wanted to prove a point? Maybe I just wanted to prove that I could? I don't know . . ." She paused, and waved a hand at the clippings. "But then it all turned into that, more hype."

"Mm."

"And then my dad wanted me to train for the Olympics. The next Eleanor Holm."

"Why didn't you?"

"Oh, I don't know . . . too much work? Too much pressure? I panicked?" She shrugged. "I went to Berkeley on an athletic scholarship, though."

"That's wonderful."

Anna shrugged again. "Now I'm a secretary. With a few swimming medals from Aquatic Park and a lot of fucking pieces of paper. You were right, you know. Pathetic." She waved the clippings at Vivian, and stuck them back in the scrapbook.

"So quit. Do something else."

"And give up blue jeans?" They laughed, silly again. "*You* do it. *You* quit."

"I did!" Vivian giggled. "No, I'm just, I've just taken a . . . leave of absence." They collapsed on the bed with laughter. Olivia laughed, too, happy, drunk on her milk.

"So is Arthur going to give you severance pay?!"

"Not if I mutiny. There's a clause in the wedding vows."

"Well, we know he can't shoot you. Maybe he'll just throw you in the Hole."

"You know . . ." Vivian drained her glass, wiped her mouth, and lifted Olivia up so the baby could stretch her legs, play-walking across the bed. "There was a second, I mean *just* a second . . . oh, no, this is awful."

"Now I really want to hear it."

"Well, just an instant, when the siren went off today, and you and I were sitting there in the coffee shop . . . even way before I got to the dock . . . just an instant when I heard the siren go off and you told me what it meant, that I thought if something *did* happen to Art . . . it would kill me, I know that, but for just an instant I thought . . . wouldn't that be great? Arthur *gone? Poof?*" She giggled a little. "Arthur, picked off by Al Capone, or something?"

"Capone got off the Rock years ago," Anna laughed.

"Well, like in the movies! Edward G. Robinson, you know, or Cagney. I mean, something really glamorous—"

"Oh, of course!"

"—not shot, you know, in the *foot* something!"

"Going in a blaze of glory! For truth and justice in the American way!"

"Right! A hero! And it would all be over! The world free for democracy! Free from . . . everything. It would all be over . . . and I'd be . . . free." She gulped, and hiccupped. "Footloose and fancy free." She laughed, a short, breathy burst, then gulped again, looking at Anna, somber. "But I don't mean any of that, I really don't." She started to cry. "I love Arthur. I love my children . . ."

"I know you don't mean it," said Anna. She put her arms around Vivian, smoothing back her hair. "I know . . . that's just the loony kind of thing you're allowed to think sometimes, that's all."

"I don't believe this, here I go, I'm . . . *fucking crying* again!" The word made her laugh, and Anna laughed, too.

"Excuse me, that's very rude! You're supposed to be setting an example for your daughter, lady!"

"More wine! We need more wine! This is a party, right!" Vivian flopped back on the bed, releasing a big sigh, and examined a lock of her hair. "I didn't mean it. What an evil thing to say . . . I think I have pizza in my hair, you know that? I've never eaten pizza in bed."

"That doesn't surprise me. Only overage children eat pizza in bed." Anna uncorked the wine jug again.

"I didn't mean that, either . . . you don't look like a child."

"No?"

"No . . . but you look like a girl, though. With the nightgown, and your hair like that . . . you look like one of those neoclassical paintings of Greek mythology. 'Young Girl Pouring Wine.'"

Anna laughed. "Right."

"No . . . like a mermaid. They were right, you look like a mermaid."

"So do you. You can be a mermaid, too." Anna ran her hand through the lock of Vivian's hair, and raised the wine over Vivian's glass, smiling. "Are you sure you want more?"

"Yes . . . what the hell, I'm sure I want more."

Friday morning Anna called in sick, as did most of the other employees; Levi-Strauss gave up and declared it an unofficial day off, a Go Watch the Battle of Alcatraz holiday. Vivian and Anna went shopping, sweeping past newsstand headlines reporting ONE GUARD KILLED, NINE INJURED IN ARMED REVOLT

ON ALCATRAZ. Vivian telephoned the Stewart Hotel from a pay phone in North Beach: Yes, dear, Arthur's still fine or I would've heard . . . Stella and Jerry asked about you, but they went off to school, they're fine . . . well, we're here another night at least . . . are you *sure*, Vivian? Of course I'll watch the children, but . . . well, all right dear . . .

They took Olivia to Golden Gate Park and let her romp, climbing up on the swings themselves, and had tea at the little Japanese garden. Anna talked Vivian first into going out in a pair of her blue jeans (Vivian, those stockings are ruined, it's either this or barelegged!), and then into cutting her hair, raising its blond curtain to just below her chin (Viv, you can get away with it, you have that kind of face! Didn't you ever have short hair?). They returned to Macondray Lane with bags of groceries, the type Vivian always admired, but never dared attempt: whole cloves of fresh garlic, mysterious Pacific Island fruits, tiny jars of marinated mushrooms. They switched the radio from news to swing and Olivia crawled around on the floor bouncing to music, naked except for a dishtowel diaper, while they filled the tiny apartment with music and heat and the smells of cooking food. Everything was delicious, better than Sylvia's food, which to Vivian seemed a miracle; at home her dishes were seldom more than edible, she knew, despite Arthur's sincere praise, his pats on the back. They gave Olivia a bath in the kitchen sink and rubbed her dry in front of the fireplace. Long after midnight they all fell asleep tucked inside the alcoved window seat below the view of Alcatraz, Vivian curled around the baby like an oyster shell, Anna's arm around them both, resting across Vivian's waist, her cello curve.

For two days the papers had reported that eighteen inmates with machine guns were involved; twenty officers were held hostage, or "most" of the island's guards; that the killing of Officer Stites was a revenge job—Officer Stites had been the Model Tower guard attacked by Limmerick, Lucas, and Franklin in 1938, who shot and killed Limmerick. The official toll counted five dead: two officers, three inmates; fifteen officers wounded; one inmate "officially" wounded.

Early investigation results, including a coroner's inquiry in which not a single inmate was questioned, concluded the officials had carried out their duties flawlessly. James Bennett, who arrived on Alcatraz a few hours after the inmates' dead bodies were removed from the utility corridor, formally praised Johnston for his handling of the battle: "There was not the least indication of negligence or carelessness or inefficiency in this affair. The felons found and took advantage of a weakness which not the most experienced and able prison man could anticipate," adding that "after the first half hour or so there were no casualties, except among the rioters." In assessing injuries to "bystander" inmates, Warden Johnston said "a number of convicts were splattered by bullets, but all injuries were superficial and no record was kept of them."

Although the inmates' perspective would carry no weight in the official reports, the internal investigation wanted as much information from them as possible, and federal investigators were frustrated by the inmate "wall of silence" they encountered. Johnston reassured them that "convicts always refuse to talk. But we always manage to find out what we want to know. It merely takes a little time and patience."

"Where the hell have you been?" Art snapped at her as she came in, dressed in her gray suit, carrying Olivia and dragging the stroller, Stell and Jerry behind her. He embraced the two children—Hey, champ, howsa boy . . . give your old man a big kiss, princess—while Vivian silently settled Olivia in her playpen, and wearily took off her hat.

"Okay, you two, I need to talk to your mother. Go on in your rooms, I'll be there in a minute."

"Daddy, we stayed in a *hotel!*"

"The people gave us guns, and we hadda give 'em back, no fair!"

"Yeah, we'll see about it, go on . . ." The children, sensing danger, went to their rooms without complaint. He turned back to Vivian. "Jesus, what did you do?"

"I cut my hair." He looked horrified. "My *hair,* Arthur. *My* hair. It's not like I lost a limb."

"Don't get smart."

"Can I get by you, please? I want to change."

"No, you're not going anywhere! Where the hell were you all this time?"

"Excuse me, Arthur, would you please not use that tone?"

"Mary Beth said a 'friend'? What does that mean? Who's your *friend*, Vivian?"

"Just some woman I met on Thursday."

"Oh." Arthur was briefly taken aback, deprived of a weapon. "Okay, so some woman, you go off for two days?!"

"I don't really want to talk about it."

"I don't care if you don't want to talk about it, you owe me a lot more than that! You leave your *children*? No one knew where you were!"

"I knew where I was."

"What the hell does that mean?"

"I knew the kids were all right, I knew you were all right, so—"

"You knew I was 'all right'? Yeah, I was *dandy*, I was in a *war zone* up there!"

"You were in the Rec Yard, they said. Standing guard."

"Yeah, and we knew shit about what was going on, who was in on it, who was gonna open fire next! What is this, I wasn't in enough *danger* for you to be responsible?"

"Of course not! But—"

"Better if I were Miller? Hal Stites? Corwin got his face blown off, maybe *then* you would've—"

"That's terrible, Arthur, to think that of me!"

"So?"

"So . . . so, I knew you were all right . . . so, what's the difference?"

"What's the . . . the difference is you don't just take off like that!"

Vivian mutely unloaded packages from the stroller.

"Look, Vivian . . ." His voice softened; he took her by the shoulders and gazed at her appealingly. "Honey, when I was out there . . . I wasn't so scared for me, I was scared for you, and the kids. You know . . . in case anything happened to me." She looked away, then, pulled away from his gaze, to unwrap packages.

"That's it? You have no explanation?"

"It just seemed like . . . my only chance."

"For what?"

"Just to . . . get out. To get away."

He looked at her blankly. "From *what?*"

"From . . . it's just . . . look, Arthur, it's just sometimes. . . ."

"I don't understand you."

"I know. I'm sorry." She paused. "Do you really want me to try to explain it?"

"Yes! I mean . . ." He stopped a moment, considering. "I just don't get what you're making such a big fuss about, that's all!"

"Artie, sometimes I feel—"

"All right, it's over!" He put his arms around her, roughly, cutting her off, and buried his head in her shoulder. "You're right, there isn't anything to talk about. You're back. We'll forget it. We don't have to talk, it's over, I don't want to talk about it."

"Okay."

"So how's this, we just don't talk about it, we forget it happened!"

"I got you your socks."

"You're back, everything's fine now."

"I'm sorry."

"You can't do that again, Vivian. Leave like that."

"All right."

"You won't do it again?"

"I said I won't." His grip on her tightened. "I won't do it again! All right?"

"All right!" He released her, and left to go see his children, smoothing his hand over Olivia's head as he passed her.

Reports were filed, and investigations were closed. Gun gallery guards would no longer be armed; holes were bored in the cellhouse walls to allow in a machine-gun muzzle from guards on catwalks outside, and steel mesh wire was installed over the gun galleries—now the prison was, really and truly, "impregnable." A judge announced that Marvin Hubbard's appeal had merit, and, if he had proceeded through the courts, he quite possibly would have gone free. Miran Thompson, Sam Shockley, and Clarence Carnes were tried and convicted of murder in Officer Miller's death;

Thompson and Shockley were executed in San Quentin's gas chamber, while Carnes, due to his age and perhaps the hostage officers' testimony, was merely given another life sentence and returned to Alcatraz. Thompson, before his execution, offered his eyes to the blind, but no one wanted them.

Josephine Miller and her children escorted her husband's body back to Philadelphia for burial. She would receive a widow's pension of $61.25 from the federal government, plus $17.50 a month for each child until the age of eighteen, but the government refused to cover the cost of the funeral; it was not government policy for penitentiary employees, only for penitentiary inmates.

Mrs. Stites and her three young children would receive the same pension. It was proven conclusively, despite the rumors, that Officer Stites had not been shot in revenge by the rioters during the attack on D Block; he was killed by a shot in the back, from friendly fire.

Despite the glowing and immediate praise, Warden Johnston ultimately suffered the brunt of growing criticism—that his reacting too late, then overreacting for too long, had been, perhaps, a factor in the battle's drawn-out and bloody evolution. In his entire career he'd never lost men like this before. He reevaluated the procedures for hiring and training officers, made some changes, but it was time to go. He would retire a year and a half later at the age of seventy-three, leaving behind the ferry named in his honor, giving up the post to Edwin B. Swope, a veteran officer of McNeil, and former warden of New Mexico State Prison.

The Sunday after the battle, the *Chronicle* contained a statement from a former Alcatraz convict, a veteran of eleven years' time on the Rock for mail robbery, who described the prison as "a place without hope, a physical prison which is the more terrible because it is a prison of the mind." The former convict, unnamed, said:

> I just want to see something done so things like this riot won't happen again. I know that if they treated the prisoners half civilly, they wouldn't react like vicious beasts. You can't coop up men and take all hope away from them . . . .
>
> Look, I've been pushed around over there . . . I've been in isolation and in the dungeon—eleven days barefoot on a concrete floor, six or seven days without food—and it's tough. But not as tough as going without newspapers. Or only getting to see a show six or seven times a year. Every time we got any privileges—Johnston calls them privileges, I call them necessities—somebody had to suffer . . . .
>
> Nobody's asking them to take the guards away. Nobody's asking for them to turn the place into a country club. All the guys want is a little more consideration. I never saw anyone get smacked around over there unless he was really out of order. It isn't the physical treatment, it's the mental treatment you get. The only thing that kept me going was the thought that I could get out someday.

Steel doors slammed closed and locked, leaving the island once again cut off and soundproofed behind concrete walls and its shade of fog.

There wasn't another escape attempt for ten years.

# Last Summer

## *Olivia*

ALCATRAZ WOMEN'S CLUB: Last Monday's meeting was well attended—coffee and peach parfait swirl were served by hostesses Mrs. William Schneider and Mrs. Edward Lucey. Yum!

ALCATRAZ WELCOMES Officer and Mrs. Stanley Walker! Officer Walker is coming to us from Leavenworth, where he served 21 distinguished years; his lovely wife, Martha, was a schoolteacher and is the former Cotton Carnival Queen of Atlanta!

FAMILY VACATION: Mrs. Arthur Thornton and her three children are off to visit her parents in beautiful Pacific Grove for two weeks. Officer Thornton remains here with us due to a scheduling conflict. Have a fun trip!

*The Pelican,* July 1952

Summer means leaving the island for two weeks to visit my grandparents in Pacific Grove; my mother, Stella, Jerry, and I take the ferry called "The Warden Johnston"—he was Warden when I was a baby—to Fort Mason at the mainland, and then hurry to the parking garage near Fisherman's Wharf, where the other families keep their cars. Ours is a Chrysler Windsor station wagon with a bumper sticker Daddy put on that says I LIKE IKE. My mother gets wound up tight as a ball of Grandma's yarn before we go, and hurries us to get there—all I get of San Francisco is the smell of popcorn and Ghiradelli chocolate and kettles of crab steaming in their shells, crowds of tourists in all different colors that we make our way through with my mother's hand firmly gripping my own, and the exhaust fumes from the parking garage. San Francisco is just tall buildings with spikes and spires growing smaller, away from me, through the back window of the station wagon, the first stop on the way to Pacific Grove, where there are no tourists, few cars, and the air smells like artichokes and burning wood.

Coming home two weeks later is autumn, which for Stella and Jerry means leaving the island every day to go back to school in the City. Sometimes they don't get to go, if there's too much fog and the ferry captain says it isn't safe; those days I have to share my mother with Stell and Jerry, but that isn't too often. On usual mornings, as soon as Stell and Jerry leave—Stell pulling the last two pins from her bangs, Jerry still chewing toast—Mommy sits down with me, to teach me at home so I'll be ready for real school. She first taught me to read with a large alphabet book—A is for Apple, B is for Ball—and when we got to V is for Violin she asked me, as usual, for other words starting with that letter; all I could think of was her name, Vivian, which is loaded up with Vs. Since then I collect V words, and try looking them up in her big dictionary. Vivid, Vivacious, Vibrant; they are words I can still barely read and can't quite pronounce, but she explains their meanings, and I am right, they are like her. I have a V in my name too, but it's stuck in the middle where you can't really see it. We read books with big print and short sentences that sound nothing like how people talk; we do arithmetic that cuts up numbered fruit and gives pieces to fake people who give it right back. Mostly, springs at home we are both bored, waiting for it to end, for the summers.

But this summer is different; it is my last one, I think, because this autumn will be different. This autumn I am going to real school, off the island, in the City. So I am extra impatient to get there, too, to my grandparents—not to *be* there, but to come back home again. For this last summer to be over.

Daddy usually doesn't come with us; he always stays behind just at the last minute to work. But this summer he is very angry about it, I heard him telling Mommy through the bedroom wall, because Warden Swope wants him and other fathers to work in the kitchen Up Top at the prison.

". . . so *cons* go on strike, suddenly they don't want to work, and *we're* supposed to fill in? Cooking their food? This is crap, I wasn't trained to wait on scum."

"Why doesn't Swope just give them wages?"

"It doesn't work that way, Vivian. Look, it's one thing for men in the industry shops, trained skills, that I can understand, sure. Pay 'em their six cents an hour, or whatever. But kitchen work? Come on, it's menial! At least Swope's got the strikers in Solitary, maybe that'll wake 'em up. But if he thinks his *officers* are gonna put up with this . . . listen, you take the kids, go, have a nice trip. Say hello to your folks."

"Fine."

There is a pause, then I hear my mother call loudly through the wall:

"Olivia? Don't forget your bathing suit!"

My mother loves to drive; she eases into the front seat of the station wagon and loosens like the spaghetti she drops in hot water. We drive for a very long time, without stopping, while Jerry makes gross noises and Stell keeps yelling he's wrinkling her and my mother tries to get us all to sing along to the radio. When we arrive we fly out of the car like startled seagulls. My grandparents run outside with big fleshy hugs, breathing cinnamon and linseed oil all over us. My grandmother is tiny but soft everywhere, with fluffy silver curls around her face; my grandfather is scratchier, in rough woolen sweaters Grandma makes. He is huge—it is like hugging an oak tree—and has long frizzy white hair, with white tufts of it poking out his ears and shirt collars and cuffs. Sylvia and Harry; they look like their names, and I wonder how their parents could tell that when they were babies.

My grandparents live in a small house covered with bits of lacy wood, filled inside with warped surfaces; doors never stay closed, or are jammed tight and are impossible to open; windows gap open slanty, or are stuck shut as if nailed; floors creak; cabinet doors hang crooked. Bookshelves higher than my head line every hallway, packed tight with books that whiff dust whenever you pass. The house is called "Victorian," but a sign out front reads "Mrs. Evelyn Potter, 1897," and no one knows who this lady is. Across the street is the Pacific Ocean; the shore is rocky, full of tide pools and seaweed and fat sea lions. Pacific Grove is home like Alcatraz is home, always on the edge of the sea, but different; Pacific Grove has bigger edges. Our island is starting to feel like a cotton dress you've loved all summer but by autumn feels thin and skimpy. You want more material floating around you.

Stell goes to unpack; Grandpa and Jerry go to fish; my mother and I are given cups of pale tea and brushed into corners of Grandma's kitchen, into chairs Grandpa makes, to watch her with food. We are not allowed to help; we are to relax. My mother nervously picks up spoons with a tight smile and broken chatter, stiff again, half-making helpful gestures; I hover nearby, waiting for this thing to happen, this "relax" of my mother, hoping for the strange ease that always comes upon her here to come upon her. We watch Grandma cook, still listening for foghorns, still restless. We watch Grandma, but it seems she is watching my mother, like she always watches her on first days here, nodding at her, looking for something. My mother will look away. Only after a few hours, when the teakettle's steam has softened her skin and hair and she has unwrapped herself in the kitchen's warmth, changing piece by piece into softer clothes, things without zippers and buckles and hooks and eyes, will my mother look Grandma full in the face, with a loosened smile and what seems like a loud sigh, but is silent. Grandma will put her arms around my mother like she was me, and my mother will hug her back, arms around my grandmother's soft waist, her face pressed to the apron front, and they will breathe together a moment. They stop watching each other then, and their talk softens too, into little bits and pieces that make them laugh; they touch each other a lot on the wrist or shoulder, leaving traces of flour like a kiss. That's when I know we are relaxed.

We collect odd leafy vegetables from Grandma's garden, smelling the ripped stalks on our hands long afterward. Grandma simmers beans and onions in enormous cast-iron pots for hours and hours. She marinates meats, using spicy, foreign liquids mixed up in tiny crystal pitchers. She makes her own breads and pastry, setting bowls of rising dough in the sunny spots on the floor, moving them every hour to soak up the warmth, and rise, moving my mother and me from chair to chair as well while we nibble on leftover choppings and taste her ripening sauces. Rows of little glass bottles with cork stoppers line her shelves, all full of curled, dusty herbs or dried seeds with strong smells and no taste, or no smell and sharp taste. Every tomato is a story to her; the split skin of every bean is worth admiring. She talks, happy with her audience, and we take long breaths of her fragrant kitchen air, her kitchen that smells more like outside, like fields and growing things, than outside ever does. Her day's work produces huge messy meals that Jerry eats too much and Stella too little of, but that my mother and I linger over, unraveled and happy, feeling a kind of nourished that only happens in Pacific Grove. I think it must be that magical kitchen air, a spell of my grandmother's, our tiny silvery wizard.

After dinner Grandpa makes us root-beer floats in big glass mugs while they talk mostly about people and things I don't know. Except Mr. and Mrs. Rosenberg, whose name I recognize because they talk about them a lot, along with a Mr. Sobell. They must be friends of Grandma and Grandpa's, because they always talk of sending money to help them out. But Mr. Sobell lives on Alcatraz, up in the prison; my father talks about him, and says he is a spy, that he should get what the Rosenbergs get. My mother usually changes the subject. I think that if my grandparents want to help Mr. Sobell and the Rosenbergs then they can't be too bad, not as bad as the other men being punished. I curl up in Grandpa's lap to play string games, watching his enormous cottony fingers unfathomably twist a scribble of string into ladders and triangles and diamonds as I nod off to sleep.

Second days set the pattern of the next two weeks. After breakfast Stella sighs loudly, already bored with the magazines she has brought, and wanders into town to shop. Some boy, an older boy, will walk her home later, but she will not invite him in for dinner—she might slip out afterward, though, for a walk on the beach and bring sand back late into our bed, then make me swear not to tell. Jerry makes summer friends easily; there is always a flock of boys his age, loud and covered with summer scabs, and they disappear to be pirates, or guards and cons. Grandpa goes to his woodwork, like a little boy with blocks; I will be going home with a wooden toy, something of pieces cleverly fitted together, sanded to silk. Grandma waves us, my mother and me, off to the shoreline with more food than we say we'll ever eat, and piles of books. We giggle again, skipping out of the little house and down to the small cove where enormous smooth brown rocks curl up at the base of the cliff like sleeping puppies.

My mother is always different here; not the home mother I know well, but, again, like a bigger me, a smaller her. I think she must truly shrink a little these two weeks every year, when we see so eye to eye. We flop on the foamy sand, already finishing our lunch, amazed by every broken bit of shell or sandcrab, by the sea urchins and starfish in the tide pools and the otter just offshore. I want an otter, to have as a pet; they are like puppies who live in the sea, and maybe I can train one to swim home to our island. But I am too embarrassed to ask my mother about this. Her long blond hair brushes the sand when she bends over, rippled as a mermaid's. She reads the hard books aloud to me, books she would think too grown-up the rest of the year, and I read the easy ones aloud to her. She loves to go swimming here; I'm not allowed to even dip a foot in the water at home, in the Bay, because Daddy says it is too dangerous, but here she taught me to swim. The water is very cold and she always says we just have to get used to it, but we never do; we run out of the waves shrieking as soon as our ears start to hurt, and rub each other with towels. She taught me to swim by having me lie on top of the water with her hand underneath barely supporting me, telling me to breath, to relax, to let my body remember the water and I'll just float.

We compete for seashells, both of us with chilling fingers, slipping on the rocks and scraping ourselves, giggling, playing together in a way we are too shy of at home, where others can see, until Grandma calls us in for another dinner of strange colors and smells. We race home with our skin turning caramel, carrying fistfuls of sweet alyssum and Queen Anne's lace to stick in the Mason jars glowing bright blue on Grandma's shelves.

My mother knows things in Pacific Grove, better than just

ABC, like teaching me to swim. Things she doesn't know at home, or things I think she knows but doesn't tell, things she lets my father tell. Here she knows why a sea urchin loses its spines; stories of moons and tides and what pulls the sea around and tugs us to the earth; where sand comes from. She tells me stories called "mythology" about Greek and Roman gods and goddesses who fight all the time, like Jerry and Stell. The air flutters with orange butterflies she says are called "Monarch," and that they all meet up here before flying south where it's warmer; they are as thick as the seagulls on Alcatraz, who sometimes blot out the sun and poop on everyone. But the Monarchs are beautiful; I ask if I can keep one as a pet, in a Mason jar with holes in the lid. But she explains they don't like to be trapped like that, no sounds, no real air, no sun, no way to fly; it would fade away and die and that isn't fair, it's against Nature. Also, they are delicate; even touching one could hurt its orange skin, brush off its tiny feathers of color.

Here she can knot weeds together and make us crowns and necklaces, but at home she cannot sew me a button without little stabs to her fingers that bleed onto a blouse, and here she laughs a lot, and sometimes skips. This summer it is the same as always, but in the back of my mind I know it is different, anyhow, because this is the last summer we will both be like this, the same size. I am not so little anymore; I am going away to school.

The drive home is no different than all the other drives home—feeling trapped in the station wagon, feeling sand trapped in the cracks of my body—but, still, it is. Stell is anxious to visit with her girlfriends; Jerry finishes the last of the brownies Grandma packed us. My mother tenses as we get closer to home, rewinding in an hour and a half what has been loose and unspooled for two weeks, and watching her I start to slip into feeling little again, the child. But not for long, I know. I am seven years old, and going home this time means starting first grade in the City, finally joining my best friend Alice, who, at eight, has been going into the City already for a whole year and has stopped being my best friend, but maybe now will be again. On my lap is my present from Grandpa; not a toy this time, but a little wooden box with sliding panels and secret compartments only he and I know the workings of. He made a show of giving it to me, insisting on revealing its trick to me alone, so no one could see, sliding it open to release its faint smell of linseed oil. It is a real present, not a child's plaything anymore, but an object with a purpose. I will keep my school pencils in it. Next to me is the package of clothes Grandma has made me special for school, all of them crisp and just slightly too big and waiting to be filled out, trapping cinnamon and fresh sage smells in their folds. I stroke the dress on top, a pretty plaid jumper, and smile to myself.

The Alcatraz lighthouse winks at us; my mother parks the car in the garage and we take the ferry home, across the mile and a half of peaking and swirling water that is so dangerous. Soon, the tomorrow morning that still feels like forever away, I will be back on this boat, without my mother's clutching hand, going the other way, away from home. I hope hard there is no morning fog. I will join the other children and ride the ferry parentless, and walk the two blocks straight up from the dock, and three blocks left (left is my hand with the scar on the knuckle from this last summer's rock scrape) on blocks of pavement into a tall cement building with children who walk the same pavement squares back to their City homes. Children who maybe live in those tall buildings with spires. I am going to make a *new* best friend, I suddenly know it, and Alice can just watch as the pretty new City girl laughs very loud at my jokes and invites me home, to climb floors and floors of stairs up from the street to her tall pink house covered with white wooden swirls. My new best friend and I will play City games, using City cast-off trash, bottle caps and gum-wrapper chains, instead of seashells and sticky seagull feathers. We'll talk, talk, talk, and play in her fenced-in back yard, on a carpet of grass. And, a dog! She'll have a real puppy to play with, maybe a few of them, the puppies we aren't allowed to have on the island. Puppies to nibble our fingers and lick our faces and tumble all over us, like the puppies children unwrap from big bowed boxes on Christmas mornings in the movies. I'll have to leave my best friend and the puppies too soon to run catch the ferry home, cursing, and race into dinner almost late, breaking the rule like Stell, still breathless, still with pockets of City air seeping from my new clothing. Life will become about that ferry schedule, and I will complain about it, like everyone else—the only thing now to limit my freedom, my grown-up freedom. Yes, this time I am happy to be coming home.

"Arthur, we decided about this. She's seven."

"Yeah, I know, but Martha Walker's already fixed everything up. No one uses the Social Hall during the day anyway, except the wives sometimes. And you know, the city's getting worse, it's not so safe over there anymore. I don't even like Stella and Jerry going off everyday. So we'll keep her home with us another year or two."

"But I think it would be good for her to go. She's too isolated here. Alice leaves every day. All she has is me."

"Well, now she'll have Martha to teach her with the other kids."

There's a pause. "Martha Walker's a little young, isn't she? What is she, all of twenty-three?"

"So what? She taught school for two years before Stan and her got married. She's qualified."

"So you know all this, you did all this . . . planning, without me?"

"Honey, you were at your folks!"

I hear my mother fussing with her suitcase, opening and closing drawers in silence. She either has nothing to say, or too much to say. I am standing outside their door with my glass, my special glass with the purple grapes painted on it. I take a gulp of water, waiting.

"Vivian, I thought you'd *want* to keep her around another year. You can make her lunch at home."

"*I* was planning, too, you know. *I* had plans."

"Planning what?"

"To have more time . . . I don't know."

"For what?" My father sounds confused.

"I could go in the city more often. There's a lot to do. We've lived here all this time, across from one of the most famous cities in the world, and we act like there's nothing out there, like this is *it*, this *rock!*"

"But we go all the time! And, okay, so we'll go more! Martha told me about this Chinese place her and Stan like, right? So how's this, how's about the four of us go for dinner some night? Stell's old enough, the kids can stay alone for—"

"There's museums! There's women's groups where they meet once a week and plan things . . . like a tour or a movie . . ."

"So, go! You can go for a whole morning. Jesus, you sound like you're locked up here!"

"No! I don't know, that's not what I mean . . ."

"Look, Martha'll have Olivia till two every day, you can go in the city and be back by then. Even if she left for school she'd be back by three-thirty and you'd have to be here. What's the difference? I don't see it."

"No, I guess not."

"I think you'd go crazy with all three of them gone all day. I'd go nuts with all your free time. You can do whatever you want, you don't even have to drive the kids to school. You've got your shopping, what, maybe fifty yards away, everything you need. Would you rather work like I do? Freezing your ass up there in a tower? Hey, I told you this, didn't I, Swope tried taking the damn *stools* outta the Towers, so we'd have to *stand* for eight hours? Jesus!"

"Yes, you told me. Before I left."

"He's no Johnston, I tell you. Johnston never had a problem with morale like this. Or how'd you like shaking down those cells all day? Cons glaring at you, you're the enemy, you know, you're always the bad guy . . . you don't realize how lucky you are."

"No, I guess not." Her voice is wound up tight.

"Oh, hey, I saved this to show you . . ."

I hear the crackle of paper, then a chuckle.

"Some guy wrote an article, talks about Alcatraz . . . here, it's called 'Prisoners are People!' Yeah, brilliant. Guy calls himself an 'authority on mental hygiene,' whatever the hell that's supposed to mean, then jabbers about 'the folly of men who persist in thinking that tougher prisons *tame* criminals, when the accumulated lessons of a century demonstrate that tough prisons make *tougher* criminals.' He's big on those new 'maximum privilege, minimum security' prisons, you know, the country clubs, like down in Chino . . . listen, he says 'the feeling of freedom reduces prison strikes, mass breakouts . . . all prisoners benefit when they know their gripes will be heard'!" This is in *Look* magazine!"

"Uh-huh."

"'America's super-security prison underscores the self-contradictory penal philosophy that you can humanize antisocial individuals by caging them like animals.'" He chuckles again. "Hey, most of 'em *are* animals! I'd like to see Mister Mental Hygiene whiz up here guarding these cons and *then* talk about giving 'em a 'sense of freedom' . . . you think he's not gonna watch his back, wish he had a .45 and a blackjack with him?"

My mother clears her throat. "You know, Arthur, Olivia was really looking forward to it. My mother made her a blue jumper for her first day. She was so excited."

"Ah, come on, we talked that through. She'll survive."

I hear my father kiss my mother on the cheek.

"It's good to have you home, Viv. I get lonely when you all go away. I don't like it when you leave, I want us all together, you know? Oh, listen, he calls Alcatraz 'a grim monument to the most colossal failure in American institutional history . . .' Jesus . . ."

He kisses her again, and she's quiet. They don't talk any more. I go back to my room, quietly, clutching my purple grape glass of water.

The next morning, the first day of school, Jerry and Stella hurry to make the 7:00 A.M. ferry, swearing Charon better wait for them, anxious for their friends, their freedom. My mother has avoided my eyes all through breakfast, busily reminding my brother and sister of things they haven't forgotten, eyeing Stell's sweater, checking Jerry's ears. After they leave there is nothing else for her to look at but me. I fix her with a stony and sullen glare, for she is my enemy now.

"Well, sweetheart, hurry up. First grade! Have a good day. Mind Mrs. Walker. I'm sure she's a very good teacher. I'll see you at lunchtime. I'll make you a surprise. One of Grandma's recipes."

But she is no wizard. I slide out of my seat, I won't look at her. She's big again, back in this house, and I'm the child, but if I'm not as big today as I hoped, neither is she as big as she was. I know now that she's powerless, as powerless as I am, as little as I am, and not in the summer way.

"Olivia, don't you want to wear the jumper Grandma made you?"

I look down at my old summer dress. The collar has loose threads. The hem doesn't quite reach my knees anymore.

"No. I'm wearing this! What's the difference?!" I stomp to the door.

"Sweetheart!"

I look back, giving her one last chance. She looks like something hurts, but I don't care.

"Sweetheart, I'm going to talk to Daddy tonight, about maybe getting you a pet, for all your own. You can have a turtle here, you know, or a hamster. Wouldn't you like a hamster? To take care of?"

I slam the door hard behind me, against her, and head across the parade ground to the Social Hall, where the children have birthday parties, the teenagers have dances, the grown-ups play bridge, and most of the families went to religious services. I've spent my whole life stuck away in there, it seems, like a boxed lunch, like an orange Monarch butterfly in a blue Mason jar.

Below me, the 7:00 A.M. ferry is halfway across the bay to San Francisco.

# Rules

## *The Prison*

> You are entitled to food, clothing, shelter, and medical attention. Anything else that you get is a privilege.
>
> *Institution Rules and Regulations*,
> United States Penitentiary, Alcatraz, California,
> revised 1956

A small riot broke out early in May 1953; inmates smashed their toilets and washbowls and threw burning pillows and clothing through their barred cellfronts in protest over their housing: cells adjacent to, or opposite, black inmates. Warden Swope was frank with the press; the riot was caused by "race prejudice," he said, and the problem of further race prejudice was solved by segregating black inmates on the second tier of B Block. Homosexuals were segregated above them, on the third tier. Black inmates also sat at the back of the now-twice-monthly movies, and went to and from meals as a separate group, the natural result of always being marched in and out and around according to cellblock grouping, a well-maintained prison routine.

*Alcatraz Rules and Regulations* was issued to every convict, so there would be no confusion as to what was "expected . . . in the matter of conduct and work."

Rules governed every possible activity; how an inmate was to wear his hair and clothing; how to smoke (including how many matches and cigarettes one was allowed to have at any given time); how to eat; how to talk to another inmate in the cellhouse or Recreation Yard; how to arrange one's personal belongings (of which there were few) in one's cell; and other housekeeping responsibilities, such as how to make one's bed; how to sit in the auditorium during religious services or movies.

> GENERAL RULE: Though not mentioned in these rules, any disorder, act, or neglect to the prejudice of good order and discipline, and any conduct which disturbs the orderly routine of the institution shall be taken cognizance of by the Warden or his representative, according to the nature and degree of the offense, and punished at the discretion of the Warden or other lawful authority.

Officer Paul Madigan, bound and gagged on the floor of an industries shop, had seamlessly ended the 1941 escape attempt involving Joe Cretzer and Sam Shockley by persuading them of the futility of their actions; he took over as warden from Swope in 1955. Madigan allowed headphones installed in the cells so inmates could listen to radio in the silent evenings from 5:30 to lights-out at 9:30—musical shows or pre-taped sports events only. This began in time for the 1955 World Series, which kicked off an informal and tolerated system of betting; inmates wagered push-ups, the winner to pay up during the Rec period. The well-stocked prison library boasted 18,000 volumes, and reading prisoners averaged seventy to eighty books a year, ordered through the circulated catalog; no volumes depicting crime or sex permitted, however. Still no newspapers allowed, but inmates could subscribe to certain magazines with money earned from work details; they could also now purchase a musical instrument, but could not sing or whistle accompaniment. Eat all you want at mealtimes, but food left earns a skipped meal, or time in Solitary. Inmates could send two letters a month, and receive seven, all still censored. Cigars and chocolate were granted on holidays, and tobacco was freely distributed to reduce its value as currency. Madigan also allowed inmates to donate blood, which earned them an hour or two out of their cells in the society of the prison hospital, drinking lemonade and eating a snack. This was a good deal; at Ohio State Penitentiary ninety-six inmates were enjoying the same treat, but after having volunteered for a medical experiment in which they were injected with live cancer cells.

More riots, more stabbings. One incident landed in federal court, where an inmate who pulled a knife swore he was innocent, that he'd only been helping a buddy fend off another attacker. The jury agreed, and acquitted him.

But Madigan, after the trial, threw the inmate in the Hole and took away his 400 days of good-behavior time earned over the years. When the inmate's attorney protested and a federal judge ordered a hearing, Madigan replied that the prison's disciplinary actions were not subject to court review; for under Alcatraz law, any inmate who broke the rules must be punished, and he as Warden had every right to do so. The keeper of the castle cannot afford to be seen as soft hearted; it levels the playing field, and no man can gain control when perceived as human rather than master.

# Togetherness

## *Olivia*

> *COLLIER'S* MAGAZINE wants to thank everyone for participating in "Children on Alcatraz"—look for it in the August issue!
>
> ANNUAL BAKE-OFF: First Prize was won by Mrs. Martha Walker, our resident schoolteacher, for her yummy Southern Pecan Pie! Second Prize to Mrs. Mary Beth Shotz for her Apple Brown Betty, Third Prize to Mrs. Carolyn Dickson for her Upside Down Pineapple Surprise! Congratulations, girls!
>
> SUMMER DANCE: It seems some officers have received complaints from their wives about not being included in functions. So, a semi-formal SUMMER DANCE will be held July 28 in the Social Hall—kids welcome, too! Ready your Rumba for the Dance Contest—First Prize will be a Broil Quick Electric Appliance!
>
> *The Pelican,* June 1954

Mrs. Walker's Southern Pecan Pie is a brown brick of sugar. She brought it to school the day after the Bake-Off as an extra-special treat, which wasn't so special because she brings us treats all the time, anyway. Everything is too sugary, and I often feel sick after school. There are only four other kids in class and they are all younger than I am, six or seven years old; they eat her candied treats early in the morning and then run around in a frenzy singing "Miss Mary Mack Mack Mack" and "I see England, I see France, I see someone's underpants." Mrs. Walker herself smells like sweet rotting flowers that need to be thrown out, and has ice-cream cone breasts. She calls us all "sugar." Other than that, and her silly high-heeled shoes that stab holes in the ground, I like her; she lets me sit by myself and read. Her waist is very tiny between her hips and her chest; Stell says she wears a merry widow, but her husband isn't dead. I don't like her husband very much, although he's been so nice to me. He's much older than Mrs. Walker, and has a swoop of thick silvery brown hair he combs back from his forehead too often. Stell and the teenage girls think he's a dream—they say he looks like Burt Lancaster and giggle in long, loud trills when he's around.

Stell also hung around the men from the magazine when they were here, wearing a dress I thought needed a slip under it; you could almost see her underwear, like the rhyme. One of the men took a lot of pictures of her alone, up on the cliff by the prison. My father saw and yelled at her to get down from there; the cons could see her from the Rec Yard, the windows. The photographer grumbled and helped her climb down; Stell just shrugged, and smiled a little to herself, and took the photographer off to the southern path leading down to the sea wall, so he could shoot her with San Francisco in the background.

My mother was in the Bake-Off; her Carrot Spice Muffins were a recipe from Grandma and I thought they were OK, except the long carrot shreds felt like strings in my mouth and I spit them out afterward, to save for my hamster. I didn't know if it was a he or a she, it was just a hamster, like mixing a bunny and a rat. I cleaned out its little cage twice a week—otherwise Stell complained about the fur, the poop smell—and gave it fresh wood shavings to sleep in, and bits of torn newspaper, but I didn't play with it much. I fed and watered it, but mostly it just ran around and around on its little wire wheel, never getting anywhere. It spun around so much that one of the wires snapped; I tried fixing it myself, cutting my fingers, but then Jerry came in—I tried to hide what I was doing, but he just took the wheel away and fixed it for me, rolling his eyes. He even put the hamster back in its cage, very gently, and scratched its little head, making friendly hamster noises.

The Carrot Spice Muffins were a big project for my mother; she dragged the TV into the kitchen to watch men yelling in a show called "The McCarthy Hearings" while she furiously shredded carrot and complained to the air how Wisconsin could have possibly produced such a monster. Her fingers were stained orange for days, and Daddy made a joke to her about it—Don't tell me you're turning *red* on me, Vivian!—that I didn't think was funny. But he didn't seem to think it was funny, either, and told her to stop it, stop shredding all that carrot, why didn't she just use canned carrots, why was she making so much work for herself? She said It's not like I don't have the *time*, Arthur, and besides, it's not worth the bother if you substitute. So she kept it up, excited, and for weeks she made batches and batches of carrot muffins until she thought they were perfect, but Mrs. Walker won the Bake-Off anyway. People like things sweet. My mother had to freeze all the leftover muffins, in the big Admiral freezer we share with Mr. and Mrs. Shotz. When the Bake-Off was all over she started getting more headaches, she said from all that baking, and would sit or lie on the sofa, being quiet. I've never had a headache, it's something only grown-ups seem to get; she told me it's like my hamster on its wheel, spinning around and around, but inside her head. They mostly started last year, when she was upset because the Rosenbergs died. Now she takes a little pill for headaches the doctor gave her, called Miltown. I liked watching her bake, even if she didn't win; she isn't so Vibrant and Vivacious anymore—I still collect V words, but they don't fit her as well—but the contest and the McCarthy show made her seem Valid and Valiant for a while.

I have a new dress for the Summer Dance, very grown-up, with straps that cross behind my shoulders, and new sandals with silver stars on them, new socks and underpants all rimmed with thin white lace. My mother took me shopping in the City, after her doctor's appointment. Dr. Gibbons is a psychiatrist, a kind of doctor to help with her headaches, but my father says that's our private, family business and I shouldn't tell people. I like going to Dr. Gibbons with her because there are wonderful magazines to read; it's very quiet while I wait for her, like being in a library. Sometimes there is a woman leaving just when we arrive, or one who comes in and sits with me reading a magazine before my mother is ready to go. There are two kinds of magazines there: the kind for women, like *McCall's*, with recipes for casseroles, advertisements for underwear and appliances, and articles on getting whites whiter and "Togetherness"; and the real grown-up kind, with longer articles and smaller print and pictures of foreign people living in grassy villages, or men standing with test tubes and diagrams of cells, or President Eisenhower. I like these magazines the best; I don't understand all of what I read, but they make me feel important anyway, as if all the layers of lines with little print and big words are stacking up inside of me and making me more solid. There are plants, too, and special articles in frames hung on the wall. One of them is about a man named Dr. Menninger, and the difference between a psychologist, who isn't a doctor, and a psychiatrist, who is. I think this means a psychiatrist can give shots because sometimes my mother is crying a little when she leaves Dr. Gibbon's office. The Dr. Menninger article says psychologists can help psychiatrists make people feel better;

the article ends with him saying in highlighted yellow pen that "There is no longer need for anybody to be unhappy."

Dr. Gibbons must be a good doctor; my mother is looking forward to the Summer Dance, too, and hasn't had a headache all day. She bought Jerry a new tie, but he refused to put it on until she said he didn't have to dance, he could even spend the whole evening downstairs bowling if he wants. He probably won't wear it at all; he gets to do whatever he wants.

I'm mostly afraid of Jerry, and he knows it. He's very big, bigger than fourteen—his wrists are wider than my knees—and thick fleshed like Grandpa, but without all the hair; Jerry wears his in a crew cut, so the top of his head looks like the edge of a broom. The day he grew taller than Stell I thought he'd scare her, too, but he leaves her strictly alone; she has crossed the line from being a sister to being a kind of woman, and I think he is scared of *her* now. They are closer in age, but around her he still seems like a little boy. I am smaller and younger than both of them, and not a woman, merely female, and so I have the disadvantages of this, and none of the benefits. I am not entitled to special privacy in the bathroom; there are more rules for me, although he makes more trouble; my weakness is not something he wants to protect, but to use. He trips me, he blocks my path tauntingly, he wipes disgusting things on my arms and laughs. He sneaks off with his buddies to the bomb shelter to smoke cigarettes, so now he stinks all the time—I don't understand why Daddy never notices how bad he smells, but it's like with the TV; he only sees it when it's tilted perfectly in front of him. Jerry hurries home sometimes with a mouthful of smoke and blows it in my face because he knows it makes me sick. His favorite torture, one that leaves no scars, is to stand in the hallway outside my bedroom door when we are alone in the house; he stretches out his arms, with one hand on the wall and the other on my gaping door so I cannot shut my door no matter how hard I try. Usually I don't care if my door is left open, but this sends me into hysterics. I start crying until I choke, and he finally walks away in disgust; I am disgusted with myself, too, that this is my only means of self-protection. I am only safe when my parents are around—Jerry, leave your sister alone!—but then it is only temporary; he will get me later. They often assign him to protect me from something—Jerry, keep an eye on your sister!—which leaves me at the mercy of my keeper, and no one to appeal to for help. But they never had any brothers or sisters, so maybe they never needed help themselves.

On the Fourth of July we had our usual Watermelon Party on the dock. Jerry and the boys like to pretend the watermelons are bombs; they grab the melons and throw them with whistles down from the cliff onto rocks, smashing them open hard, before the grown-ups can stop them. They spit the sticky seeds at the girls, who walk around afterward with their bare legs and shoulders spotted black; the seeds stuck to their skins are a badge of something. The parents are happy and indulgent and let us make a juicy mess. When it gets dark we all sit on the dock and watch the fireworks; the explosions are mirrored in the water, so there's bursting lights all around us, like being trapped between two armies, my father says. Sometimes the older kids get sparklers to run around with, but they make me nervous and I always drop one as soon as it is handed to me.

I walked up to our cottage to go to the bathroom and saw Jerry coming out, cupping something in his hand, followed by other boys holding sparklers that burnt bright arcs in the darkness ahead of them. Something wasn't right, they had that kind of harsh hum building up around them. Jerry spotted me and grinned, and held up what I then saw was my hamster, swinging it a little by its tail. The other boys waved their sparklers at it, and I yelled at them to stop, but they ran past me, shoving, to the empty parade ground. They set the hamster loose on the wide, empty cement and circled it, poking at it with sparklers while one of them held me back. Jerry swooped in on it, screeching like an evil seagull prepared to attack. When I couldn't stop screaming and crying they finally poked their sparklers at me, to get me to shut up, but I screamed louder, afraid of being burnt, waiting to catch on fire. Then there was a shout, deep and adult—Mr. Walker came up and grabbed the boys away, pushing them aside until they scattered. He very nicely gave me back my hamster, trying to soothe it; it was twitching and stiff, its heart pounding through its thin chest. We put it back home in its little cage, where I used to think it was safe. It burrowed deep into its wood shavings. Mr. Walker escorted me back to the dock without telling anyone what a crybaby I was, and made sure I got another piece of watermelon. I'm glad he was there to save me, like a prince riding by in a story.

But late that night I took my hamster and snuck outside, to let it loose in the bushes. I couldn't protect it anymore, even at home in its cage, so I didn't deserve to have it. It scurried off, little wood shavings stuck to its fur—it was safer without me, I thought, even outside in the real world; it would take better care of itself, be better off, on its own.

But I will be safe tonight at the dance, and I am excited. Stell is across the hall in the bathroom putting on the makeup she's not really allowed to wear; she slips a little more on each time, so my parents won't notice. I know that my mother notices, because she's started handing Stell a napkin, silently, when she comes in before dinner to wipe off the lipstick; the wastebasket in our bedroom is often full of these old mouths of hers. Revlon Fire 'n Ice. She brushes her eyelashes with Max Factor mascara. It comes in a tiny case, harder than mud, and she spits at it to make it runny; after it goes on her lashes wet, like she's been crying, it dries hard again. To me it looks like dirt stuck on her eyes.

I'm in our room trying to button the straps on the back of my dress—I think I need my mother to help me, or Stell, she usually does that kind of thing for me now—when I hear my father come in the living room; the front door slams hard behind him, and I know something's wrong. Something's been wrong a lot; my mother told me that Daddy is just worried because men in Washington who don't know what they're doing are talking about closing down the prison, and we might have to move. Daddy's angry because even Warden Swope thinks so, he thinks running the prison costs too much money. Daddy says Yeah, and what costs so much is the thing that makes it so good, us being way out here on an island, Alcatraz *always* cost a lot, what's all the fuss about now? I just think if we move I can maybe get a dog—a big one, shaggy and fierce, to protect me.

But now Daddy starts yelling at my mother—Damn it, Vivian!, Arthur, calm down, what is it?—so I look out my door a peek to listen, and see him toss something at her.

"You want to explain *this*, Vivian?"

"What?" The thing, a soft scrap of something dark, almost hits her in the face, and she snatches it up in her hand. It's black and lacy, a pair of women's underpants. I've seen advertisements for those kinds of underpants, in the back of the women's magazines at Dr. Gibbons's. My mother laughs a little, like she does when she's confused. My eyes meet Stell's across the hall in the bathroom; she silently closes the bathroom door.

"I don't know, Arthur. Maybe it's something *you* want to explain to *me*?"

"They were being passed around up there, like some sort of goddamn trophy! How the hell am *I* supposed to keep order up there, get *respect*, when I've got cons sniffing at my wife's panties?!"

"What makes you think they're mine?"

"They went through in our laundry!"

"They're not mine." They glare at each other a moment in silence. My father yells "Stella!" I close my bedroom just before my father heads down the hallway; I hear the bathroom door thrown open, and more yelling, overlapping like blankets:

"What the hell?—"

"Just a joke, Daddy!—"

"Arthur, let her!—"

"And where were *you*, Vivian? How could you let her do—"

"Oh, stop it, you can't blame me for—"

"Look, *you* can't handle things around here, fine, I'll have to—"

"Daddy, you're hurting me—"

"A goddamn tease, that's what she is, I have to be ashamed of my own goddamn daughter—!"

And then a sound I've only heard on television, usually in movies where a man and a woman are fighting, and right before they kiss, the sound of the man slapping the woman, or girl this time, across the face. My mother is yelling Stop it, Arthur, and I hear Stell crying. Her mascara is going to smear, and go from hard to runny all over again.

Mrs. Walker loves to dance; when I come in the Social Hall with my parents she grabs my father by the hand and drags him out on the floor, laughing: "You don't mind if I steal your husband now, do you, Vivian?" My mother shrugs, and my father sheepishly dances with Mrs. Walker to "Mr. Sandman." He doesn't like to dance, I know, he thinks his bad hip makes him look stiff. I don't understand how *she* can dance, though, balanced on those little shoe points, or in her narrow white dress. It is all white lace, over some material the color of her skin. Mr. Walker winks at my mother and me, and pulls me out by the hand, spinning me around. I'm surprised, and laugh when I feel my skirt twirling up my legs. I forget that I ever didn't like him; I wish Stell were here to see this, Mr. Walker dancing with me, but I know her friends will tell her—Mr. Walker asked *Olivia* to dance!—because they're watching us, envious. My mother smiles, looking tired, and drinks punch. The music changes to slow but my father keeps dancing with Mrs. Walker; my mother goes to sit down in a folding chair by herself. Mr. Walker bows to me, overly dramatic, and everyone applauds us; I feel proud, and grown-up, but also a little embarrassed, so I take him back to sit with my mother.

"You're not dancing, Vivian?"

"Oh, no thanks, Stan. Looks like Martha's taking good care of Arthur."

"Yeah, she'll keep him hopping." He sits, and quickly runs a comb through his wave. "Haven't seen you around much, Martha'n me."

She simply nods.

"You hear about Congress? Art tell you? They finally voted to keep us in business. Finally. Whew . . ." He's breathing hard, from the dancing.

"I heard." She paused. "You'd think, though, I mean, the Bureau of Prisons *and* the Justice Department flat out say we should be shut down. Even Swope thinks the island's not properly designed for what it—"

"Yeah, but he also said the country needs a place like this. He's on his way out, anyhow. Don't you worry. There'll always be an Alcatraz." He looks around. "Where's Stella?"

"Home. Not feeling well." This, too, is private, and I

don't say anything. My father dragged her out of the bathroom and shoved her into our bedroom; my mother pulled me out of the way as he threw open our closet and dumped out all our things from dresser drawers and nightstands, looking for something to keep him angry, still yelling at Stell. He finally finished shaking down our room and left, left Stella crying, to clean up. She is grounded for a month. My mother didn't want to come tonight, after that, but my father insisted the rest of us all go, he wanted us together. He wasn't angry with me, so I didn't say anything.

"Hard to believe you got a sixteen-year-old."

"Mm-hm." I realize for the first time that my mother doesn't like Mr. Walker, and, despite his being so nice and saving me, I remember that I don't either. He has been so nice to me, but now I feel his hair oil on my hands, from the dancing; I wipe my palms on the side of my dress, holding it against my legs.

He winks at me. "And *you,* kid, you're what now, eight?"

"Nine."

"Yeah, getting to be a real little lady." He puts an arm around my waist and tugs, so that I stumble slightly and wind up sitting on his knees. He pats my back and I feel his bare hand on my skin through the lattice of dress straps; something flickers across my mother's face, and I know that at nine I am too old for this kind of thing. But Mr. and Mrs. Walker don't have children, so maybe he doesn't know this.

"Mom, do you want some more punch?"

"Yes, thanks, sweetheart."

I climb off of him, but he gets up and pushes me into his chair. "You ladies just sit, I'll get the punch." He winks at me, takes my mother's cup and leaves; my mother gives me a reassuring smile.

"I'm gonna go to the bathroom." She nods, and when I go downstairs my father is still dancing with Mrs. Walker—

I hear her ask him if he's seen *The Country Girl* yet, because he looks just like William Holden, *really*. My mother is watching them, and Mr. Walker is ladling red punch into two paper cups.

Downstairs Jerry is playing pool with some of the older boys; his tie hangs loose around his neck, like a noose, and a cigarette hangs loose from his bottom lip. He lines up an elaborate shot, with much practice cue-sliding and hip adjustment before he shoots. I pass by just as the cue ball pops up a little, barely hitting its mark. The older boys guffaw and I smile, too; Jerry sees me watching and flushes, angry—he sucks hard on his cigarette, snakes his tie from his neck and flicks it at me like a whip. I flinch away, and they all laugh again, Jerry adding a now-triumphant smirk. I try to maintain my dignity and head for the bathrooms at the far end of the room, a little nervous at their presence, the smell of their smoke and heated laughter. I think it is always worse when there is a group of them; it is like how the Indians boiled water. Mrs. Walker taught us this, how the Indians would heat stones in the fire, then put the hot stones in a pot of water or gruel to cook it. One stone alone doesn't cook much, but a group of stones makes a lot of heat; they keep the other stones hot, and stay hot longer themselves.

In the bathroom I find one of my straps is loose, a button has come undone, or I buttoned it wrong; I'm sitting on the toilet, reaching over my head behind my back to fuss with it, knowing my mother will have to help me, when the bathroom door opens suddenly and Mr. Walker enters.

"Oh!—"

"Oh!—Hey, sorry, kid."

"Uh, that's OK . . ." Didn't I lock the door? Maybe not . . . so this is an accident, that's all, like spilling something. No one's fault, not his fault. But I feel cold, then frozen when he doesn't back up and leave, the way anybody does, or should, when they walk in on you in the bathroom. He leans against the doorway, holding a full paper cup.

"I brought you your punch."

"Thank you."

He sets it down on the sink, but doesn't move from the doorway, just stands there, watching me. I don't know what to say, because anything said will make it worse, somehow; at least the silence is thick, like a barrier between us. My brother is just outside and I want him desperately, to come in, to barge in, and help me. But no one comes.

"Yeah, you're a real little lady now. Awful pretty."

I look down and see my new white cotton underpants lying at my feet, around my ankles, blending with my white cotton socks. The silver stars on my sandals peek through. This is the most freezing thing, the most shameful; he can see my underpants. I am *letting* him see my underpants. I cannot hide them, and they gleam against the dark tile floor, so white and so dirty.

"Well, see you upstairs, kid." I nod, still looking down in shame, and he slowly leaves. I wipe myself and pull up my underpants, hard and high between my legs, around my waist, and begin scrubbing my hands. When I walk through the downstairs the boys all ignore me, engrossed in their game.

Upstairs, there is a small commotion; my mother is standing near my father and Mrs. Walker, holding an empty cup; Mrs. Walker's dress front is stained with punch, a huge blot, red at the edges, dark gray where it's soaked through the lacy white cloth. She looks like the flag of Japan. My father is attempting to hand her napkins, but she just keeps blotting the stain with her hands, shaping the wet dress against her body, wailing a little like it hurts. Other women are clustered around, fluttering their hands; my mother keeps repeating what an accident, what a shame, this slippery floor, I was a little dizzy from that sweet punch, I'm so sorry. She apologizes but then starts to laugh, at first deep inside, rumbling, but then it explodes like a watermelon on the rocks. She laughs louder and louder, and my father tells her to be quiet, that she sounds crazy. Mrs. Shotz tries pulling her away, patting her hand. Mr. Walker turns away when he sees me, and I feel my loose, unbuttoned strap again; I know this is another thing my mother can't help me with. I will have to start learning to do things, to take care of things, myself.

# Hellcatraz

## *The Prison*

> Men go slowly insane under the exquisite torture of unrestricted and undeviating routine.
>
> "20 Months in Alcatraz," Bryan Conway (AZ #293) to T. H. Alexander, *The Saturday Evening Post,* February 1938

> Alcatraz is hell, all right, but it is a psychological hell. . . . Why, they don't treat you like a man over there. They treat you like a child. The guards are like big schoolteachers, herding around kindergarten children.
>
> John Stadig, Alcatraz inmate, in the *San Francisco Chronicle*, 1934

The year after Warden Johnston retired he published *Alcatraz Island Prison and the Men Who Live There,* in which he reports only one inmate suicide occurred between 1934 and 1948. Every community has its "mentally defective" persons, he points out, and prisons, of course, are no exception—they boast an even higher percentage of persons suffering mental and emotional strain, but prison more often was the unfortunate and exacerbating end result of such strain, not the primary cause.

> Mental difficulties of prisoners are deep seated and originate from past maladjustments and inner conflicts that may have

> been in process of incubation over a long period rather than from imprisonment, but they can be aggravated by brooding over long sentences, hopeless outlook, and the situational difficulties of the restricted prison environment.

If an inmate's "conduct was bizarre," or he showed signs of "growing demented," he was placed in the hospital for a period of observation under one of two psychiatrists on consultation status—a clever con might devise an act to fool even an experienced guard, but he could not deceive the psychiatrist for long.

Johnston allowed inmates suffering physically or emotionally rather liberal access to medical attention, for "sometimes worried men, suffering a brief spell of despondence, would benefit by a short period of hospitalization and return to their assignments." If that didn't snap a guy out of it, a board of three psychiatrists would examine the case; if the inmate were judged truly insane, it warranted a transfer to the U.S. Medical Center at Springfield, Missouri.

Attorney General Murphy inspected Alcatraz in 1939; while he praised Johnston, he called the Rock "a place of horror," which exercises a depressing and wicked psychology on the inmates. In his opinion, "conditions tending to make prisoners 'stir crazy' were more evident at Alcatraz than elsewhere."

Bryan Conway's 1938 account of his "Twenty Months in Alcatraz" told of his being sent to the Rock—while eligible for parole at Atlanta, with a spotless record—after being "certified as an incorrigible," due to his refusal to testify against a buddy in a prison murder case. According to Conway:

> The undeviating routine is what kills and maddens prisoners . . . out of a total population of 317 prisoners, fourteen

> went violently insane during my last year on the Rock, and any number of others were what we call 'stir crazy,' going about their familiar routine like punch-drunk boxers. Of course, they do not formally declare them insane, but they isolate them.

Conway was present when Rufe Persful chopped off his fingers with an ax and subsequently disappeared from the general population; he also knew Joseph Bowers, the first inmate killed during what was called an escape attempt, and that everyone knew old "Dutch" was mentally unbalanced. He states that "next to routine, one of the worst forms of mental torture at Alcatraz is the target practice of the guards . . . this is calculated mental cruelty." He describes it as a nightly occurrence so that men in their cells cannot sleep, then in daylight must walk past the human dummies "sprawled along the walkways," as a constant, silent lesson.

Roy Gardner, one-time Public Enemy Number 1, served two years at Alcatraz before a final transfer to Leavensworth, and then release. He earned a brief celebrity in 1938 when the sale of his story was published as *Hellcatraz: the Rock of Despair,* in which he calls Alcatraz "the tomb of the living dead":

> Hopeless despair on the Rock is reflected in the faces and actions of almost all the inmates. They seem to march about the island in a sort of hopeless, helpless daze, and you can watch them progressively sinking down and down.

He describes the "hell nights" of inmates unable to sleep, picturing women, families, the lives they've lost. An inmate knows when Alcatraz "has really got him—when the mind pictures don't fade away with the daylight."

Two years later, in a tired San Francisco hotel, Gardner dropped cyanide pellets in a glass of acid, put a towel over his head like a little old lady hoping to clear congested lungs with a cloud of steam, and took deep, mortal breaths, finally clearing away the mind pictures, the hell nights, once and for all.

# The Ferry

## *Olivia*

I have my bed stories to help me go to sleep at night, some nights when I'm scared and my thoughts spin around on a hamster wheel, or nights before a special thing, like tomorrow, my first day at real school. It's for sure this time—my parents decided after the Summer Dance not to have Mrs. Walker teach me anymore. I'm going to fourth grade at Sherman Grammar School, a big yellowish building with Mexican tile on the walls. I think it looks a little like the old California Missions Mrs. Walker showed us pictures of, where wandering soldiers went to pray or rest. There's a tall churchlike tower attached to the main building, and I hope it holds a bell. My mother took me there a few days ago to enroll me—when she was feeling "Up To It," as if she needed to be tall enough for the task—and to show me the school so tomorrow it won't feel too new. Stell and Jerry are supposed to walk me there the first day, out of their way, all the way up to Union Street, but after that they can meet me at the Bay Street corner. I'm not supposed to get lost. She also bought me a brand-new lunch box, with its own Thermos and Howdy Doody on the front, which I hope I'm not too old for.

My bed stories aren't the baby fairy tales Mrs. Walker tells the little kids, or like stories Stell reads me now from her magazines, the ones my mother doesn't like her reading; she smuggles them home and hides them under a flap of carpeting, in case there is another shakedown. Stell gets in more and more trouble, although I think now that she's sixteen, almost a grown-up, she should get in trouble less. She loves these glossy magazines with women on the covers looking anguished and hopeful; they are called things like *True Confessions* and *Real Love*, titles that sound much more serious than fairy stories like "The Frog Prince," but the girls in all of them seem the same. They have long hair that cascades, there is aching and swooning, and they always fall sick and are pale, sometimes at the creaking door of Death, until the PHONE RINGS—it's *HIM* calling!—or He arrives at the door with flowers, his white car or white horse in the background, ready for sweeping away to another End, one as hazily defined as Death, but always HAPPY, a desired END. Snow White and Sleeping Beauty, lying still as butterflies in resin, hands pressed to their breasts, are rewarded for their goodness, their dormant hush. Being quiet is good; the magazine girls are rebuffed when too shrill, and men turn away to leave them collapsed against a closing door, pounding their fists, still screaming at the pain of TRUE LOVE. The little Princess in "The Wild Swans" gives up her voice while she weaves shirts from stinging nettles for her swan brothers, to release them from an evil spell cast by an old and ugly and unloved witch; the Prince discovers the Princess in a cave, with blistered and bleeding fingers, resolutely mute, and falls in love. The Little Mermaid, too, gives up her voice for a pair of painful legs and crawls up on land from the sea to dance cripplingly for the Prince, who is also enchanted by her inaudibility, her whispering, bleeding feet. My mother doesn't read fairy tales; she likes mythologies better, where young human girls are always turned into trees or stars or mute animals by lovesick Gods, who can keep the girls trapped in silence forever, loving them all the more. In one mythology a sculptor falls in love with a stone girl he's carved, with her dusty, marble skin. I think she gets to be alive for a while, but winds up in the end being a piece of stone again.

I have made up my own versions, stitched together from other bits and pieces. One of my bed stories is that I am a maid living in a castle with a famous Prince, although I really am a Princess myself, I just don't know it and no one else can tell because I work in the cellar. The Prince gives a big dancing party for other Princes and Princesses and I creep up to watch the swirling dancers and listen to the music my mother calls "classical," the kind of music that is boring anywhere except in my story. While watching, I faint from something and crumple to the ground. The Prince makes his way through the crowd, picks me up in his arms, and I wake up later in a beautiful bedroom upstairs. I think I'm not wearing clothes, something to do with my illness means they had to take off my ragged dress, but I'm covered by a heavy satin coverlet. The Prince comes in to visit me as I lie pale and sick, too weak to speak more than a questioning word or two, conveying my fear and unease at being in such a grand room. The Prince takes my limp hand and kisses it, telling me to go back to sleep, I must get well, and then he will take care of me. He is fascinated by my meek beauty, and my lack of typical Princesslike airs, and when I am well he will marry me. Thinking this, I usually drift off to sleep feeling safe and comforted.

My other favorite is I am lying in a wagon along a country road, soon to give birth, a condition that seems merely like another way of being sick, while my husband drives us to shelter and safety in some very far-off place. While I lie there I weave large mats from grasses my husband collects from the side of the road, to protect us at night; I am ill, but industrious. He admires me for my quiet bravery, my lack of shrill complaint.

These stories lull me to sleep at night, lull me off somewhere it's easy to be a good girl. It's getting harder, in real life. Look at Stell. I thought getting older would make it easier.

On the first day of school I ride the morning ferry with the other kids, proudly holding my lunch box. There's nothing special about the ferry anymore; my mother and I ride it twice a week now to go to her doctor. Once coming home she told me a new mythology, during a life-jacket drill—we have them once a month, so we all know what to do if the ferry sinks, so we don't drown in the dangerous Bay. We hooked on the rubber jackets and stood at the rail watching Alcatraz dip and sway toward us, and she told me about a ferryman just like Captain Pearson, who pilots our little boat back and forth all day from his windowed cabin, waving at us. In the mythology the ferryman isn't nice; he's called Charon, and he takes the dead people across the river Styx to the Underworld, which is really Hell. She lets me say "Hell," too, this time, although I'm usually not supposed to swear. Apparently you can say "Hell" when you're telling a mythology, or being religious, which we aren't—my father is Lutheran and my mother is Jewish, but neither of them cares about the religion part; they cancel each other out, and so we're nothing. Stell and Jerry and I all call Captain Pearson *Charon* now, giggling, although my mother says we mustn't say that when he can hear. I bet the people on the real Charon's ferry don't have to bother with life-jacket drills, I told her—because they're already dead, get it?—and she laughed a little.

Stell has also brought me with her into the City on the ferry. She likes it when there's a woman we don't know, coming or going; these strange women are always "dolled up," Stell calls it, with veiled, feathered hats and strips of fur around their throats, all dressed to kill to visit a husband in the cellhouse. Stell usually sniffs and says these women have bad taste, but they fascinate her. When they are coming they stand up very straight and examine their fingernails, and clutch at their little hats in the wind, but when they are going they look weary and smeary-eyed. We giggle, sometimes, about the story of one lady who set off the snitchbox and had to take off all her clothes for the guards; they found metal in her corset. She was the mother of a gangster convict, a long time ago, named Capone. I giggle, but this story makes me uncomfortable; I don't like the part about the guards looking at the lady in her underwear, but this is what Stell dwells on—also that the gangster got sick and died later of V.D., but she won't tell me what that is.

Stell is supposed to come straight back to the island after school now, it is a new rule; there is a shadowy threat of something if she misses curfew again. But my father finally agreed to let her take me into the City for a movie on Saturday afternoons. Or perhaps I am taking her; it is unclear who is supposed to be guarding whom. She spends much of the movie in the bathroom and returns with half-eaten bags of popcorn she gives me the rest of. Afterward she installs me at a soda fountain in the Marina with a tin-roof sundae while she talks to the boys always nearby, hovering, drawn to some sweetness in her I've never seen. There's one she leaves with a lot; he is a sailor, and wears a stiff bleached uniform and little bowl hat. She comes back alone a while later, perfectly timed, just as I'm eating the cherry sunk to the bottom of my dish, in a puddle of melted whipped cream. Once on the ferry home she showed me a jangly charm bracelet he gave her that I was not, *not* to tell our parents about, and if I was good and didn't say anything she'd let me wear it. The truth is, I don't really care what she does, but I don't want her to get caught breaking rules; it somehow gets my mother in trouble, too. At home over dinner, if we all have dinner together that night, Daddy will ask Stell a lot of questions about the movie we saw; she always remembers details from the beginning, and how it ends, and he is satisfied. But the stories in movies mostly begin the same and end the same, anyway. My father doesn't see a lot of movies, so maybe he doesn't realize this.

The classroom at Sherman Grammar School has long wooden tables we sit at in twos; my partner, who I assume will be my new best friend, is a pretty girl with chalky skin and a kind of dark hair I've never seen; a short fringe cutting a harsh line high across her pale forehead, then hanging straight as black glass on the sides to her shoulders. It's odd on a little girl, too severe—even the Chinese girls wear braids and bows—but on her I think it is that desirable thing to be, sophisticated. She is what Stell calls "blasé," and now I understand what that means. The girl shrugs at me then complains to the teacher that she wants to sit next to her best friend Wendy, but the teacher makes her sit with me because our names are in that order. It dawns on me that everyone has their friends made already; they have spent first, second, and third grades figuring it out. I'm starting late, and Monica looks at me like I'm doing something rude. I will have to give her time to get used to the idea of being my new best friend.

Our teacher Mrs. Marsden is older than Mrs. Walker and not as pretty. We stand up to say the Pledge of Allegiance, like we did with Mrs. Walker, but now there's a change; Mrs. Marsden tells us before we start that Congress wants us to add "under God" to part of it, after "one nation" and before "indivisible." The kids here aren't used to it, either, and we all fumble "under God." She says we'll get better with practice. Then she takes roll and when she gets to my name, just after Monica's, she looks worried and asks if I have an older brother Gerald; when I say yes she frowns, and moves on. I try to smile and look sweet to reassure her, but I get the idea I'm not exactly starting school with a gold star on my chart. Jerry used to come home all the time with notes from teachers and I guess Mrs. Marsden was one of them. I am guilty by association. Monica looks at me, wondering what is wrong with my family.

We file out to recess together to drink our juice—after she stops to wash her hands—and she asks me where I live. *She* lives in the Heights, which I think is supposed to impress me, so I raise my eyebrows. I ask her if they have puppies; No, she says, dogs carry *germs*. They have a cat. She asks me again where I live; when I tell her, she raises *her* eyebrows, and starts asking questions.

The *Collier's* story made us famous, the "Children on Alcatraz," as if no one ever knew we were there. They ran the "First Pictures" of us, and when I opened the magazine I thought they would be our baby shots. But it was only regular pictures of the kids on the ferry, at the Social Hall, on the parade ground. I secretly had wanted to be on the cover; I would be a magazine girl. I hung around near the men taking pictures, mutely smiling, hoping my hair would cascade. But they chose Cupie Mitchell, who's only five, and put a watercolor sketch of her clutching a doll in front of one of the Towers on the cover. Inside there's a photo of kids running on the parade ground; I'm in the back, blurred, running beside Jerry. They didn't use any of the pictures of Stell; my father wouldn't let them, he said the wind was blowing her skirt up. She keeps a copy of a picture the photographer sent her in a scrapbook; she calls it her "portfolio," and says the photographer told her she was destined to be a model. The article talks about how normal and happy we all are, then mostly about the prison.

As usual the other Alcatraz kids are a grade above or

below me; I am the only one in this class, so Monica has no one else to ask her questions or verify the information I give her. I don't like her questions, about barbed wire and electric-shock fences and can I hear the beaten men screaming in the cellhouse at night, but I know if we're going to be best friends I have to like her a little, and I want her to like me, so I try to answer without lying while still making it sound like a thrilling adventure. Sure we see the convicts, all the time, well, sometimes, but no, none of them have asked me to help them escape. No, I've never been taken hostage, and I've never seen the Birdman. No, there aren't any bloodhounds; the only dog on the island is Warden Swope's and he's just an old, droopy-eyed setter. She seems disappointed, and so I tell her that sometimes gangster convicts get sick with V.D. and die. She raises her eyebrows again, enthralled, and says that's dirty. I'm glad I have all this to create a kind of glamour about myself for her, to be attractive as a new friend. She thinks living on the island is a riot, which is a word I know is not good, and washes her hands again before we go back to class.

Mrs. Marsden is very serious about the Purpose of Education. She announces that the U.S. Supreme Court says we can't violate the Fourteenth Amendment, so we're all going to be together in the same classrooms now. This makes no sense to us and we all look at each other, unimpressed, until she explains that the Negro children will be with us now, just like the Chinese children and the Mexican children, everywhere in the country, even in the South, because the important thing to remember is that under the eyes of God we're all *American* children, isn't that so? We all nod. The only Negroes on the island are what Daddy calls segregated, in part of B Block. I've heard my mother argue with him about it; he always ends the argument saying that it's for their own protection, they like being with their own kind. There is a Negro girl at the table next to me, and I suddenly wonder if she won't want to be my friend, but she smiles at me, and slides open the little drawer in her desk to show me where I'm supposed to put my pencils. Monica wasn't so helpful. Now I wish I was sitting next to this other girl; she is starting everything late, too.

Mrs. Marsden then talks about what fourth grade has in store for us: mostly, projects. We're going to learn about Electricity and Currents and make our own battery; the Planets, the Solar System and Man's place in it; California History and the Indians; and division and putting fractions together. The textbooks handed out are impressive; scuffed and thick, with plain hard covers, the tips softened with wear. We are told to make covers for them out of shopping bags at home, which we are allowed to decorate however we want. I've seen these covers on Jerry's textbooks; his have bloody dinosaurs ripped apart by saber-toothed tigers, and jagged concentric circles meant to be nuclear explosions, all drawn hard in waxy crayons that leave shavings. He likes anything nuclear, especially *thermo*nuclear, which is much better than the old kind of bomb. The other girls in my class whisper; they are all planning flowers. I realize this decision is going to be important. Maybe my mother can help me, if she's feeling Up To It.

At the end of class Mrs. Marsden tells us we will all be getting the brand-new polio vaccination soon, and that we must bring this signed letter back from home giving permission. She says Science is a wonderful thing for Mankind, and we are very lucky and should be grateful to Dr. Salk because now we won't all get sick and be put in iron lungs like more unfortunate children who can't get the polio vaccination. Tonight we're supposed to pray for Dr. Salk's health, and all the other sick children in the world, especially the poor Soviet children who don't have God.

My brother and sister are waiting for me after school at the prearranged corner, then ignore me and each other when we meet up with the other kids at the ferry. Stell and Jerry are both used to first days at school and it doesn't occur to them to ask me how mine was. I act like I don't care, like my own thoughts are so absorbing I don't even notice them. Anyway, it's better when Jerry just ignores me. Alice, my old best friend, is on the ferry, too, but we're out of the habit of being friends now and just feel a little embarrassed with each other.

The ferry scrapes the Alcatraz dock, and dips. We let the adults go first, then the older girls, who make the most fuss, then the rest of us take our run-run-leap from gangplank onto the floating platform, then up on the dock—the fewer steps, the more reckless we are, the better. The most daring usually earns admiration from the others and a rebuke from the boat linesman on duty. Today it's Mr. Lucey, Alice's father; it's his job to grab the wet line from the dock and struggle to tie up the boat. I'm not used to the run-run-leap with an armful of books and a lunch box, and my final thud onto the dock is clumsier than I'd like; Mr. Lucey grabs my elbow, steadying me before my books can plunge into the water, and shakes his head good-naturedly. Most of the families have dropped something of value into the sea this way; the Lupianos lost a brand-new television set in the water, and Mrs. Lupiano cried in front of everyone while Mr. Lupiano tried to joke that Well, we all know nothing's gonna survive a swim in this Bay, right? Jerry dropped a new football once and jumped in after it, getting his head smashed between the boat and the dock platform; he had to stay in bed for a week, but saved his football. He was happy, but my mother and I had to wait on him, bring him things every few minutes and do most of what he said.

When cons come to live on the island there's a special ferry only for them, but when just a few of them are coming or going to talk to a judge at the courthouse in the City, they ride with us. During the trip they are chained in a little room inside the main cabin, away from us; we aren't supposed to hang around, but the boys always gather up the road to watch them being marched up to the cellhouse. There aren't any today, just regular people. Stell goes off to the soda fountain with the other girls; Jerry heads for the canteen with his friends. I walk home with my books, my lunch box.

Martha Walker hurries across the parade ground on her clicking heels, heading for the dock. I haven't seen her in a few months, since the Summer Dance and the spilled punch on her white lace, the dancing with my father. She loses her clicking rhythm in a stumble when she sees me, then stands too theatrically with a hand on her hip, as if her venture out was only an excuse for us to chat.

"Well, hi, sugar!"

"Hi, Mrs. Walker."

"They don't lose any time loading you up on schoolwork, do they! Look at all those books! And on your first day! So, so, how was it? You have fun?"

"It was OK."

"Well, *that's* good . . ." She glances past me, toward the dock, at her watch. "Well, *I'm* getting my hair done. Better hurry if I want to grab the three-fifty!"

I stand aside, theatrical myself, to let her pass.

She hesitates a moment. "How's your mother doing, sugar?"

"She's fine. My mother's fine." She gives me a big sweet smile and clicks off, stabbing the ground. I find myself thinking that if Mrs. Walker got polio, or maybe V.D., she wouldn't be able to balance on shoes like that anymore, but that's a nasty thought, so I head home.

It's a dark day, though; the shades are drawn and my mother is lying down on the couch, in front of the television's grainy flickers. My father must have fixed it, then. Last week the current from the power plant blew out the set and he said the generator's current is too strong—we need a converter, something about AC and DC; my mother said she'd told him that before, the toaster *still* doesn't work. He looked annoyed then and said Can't you fix it, can't you do it yourself, Vivian? She just sighed, But you said *you* wanted to do it, Arthur, you were going to— Yeah, all right, he said, and took it up with him to the prison, to have a con fix it. When Mrs. Marsden teaches us about Electricity and How it Helps Us, I will understand it all better, how it works. My mother read for a few days, but now she has television again; she watches anything, all day, and we'll probably have TV dinners tonight. I like them, the tidy compartments of meat, vegetable, potato, dessert. Whoever makes them is a better cook than my mother, although I bravely kicked Jerry under the table when he said the same thing a few nights ago—a mistake, as he later gave me an Indian burn so bad I thought my skin would tear. I'll probably learn from Mrs. Marsden now, too, why it's called an "Indian" burn. Maybe some kind of savage warfare. Daddy wasn't eating with us that dinner; he's been working more night shifts, and eating his dinner at the prison. He says the food the inmates eat is better than most restaurants in the City.

"Mom?"

She stirs, fumbling to get her slippered feet on the floor. "Oh, hi, sweetheart. How'd it go?" She peers at her watch, and smooths back her blond hair from one flattened side.

"It was OK. We're going to make papier mâché planets, the teacher said. Mrs. Marsden. And at Thanksgiving we're going to have a pageant about the Indians. She likes projects."

My mother smiles. "That sounds good. Sweetheart, could you get me a glass of water?"

"Sure." I put down my stack of books and fill my purple grape-painted glass from the kitchen faucet. "Here." I hand it to her very carefully because she is always breaking things now, dishes and glasses slip out of her hands all the time. I sit at her feet, wanting her to touch me. She fumbles instead with her small silver pillbox. Mother-of-pearl inlay on the top. She taught me once in Pacific Grove how mother-of-pearl is made, not just from oysters but from any mollusk shedding the insides of its shell. On the beach she opened up an empty, drying mussel shell to show me its glittery rainbow side. Its insides were gone, scooped out and eaten by a larger animal. But only an oyster can make a pearl, she explained; the oyster takes care of the pearl inside it, covering it in milky layers, until it grows big enough to be jewelry. Like you, she'd said, fluffing my hair, You are my pearl, so . . . *You* are the mother-of-pearl! I finished, giggling. We thought this was extremely funny in that nonsense way, and spent a summer laughing about it, singing loudly—You are my oy-ster, my only oy-ster . . . you make me hap-py, when skies are gray . . .

"I made a new friend, I think. Her name's Monica."

"Mm-hm?" She swallows a Miltown pill. Maybe they are for her like my bed stories are for me. Her pillbox clicks shut.

"She's pretty, but sort of in a creepy way. Like her hair's too black and her face is too white. She lives in the Heights." A beat. "She thinks living here is a riot." My mother laughs a little, the kind of laugh where you don't open your mouth. "I guess I'll go start my homework," I tell her.

"Homework so soon?" She stretches out on the couch again, pale, pretty. Or Vague, Vapid.

"Yeah." A beat. "I'm in fourth grade now," I say, as if we've just met.

She smiles. "My big girl."

I go to my room, thinking I will try to make my book covers myself, humming a little in my head. You'll never know, dear . . . how much I love you. Please don't take my oy-ster away . . .

I forget to cover my books, I forget to get my polio letter signed, and the next day, during the Pledge of Allegiance, I forget to be "under God," too. When Mrs. Marsden asks if we remembered to pray for the sick children in the world, and I realize I forgot to do that as well, I wonder what is wrong with my head. But I don't pray at night anyway, even though my mother once said it isn't really about religion, Lutheran or Jewish, it's just God. But God always seemed too important, like the Warden, too huge to care about me, to hear me; he has wars and countries, and I used to think there was maybe a Mrs. God who handled the little things, like children and presents and when you lose something or don't want it to rain, sort of a mix of Mrs. Claus and Mother Nature. So I tried it once, this last summer, praying to Mrs. God. But I think praying is something you have to start when you're really little, like ballet. It's too late for me.

Mrs. Marsden says whoever remembered to pray, raise their hands. Monica raises her scrubbed hand instantly, and mine hovers somewhere over my head, but she could see that I didn't immediately raise it, not with her own virtuous certainty. Mrs. Marsden then explains it's a sin to lie about God and praying, it's very bad; now good children will keep getting sick, and the bad children will go straight to Hell. When she says this, Monica looks sideways at me like going to Hell is contagious and she hopes I go soon. Like I am a Godless Soviet child, full of dirty germs, full of V.D. She looks at her best friend Wendy, and rolls her eyes at me. I know I will need a lot more glamour to win her back, if it's even possible.

I trudge along to the pier behind Stell and Jerry, frightened. It's true, then, that I really am bad, in a serious way, that hurts other people. I'm going to be punished for it, for what I've done, really punished. I'm going to Hell. For the first time it doesn't seem like just a story, it seems like a real place that has always been there, waiting for me, that I simply have been lucky enough to avoid.

At the Fort Mason dock Stell and Jerry board the ferry and I'm about to, when Captain Pearson waves at me from the window of his little cabin, and I freeze, both feet still on the dock. This is it, then, it all suddenly clicks into place like the lid on my mother's pillbox; he *is* Charon, the Ferryman, and this is the boat to Hell, like my mother said once, and he's going to take me there. Maybe it *is* the prison; Daddy has said before it is Hell up there, I remember, and now it's time for *me* to go.

I won't. I won't get on the boat. Stell and Jerry look back impatiently, and yell at me to come on; Charon doesn't like to wait. I shake my head, No, I'm not going! Stell comes back and grabs at my coat, tugging—Come *on*, Olivia, why are you being such a baby?—and I drop my books and wrap my arms around a piling to hang on. I'm not going, you can't make me! No! I howl at her, kicking her away, not caring that all the other kids, the safe ones, the good ones, are watching me curiously. Stell lets go, gets on the ferry and comes back with Captain Pearson, who reaches for me, smiling. I start to scream, not caring how loud I am, or that I'm acting like a baby. It's my last chance.

They back away, and I stop screaming. They huddle together, talking. Stell shrugs a lot, shaking her head. Jerry is brought in. Then they all board the ferry except Jerry, who stands at the edge of the dock; he is being left to guard me. Glaring, he kicks at a piling like it's my face he wants to break, my stupid, baby face. I may survive this day, but I am not so sure I will survive his rage at me later. The ferry chugs off across the water, and I think I'm still safe, for a while, before they come back for me. Jerry realizes he's safe, too; he takes a forbidden pack of cigarettes from his jacket pocket and lights up, blowing smoke in my direction. The wind merely whisks it away, it doesn't even touch me.

The ferry returns what seems like a long time later; the fog has almost blanketed the island and I think when it reaches me I can run off with it, hiding in it's folds. My fingers, still clutching a piling rope, are a dark, bluish white, like raw oysters. My teeth are chattering. The ferry docks and my mother gets off, helped by Captain Pearson. She comes toward me, alone, shivering, and I can see she's not dressed for this: a coat hastily thrown over a housedress, no sweater or gloves.

"Olivia?" She says this gently, bending over toward me. "Sweetheart? What is it?"

I can't tell her. She's betrayed me before, hasn't she, failed me, by being so powerless? Maybe they've gotten her to come, just to take me to Hell. She reaches out and takes my face in her hands, so softly, and I know suddenly, for sure, that she loves me.

"Can't you tell me, Olivia? Can't you tell me what's wrong?"

How do I tell her how bad I am? That I'm too loud, I lie, I break rules, I'm not pretty enough, not good enough, not under God. I think about my sinning, and being bad, and polio, and germs, and that I'm dirty. That home is Hell now, but how can that ever be bad, be Hell, when she is my home?

"What's wrong with you?" I ask. "I want to know what's wrong with you."

She's unsure what to say. "Well . . . nothing that can't be fixed, sweetheart. I just need to—"

"It's because of *me,* isn't it?"

"What is, Olivia?"

I struggle to say it. "It's because of me, because I'm bad. So God's making you suffer. That's why you're sick."

Her mouth drops a little, and we stare at each other, then she gulps air. "Is that what you think, Olivia, really?" I nod, and start to cry again. She looks around, wildly, not at me, then gets down on her knees. I let go of the piling to hug her, to hold on. She rocks me a little, holding me like Grandma holds her, like she hasn't held me in a long time. "Oh, no . . . no, sweetheart, that's not true. That's not true. Listen to me, all right? Stop crying." I bury my face in her neck. "Listen, when you were born, when I was in the hospital, after having you . . . well, your middle name is Claire, right, for your daddy's mother?" I nod into her shoulder. "And everyone kept asking me 'What's "Olivia" for? What's "Olivia" for?' And it sounded like, what am I planning to *do* with you, why did I have you, what's your . . . purpose. 'What's "Olivia" for?' . . . you see what I mean?" I nod again, I just want her to keep talking, not because I understand, which I don't, not really, but because it feels good. "And I thought, well, Olivia's for me to do it all right this time, like another chance. Something to hold on to. She's for me, now, like a present, that I didn't even know I wanted . . . —oh, do you understand any of this?" I shake my head and sniff and she takes my face in her hands again. "Well, that's what you are, you're like a wonderful present to me, that I think I don't even deserve sometimes. So it isn't you, what's wrong is *me*, there's something . . . wrong with how I feel about everything, it's all too sharp, around me, sort of. Like trying to hold something back, off of you so you don't get cut, but then your hands are just going to get cut, so you pull away, you turn away . . . but that makes anything I do not *work*, you know, if you can't *touch* anything, but I can't seem to hold on . . ." She stops what she's saying, trails off, and just hugs me again. "Never mind all that, Olivia, listen to me, you're not bad. I'm not sick, or anything like that, because of you. And it has nothing to do with God, even. I'm just, I'm going to get better, sweetheart. It's going to get better, I promise, for you, too, but don't ever, ever think you're anything bad. I love you, you make me so happy. All right?" I nod. "You're my pearl, right?" I smile and she kisses the top of my head, a long kiss. "All right, come on, it's so cold. Let's pick up your books. We have to make covers for them, don't we? I can help you with that. Are you ready to go home?" I nod again, clutching at her hand like a little girl, not wanting now, or ever, to let go.

# Hysteria

> VISITORS: Just a reminder: family visitors are always welcome, but must be registered in advance and informed of the appropriate rules and regulations! We want everyone to enjoy a safe and happy visit to our island!
>
> AVON PRODUCTS: Our new Avon representative will be here the first Saturday of the month! This month's special: stick cologne! 75 cents plus tax.
>
> GRADUATION PARTY: for our High School Seniors in the Social Hall, June 12, 7:00! Let's show how proud we are of our grads!
>
> *The Pelican,* June 1956

## *The Escape*

Floyd P. Wilson was an unemployed carpenter with no criminal record, five freezing children, and no heat in his Maryland home in winter of 1947. He went out to get coal and in the end shot the manager of a small grocery store, who was sitting in his car outside the shop totaling weekend receipts. Wilson fled in a panic without the $10,000 and on his arrest swore he had not intended to kill the man, that the gun had fired accidentally. He was convicted and sentenced to die in the electric chair, although his jury had recommended leniency. His sentence was commuted to life imprisonment by President Truman, and in 1952 he was transferred from Atlanta to Alcatraz. Four years later he was working on the dock, where his job was to secure bundles with sash cord in preparation for their shipment from the island. Over time he had hidden twenty-five feet of cord in the dock area, and in the afternoon hours of July 23, 1956, he retrieved his cord, casually strolled to the edge of the dock, and dropped down behind several large boulders that formed a crevice between the island and the sea. His absence was noticed within a few minutes and quickly reported; for the first time in ten years the prison siren began its throaty scream.

## *OLIVIA*

"Hysterical" is not an attractive label, and unfortunately it is the one they stuck on me. I only dimly remember making a scene a long time ago at the Fort Mason dock—something about Hell and the Ferryman, and the fear of losing something, being taken away or having something taken away from me—and I don't think it's fair that for two years everyone at school still uses this as an example of my character. No matter what I do—if I prefer chocolate milk to plain, and privately switch cartons; if I quietly point out to Mrs. Nitrini that she added up my math score incorrectly—it is seized on by my classmates as my Making a Scene, Olivia Being Hysterical, it is understood I Get That Way. This is despite what I think is magnificent control on my part; I haven't cried in two years, even when I hurt something. I am so good that I hardly laugh aloud, and barely even blink when I'm surprised; I have perfected a stoic shoulder shrug in response to everything, which makes me impervious. Monica whines all the time but still somehow comes off as terribly blasé; she must have done something, once, truly and indelibly blasé for that idea of her to hold on to its power. There are still girls who burst into tears when the boys tease them, or won't touch a battery with their tongue to test for energy, or whimper when we duck and cover under our desks during bomb drills, protecting ourselves from pretend glass flying overhead during a pretend Soviet blast. But they are excused and merely called *Girls* in a way that sounds both approving and contemptuous, while, despite my cultivated calmness, what I appreciate as a kind of grace, I am dismissed as Hysterical, which is much, much worse. I realized too late that protest over their misjudgment was pointless, for it only proved their opinion, not mine. Protesting is like the bomb drills; I read in an old *Collier's*, the one that has us in it, that an atomic blast won't burn you if you duck within 1/25,000th of a second. So all that ducking and covering is pointless, but you still do it, you duck and cover anyway, thinking that will make everything OK.

For two years I've asked my father, unsuccessfully, to send me to a different school, a new place where I can start over fresh, where no one knows me and I can recreate myself. I start Marina Middle School this fall, which my father thinks is the answer I've been looking for; he doesn't realize that the same kids from my grammar school are also going to Marina, that they are following me, bringing with them the rap sheet of my mistakes I cannot wipe clean.

I have tried for the same two years to win Monica over—if I even want her at all, that question to myself I ignore. We are still continually lined up and seated next to each other due to the alphabetical order of our names, which has created a grudging friendship by default. But despite my being Hysterical, I am not a huge liability to her; when she rolls her eyes dramatically at my behavior, which inflates whatever I do so that she can mock me, tell her other friends what a riot I am, it highlights her own cool and powerful pose. A riot, after all, is something that must be controlled.

Of course I still have my trump card, the thing that sets me apart. We are not going to Pacific Grove this summer—

my grandparents are in Israel, which my father says shows they are crazy—and I call Monica up from the phone in B Building to ask her if she wants to come visit me on the island. I will show her Alcatraz. It is my last-ditch effort to get her on my side before we start at Marina, to bind her to me. She hesitates, tempted; her mother insists on speaking to my mother first, for reassurance that it is safe.

I met Monica's mother once, last winter, when I went to return some books. Their house in the Heights is very old and Victorian-fancy, but the furniture inside is angled like geometry, and everything is pink and gray, or "salmon" and "charcoal" as Monica describes it; it is a color scheme. Mrs. Thompson looks like an older version of Monica, with the same severe black hair and white skin showing her veins, but her lips are a dry dark red, while Monica's are always just normal dry skin. She is artistic, and does something involving a gallery and many young male artists who Monica says are geniuses. She wore a straight black sleeveless dress, the kind Stell always wanted, and black eyeliner, and carried a burning cigarette with growing ash on a long black holder. I expected her to have an exotic accent, something Slavic, with languid *shka* sounds, but her voice is flat and tense. Monica's father wasn't there; there has never been any mention of him. A Negro maid only a few years older than Monica and I came in to announce dinner, but I was not invited to stay, as I'd hoped; I had wanted to see if even their food was pink and gray. When their Siamese cat jumped across Monica's mother's lap, a gray worm of ash fell onto her black dress; I didn't say anything, hoping ash stains. Like Monica she seems nervous and blasé at the same time, and I don't know how she does this.

It is agreed Monica can come over for lunch, but will be returned to Fort Mason before dinner, before it gets dark; my mother or father must accompany her to and from the ferry. I think this is babyish; I have been riding the ferry unescorted since I was nine, but, again, with Monica such girlish frailty is accepted without question.

I have saved this final ploy because I know that once I use it, once it is familiar, its attraction will fade. A change in my mother has also decided its timing; she is taking a new pill called Equanil, which maybe is supposed to equal everything out. These have been added to the rows of her pill bottles kept in the spice cabinet in the kitchen, alongside the cinnamon and paprika and minced onion, and she seems to handle everything better now. She got them right after Stell left, last month. We were all having dinner—a night that Daddy was home eating with us—except Stell hadn't come home; it was past curfew and her empty chair was very loud. I started chewing my food extra hard and slowly to keep my mind off it, off my father getting angrier and angrier, drinking a fourth martini. Dinner was charred meat that bled inside, and potatoes *and* rice—you'd think my mother would have learned to balance it better, after all those TV dinners—and flabby Jell-O. But I was glad my mother had cooked, because there was such a huge mess to clean up; after only a few bites my mother and I escaped to the kitchen and washed dishes more thoroughly than ever. She wears bright yellow gloves to do this—Dishwater is very harsh on your hands, she says—and first takes off her pinkish gold wedding ring, setting it on the windowsill. She broke a dish, of course—These gloves make everything so slippery!—and that gave us more to clean up. She finally just sat in a chair, her mouth pressed to her hand, her eyes dull, while I finished. Mrs. Shotz knocked much later, with a message—their apartment in B is right near the telephone; Stell had been studying at a girlfriend's house and missed the last ferry, and so was spending the night in the City. We all went to bed. My sister came home at 6:30 the next morning; I woke up when she came in our room and watched her lie down very carefully and stiffly on her bed, fully dressed. She looked gray and used, as if blood had been squeezed out of her like toothpaste. She must have not slept well, at her friend's house.

"Are you OK? Stell?"

"Yeah, just go back to sleep." She wiped sweat from her upper lip.

"They were all worried."

"Yeah, I bet . . . Daddy call out the Coast Guard?" She drew her knees up very carefully, pressing them together, and tucked a hand between her thighs. I thought of when my mother glues a broken plate, holding its cracked edges together hard. "'Help, help, my little girl's gone!' Please!"

"Are you hurt? What happened to you?"

"Nothing!" She took a deep breath. "I swear, Olivia, I'm gonna get out of here. I'm leaving, I'm not a kid anymore, Daddy thinks I'm some, I don't know, little tin wind-up toy he can just spin around, lock up when he wants, Yes, Daddy, No, Daddy, whatever you say, I can't stand it! I'm a woman now, he doesn't even *know*, he'd flip out if he knew what I—" She pulled her hand out, looked at her fingers. "Oh, God . . ."

"What is that? Are you bleeding?"

There was a pause, and then she sounded scared. "I'm fine, they said I might, a little. It's OK. Look, just do me a favor? Go in the bathroom, but don't wake them up—"

"What happened?"

"Just go in the bathroom, I need you to get me—" but then we heard my parents through the wall when the fight started, the usual kind: my father's booming voice, that it was his house and we were all going to live by his rules, and my mother saying Will you please calm down, Arthur, calm down, and my father saying You know how she's gonna wind up, don't you? Bringing home some little bastard, that's what! I heard Stell laugh then, a harsh gasp of a laugh. Then we heard, loudly: Stella, get in here!

Stell slowly dragged herself up.

"Tell Mom you're bleeding, you better—"

"No! Just forget it, Olivia! Don't say anything about it!" She left our room. I had to put the pillow over my head to drown everything out, wishing the foghorn would scream and yell instead.

A few days later Stell was gone, right after her graduation. We were all supposed to go to the Grad Party in the Social Hall, but my parents found her note instead. There was a lot more yelling for a while, back and forth between them, but they finally tracked her down and spoke to her on the phone. She married some boy, they told me, and wasn't coming home. They couldn't do anything—she was almost eighteen—so that was that. Nothing to talk about.

That night on the way to the bathroom I saw them sitting on the living-room sofa; my father was holding on to my mother like a little boy, and crying. I've never seen my father cry, even when he stubs something or cuts himself. My mother was smoothing the hair back from his forehead, murmuring; she traced her hand over the side of his face very gently, and I saw his tears shine on her fingers when the lighthouse flashed through the window. He kissed her hand, and held it so tightly it must have hurt. I went back to my room. When I got into bed I found the charm bracelet that sailor had given Stell a long time ago; she left it for me, buried deep under my pillow. It is even uglier than I remembered, with its hollow hearts and four-leaf clovers dangling loudly, in very bad taste, and I put it away in her nightstand.

So everything is quieter, now, really, with Stell gone, and

the new pills. Things aren't as sharp for any of us, everything's easier, and less, to handle.

We meet Monica and her mother at Fort Mason—I was worried about this, but my mother is Up To It, very calm and even elegant; next to Monica's pale and black-coated mother she actually looks healthy and golden. I wonder if Mrs. Thompson always wears black, maybe so she doesn't clash with her color scheme. My mother assures her again it's perfectly safe, that we're going to have fun, that Monica will return here at 5:30; my father's shift ends at five, and he will escort her back on the ferry.

Monica is queasy on the crossing; my mother tells her it's merely the gas fumes, and we're almost there. We leave the main cabin to get her some fresh air; Monica peers down into the Bay for sharks, and squints back behind us at the City, trying to point out to my mother where her house in the Heights is. When she turns back to the island she sees the sign: WARNING—PERSONS PROCURING OR CONCEALING ESCAPE OF PRISONERS ARE SUBJECT TO PROSECUTION AND IMPRISONMENT. She reads it to herself, moving her dry lips. When we dock, the spray of the sea in her face takes her aback—so does the snitchbox she must pass through, so does the convict unloading a truck, who gives us a friendly nod. She tries to cover her nervousness by repeating what a riot this all is. I don't even notice these things anymore, and I realize suddenly why I invited her; it is not so that she will like me more, it is so she will respect me more. I can show off my own kind of sophistication; I can be blasé about all this, and mock her a little, inside.

I first show her our cottage, because she wants to wash her hands; I am a little embarrassed that we don't have a color scheme, but at least my mother cleaned up. There is even a big vase of wildflowers in the living room, like in a magazine. Then we wander the parade ground where other kids are playing—This is my friend from school, I say casually, Monica—the little footpath, and the main road leading Up Top to the prison. Jerry passes to go fishing with his buddies; I tense up and tug Monica away, but she stops and introduces herself. Jerry actually grins at her, friendly like someone else's older brother, or a movie version of a brother, and gives her a look I've never seen, that makes her white cheeks flush pink. His hair is very long now and he combs it back into a scraggly DA; my father keeps telling my mother to get Jerry's hair cut because he looks delinquent. He also steals; I've lost school stuff from my room, and I've seen him fumble with my mother's purse when she wasn't looking, poking in the envelope my father gives her with the household allowance. Later she had to ask my father for extra money because she couldn't find $20 and he got irritated and asked why was she getting so irresponsible. She was Vague, then, and I knew she couldn't explain herself, she wasn't Up To It. I thought about saying something, but I got mad at her, too, because she *is* irresponsible; all those dropped plates and spilled things, and the house never feels clean anymore. And if she can't see what Jerry does right in front of her then she deserves to get stolen from and confused. Later Daddy apologized for yelling at her, and gave her more money, patting her back; they are both trying to keep things quiet now, to keep things nice.

Jerry asks Monica, and by default, me, if we want to go with them; Monica squeals a little and protests she's never been fishing, she wouldn't know what to do, and does he catch a lot? She's sure he catches a *lot* of fish, doesn't he? My brother says Yeah, tons, and offers to show her how to do it, Nah, you won't get in the *way,* c'mon, it'll be fun. He even gives me a friendly punch, but I am not lulled; I sense I'm losing her and I'm unwilling to be stolen from anymore, so I launch into a description of how the girls always have to clean and gut the dirty fish afterward because the boys don't like to do it. Monica tells Jerry it sounds like a riot, but maybe she'll just see him later; I give him one of Stell's smug smiles, and one of my own impervious, stoic shrugs. I have learned that this attitude works on Jerry, better than the kids at school; he leaves off torturing me now much sooner than when I would get hysterical. My biggest fear of him is that he will kill me, but I have recently realized that his biggest fear of me is that I will laugh at him. In a way this makes me powerful, because I can laugh at him in small doses whenever I need to, but he can only kill me once.

Monica and I find a grassy ledge surrounded by wild poppies and honeysuckle and the tiny yellow flowers shaped like long bells, and sit down after she wrinkles her nose at the bird droppings everywhere, the smell of fish. We eat our peanut butter and jelly, deviled eggs, and Carrot Spice Muffins my mother packed us, from the huge store of them in the Admiral freezer. My mother handed us our picnic like she did this everyday, making a perfect lunch, smiling brightly, sending me off to play with friends—Have fun, girls!—undertreating it so much and being so normal I loved her madly for it. It is a beautiful July day, and the Golden Gate Bridge is holding back the summer fog; the City is sharp in front of us and I take pride in the view, like it is mine to show off and I am being gracious in sharing it. We talk about school—the school behind us and the school to come—and kids in our class, and movies we've seen this summer; it's an imitation of girlish intimacy we don't really have, but I hope if we repeat this dialogue enough it will feel more earned.

Monica keeps looking around the island as if expecting gunfire; when our conversation gets too boring and her nervousness too irritating, I begin to belittle her concerns—Oh, I'm pretty sure the cons are all locked inside the cellhouse by now, mostly, anyway, maybe a *few* are out wandering the island, but they aren't dangerous, you really don't have to worry, Monica, there's nothing to get *upset* about, why, we never even lock our front door here! When the fog gauzes the sun she suggests we go inside for the rest of the afternoon; I reluctantly, indulgently agree, rolling my eyes in mockery. But we are jolted to our feet by something else, a sound I have never heard in my lifetime but recognize instantly: the escape siren. I know what I am supposed to do, I know the rule, they tell us about it all the time. I grab Monica's hand to get her up, and she turns as chalky white as the sandstone cliff. From the parade ground we hear, layered under the siren, the sounds of front doors slamming shut, and we run.

My mother lets us in; she, too, is pale, but not as bad as Monica, whose mouth has started to tremble. My mother yells out the front door—Jerry?! *Jerry*?!—and we tell her he has gone fishing. Mrs. Lucey runs across the parade ground, shouting to my mother that, yes, there's an escape and the men are all on alert, starting search parties. She hurries in her own front door, and slams it. Through the window we see my father hurrying down the footpath from the prison, carrying a rifle, followed by other men. My mother draws the shade, and turns to us.

"Well!" We look at her, mutely. "Well, there's nothing to worry about, girls. We just stay put, that's all. We're perfectly safe." I nod, but Monica starts to whimper.

"I want my mother."

"I know, sweetie, but we can't go anywhere. It won't be very long." Monica is chewing her pale lips, and I am pleased to think they will start bleeding soon. There is a sudden pounding at the door; Monica shrieks, and my mother and I jump, until we hear it is my father.

"Vivian? Open up, let me in!"

"Don't! Don't open the door!" Monica wails. My mother ignores her and lets my father in, closing and locking the door behind her.

"It's just one con, we're pretty sure. Wilson, disappeared from the dock. Shouldn't take long." My mother nods.

"I want to go home!"

"Daddy, this is Monica Thompson, my friend, remember?"

"Well, sure . . ." My father leans over and pats Monica on the head like she's much younger than she is. "Hey, Monica, looks like you're getting a little more excitement than we planned for you, huh?"

"I want to go home."

"I know you do, but we can't let you leave here until it's safe. Now, you understand that, don't you?"

"Arthur, can you call her mother?"

"Yeah, I'll try to get to a phone . . . the line's gonna be jammed, though." He looks around. "Where's Jerry?"

"He went fishing, Daddy."

"But Mark and John and the others are already back home, Charlie told me. Where is he?" He looks accusingly at my mother, like she's hiding him.

"I don't know, Arthur. He knows to come home."

"Jesus . . ."

"You want *me* to go looking for him?"

"No, just . . ." He goes into their bedroom, and we hear him rummaging in a drawer. He comes back out, his face stiff. "Where's the Colt, Vivian?"

"I haven't touched it."

"It isn't there!"

"Well, *I* don't touch it! I don't even like it in the house. Did you check it at the Armory?"

"You *know* they don't—" He stops abruptly. "All of you girls, just stay put, all right? I'll be back later." He kisses her and leaves, slamming the door behind him. My mother locks it, and looks at it pensively.

"Hey, girls, I have an idea! Let's all of us push the china hutch up against the door, okay? Like a barricade?" She says this gaily, as if it's a game. Monica starts to cry.

Jerry doesn't come home, and as it gets dark outside my mother tries keeping us busy with making cookies. She picks the most elaborate recipe and we discover halfway through that we are missing key ingredients; we are left with an enormous bowl of sweet hardening slop, and sticky hands. Monica gives up and sits on the kitchen floor, weeping, wiping her hands. She is sure we are all going to be killed and she will never see her mother or cat again. Her terror actually calms us down, my mother and me, by allowing us to feel brave. My mother tells the story I've heard many times, about being caught in the City with me when I was a baby during the Big Battle of 1946. It is meant to be comforting, but when she gets to the part about officers being killed she suddenly stops talking and peers out the window again, twisting her pinkish gold ring around on her finger. Finally she brings the vase of wildflowers in from the living room and begins pulling the flowers out, snipping off the dead ends of stalks, although she must have picked them just this morning. I am not concerned at all for Jerry—part of me hopes he is taken hostage, or killed by a desperate con—but I am worried for my father, and, most of all, for my mother, although this makes no sense; she is as safe here in the house as I am, isn't she? It is obvious Monica must stay here overnight, and my mother stops fussing with the flowers to put TV dinners in for us; Monica has never seen TV dinners before and she asks if freezing the food really kills off all the germs. Her fear does not wear her out as we thought it would, but feeds on itself;

she is now crying loudly and having trouble breathing. She finally gets hysterical, moaning and choking, which delights me, and I ask my mother if I can slap her the way you do to hysterical women in the movies. Instead my mother gives her some of her Equanil pills to swallow, telling her they're aspirin. Monica curls up on the sofa clutching a pillow, quiet at last. She barely stirs when my father comes in very late, and I am almost asleep as well.

"He hasn't come home, Arthur."

"Look, if anything was wrong there, we would've heard by now. He's fine. Probably just running around, excited, that's all. He loves this stuff." My father reaches far back in the cabinet for the bottle of gin and pours himself a glass, no olives or anything.

"Go look for him, *do* something, then!"

"The whole damn island's being searched!"

"You let him get away with anything he wants!"

"Jesus, Vivian, don't start arguing with me. *You* let him take off!"

"To go fishing!"

"You have one thing to do, *one* thing, that's keep an eye on the kids, you know that?"

"Excuse me, he's sixteen years old! It's not like he comes home every three hours to nurse!"

"Don't get smart, I hate that! I'm telling you, we have to do something, I'm not raising some goddamn juvenile delinquent!"

"You're not raising him at all!"

"Oh, come on!"

"You call him champ, you pat his head, you get all puffed up like he's some little *you*, but have you *looked* at him? He's four inches taller and sixty pounds heavier than I am, for God's sake, you want me to control a grown man? Why should he listen to me, anyway, *you* don't—"

"Yeah, that's true, you couldn't even control Stella, she got away from us, didn't she?"

"You're blaming me for that?"

"Hell, no, what's wrong with my seventeen-year-old daughter running off to get married? Hey, better than I thought she'd turn out, right? I would've bet she'd—"

"All right, fine, so Stella was all my fault, I'm the worst mother in the world! You can have Jerry, then! He's all yours, do what you want with him!"

"What the hell're you—you're being neurotic, that's what that doctor of yours says. I'm gonna have a talk with him, that's what we'll do, he's doing jack *shit* for you—"

"Stop it, Arthur!" My mother stuffs the flowers back in the vase, the petals sticking to her wet fingers.

"You're either a zombie, or you're hysterical half the time!"

"Please don't say that! I'm trying—"

"I don't get you, you've got a beautiful house here, a couple of kids, I earn a good living, don't I take good care of you? I'm paying a fortune for that doctor, just to sit and *listen* to you—"

"Then, don't! He doesn't listen, anyway." My mother clutches the damp vase to her chest, gripping it hard.

"Oh, I get it, so he's a bad guy too, right? We're all in it, big bad wolves, some conspiracy to make little Vivian's life miserable!"

"Why do you do that? Why do you like making fun of me?!"

"You're not doing your job, that's the problem! Always throwing fits, always screaming at me, letting things go, I can't live like this anymore, Vivian, I swear to God—"

"I don't know what to do anymore!" Her voice is shaking.

"All right, just calm down! Let's not start all this, let's just have some quiet!"

I don't know if Monica is awake or not, listening to this, and I don't really care. I can feel the swelling inside my chest, trying to lure and coax me into hysteria, and I pack it down like a paper cup, flattening it. They are going to keep saying these things to each other, my mother is going to shake more and then the vase will break, the flowers will spill all over the floor, and my father will clean it up, swearing. But they cannot make me cry anymore over this, over anything, because I have my magnificent control; I can dig my nails into it, and stay very, very quiet. I slip off the sofa and go to my room. I won't sleep, I know that. With the door closed I can still hear them, but I don't hear the actual words, and sometimes it's easier that way, when it's just the sounds.

## *THE ESCAPE*

Floyd P. Wilson hid among the wet rocks for almost twelve hours while tired and frustrated officers continued their search; he was finally spotted and captured near the seawall, trying to gather driftwood he could tie up with his sash cord to make a raft.

At his trial he said he couldn't even swim and that his attempt was merely a ploy; he'd wanted a public hearing in open court, where he could get his case heard. The jury listened, then let the terms of his original crime and punishment stand. They acquitted him of the escape attempt, however, refusing to add anything on paper to his existing sentence. A vindication of sorts, but worthless in value; he was in for a life term, anyway, and was returned to Alcatraz to serve a portion of it, on Warden Madigan's direction, in the Treatment Unit.

# The Monarch

## *Olivia*

MERRY X-MAS! A group Christmas Tree run into the City will be December 22, so all the children can join in. Also: caroling begins on the lower balcony of 64 Building, 5 P.M. X-mas Eve!

HOLIDAY FORMAL: December 20 at the Rowing Club, Aquatic Park.

ASIAN FLU: Mrs. Arthur Thornton is still over at Saint Francis Memorial with that nasty bug! Officer Thornton says she's improving and will be home soon; their youngest, Olivia, is spending the holiday with her grandparents in Pacific Grove. Get well soon, Vivian!

*The Pelican,* December 1958

"The Monarch butterfly is a large, migratory American butterfly (*Danaus plexippus*) having orange-brown wings with black veins and borders and larvae that feed on milkweed." The caterpillar spins its own cocoon, trapping itself inside; this is a "chrysalis, where it passes its pupal stage in a quiescent state enclosed in a firm case." Then it breaks free from the chrysalis and flies off as a butterfly. There is a drawing of one in the book that doesn't do it justice, a black and white and gray sketch. The real ones have such rich color; they are very vivid, and velvety.

There aren't any real ones left, though, only the fake ones

of orange plastic or glass that people hang in their windows. I've never been in Pacific Grove when there weren't butterflies; we usually arrive just as they do, at the end of summer, before beginning their migration all autumn to the south. They've already left, and Pacific Grove seems duller without them, colorless. The fake ones aren't the same. I imagine them in Mexico, maybe, in the sunshine. I don't understand why they can live trapped in a cocoon but not in a Mason jar; a jar even has air holes punched in. Maybe the difference is that they've spun their cocoons themselves, but I think that would make it even worse.

It is raining here now, and gray; the sea whips up like egg whites, and the trees are piercingly bare. There is little to do; I stay away from the beach, it is too empty and cold to swim. Everything feels damp, anyway. My grandparents' house still smells good, though; it's a winter version smell, more of burning wood and cider and less of fresh vegetables and sunning grass.

I'm reading the *World Book Encyclopedia*—I'm in the late Ms. They take up an entire row on the bottom of a bookshelf in the hallway; Grandpa says they used to be my mother's. They are full of penciled notes and arrows, to herself, I guess, when she wanted to remember something. When my grandparents aren't around I sometimes pull volumes out just to smell them; I know this is silly, but I wonder if the smell of her hands is caught somewhere in the pages, blotted up like ink. I wind up just sneezing, and Grandma will hand me a sweater and ask if I want some tea. This is the only place in the entire world I ever drink tea, and we drink a lot of it. Nothing as mundane as Lipton's, of course; they are herbal teas that look like tinted water and smell a little bit like how Grandma's odd food tastes.

When my mother went into the hospital a lot of the other wives and mothers brought us food: mostly magazine casseroles they said they accidentally made extras of. I usually ate the casseroles alone after school, when my father went up to the prison. Once we had a real dinner at Mr. and Mrs. Shotz's, with courses. I like them, but Mr. Shotz is retiring and they are moving to Florida. Mrs. Shotz kept asking my father if she could go visit my mother at Saint Francis to say goodbye, but he didn't think it was a good idea. The worst was when Mrs. Walker brought food over; she stayed to eat with us because Mr. Walker was on Tower duty and she said she felt lonely, that we must feel lonely, too. I hate her food even more, now; even the chicken was too sweet, and the carrots had a glaze on them like melted caramel. I don't want anything from her, but my father seemed happy to have her there, have her food. She has started wearing her hair in a big bubble and I picture Mr. Walker blowing it up every morning from the back of her head. I left the table to finish my homework and didn't come out of my room again; I could still hear them laughing, though, until it was late. She laughs in long trills, like curling ribbon, just how Stell used to giggle with her friends around Mr. Walker. I was glad to come stay with my grandparents over Christmas holiday.

In a way I was right about Marina Middle School—most of the groupings of Sherman kids still stuck, especially the Negro kids and the Chinese kids, but I forgot there would be new kids coming in, too, from other grammar schools, like streams feeding into the bigger middle-school river. The school is a huge stone building that looks a lot like the cellhouse but the top of it has a border of names carved in: DARWIN, EDISON, MOSES, SHAKESPEARE, MICHELANGELO, and so on. I already know who most of these men are, and I assume we won't be allowed to graduate this spring until we know all of them, what important thing they've contributed. There aren't any women carved in, unless I'm wrong about some of the names. I'm not absolutely sure who Wagner is, and I'm almost positive Pasteur is the milk scientist, but I think they're both men. I have to look them up in the encyclopedia, when I get to the Ps and Ws.

When we started sixth grade at Marina I was nervous to see what Monica would do. She was gone when I got up that morning, two years ago, after the Wilson escape. My mother was dingy and dull, sitting at the kitchen table like she hadn't slept all night, and told me my father had taken Monica back to her mother early in the morning—Mrs. Thompson had called the police when she heard the siren, saying that her daughter was being held hostage on Alcatraz. They finally got her a message from my father. I had almost fallen asleep, but around midnight Jerry banged on my bedroom window, startling me awake, making threatening motions if I didn't open up. He smelled like cigarettes and beer, and other boys. He told me he'd been helping the guards search for the missing cons, and I better put this back—he handed me our father's gun from the war, his Colt. I didn't want to touch it, and he got angry—Just *do* it, Olivia, you better do it!—then he dropped it through the window onto my bedroom carpet and said now I had to, or it would all be my fault, and if I said anything he'd really get me. I thought for a moment about killing him right then; I could, I could say I'd stolen the gun because I was scared when the siren went off, and when Jerry knocked on my window I thought he was the escaping con so I shot him. I'd get in trouble for stealing the gun, but they couldn't really blame me for killing Jerry if it was an accident, and then he'd be gone, and everything would be easier. But Jerry took off while I was thinking this through, and in the morning I put the Colt back in my father's nightstand before going into the kitchen. My mother told me Jerry had been found hiding up on the cliff by some guards; he swore he'd been fishing when the siren went off and just stayed where he was for fear the guards would accidentally shoot him. My father didn't do anything to him, really, except send him away to military school. So he *is* gone, anyway, his stink is gone, but I bet he gets to play with guns there and likes it. Dead would be better. They cut off his DA, but that just isn't enough.

I had expected Monica, in her stories to people, to play up the drama of it, and her own girly-girl terror, but she didn't—maybe she sensed her hysterics were too real to be charming. Instead, she was the heroine of the piece, assuring everyone there really was no danger at all, it was sort of exotic fun being trapped on the island. But I wasn't cast as the weakling; she often, smartly, I thought, stressed how much fun we had *together*, that we were both brave and bold, that I was especially cool. I think she knew I would let her own false heroism slide but would not, in this case, tolerate it at my expense, that I would expose her—and, on this one topic, Alcatraz, I would be seen as the authority. We cannot really be friends, however, without acknowledging her lie, which neither of us has any desire to do; we have been quite happy to sacrifice each other for the sake of the story. So in a way we are finally bonded together without having to fake being friends any more at all. She said nothing about my parents, or the pills my mother gave her, and I am silently grateful for this—it's possible she doesn't remember that part at all, or that she is smarter, or more worried, than I give her credit for. Also, she doesn't have a father, so maybe she has nothing to measure the reality of mine against.

And so, at last, I am no longer Hysterical, through no doing of my own. I don't have to try to prove it anymore by deliberate dispassion, but my magnificent control has finally taken root, anyway; it is as natural now, as webbed through me as the black veins of the Monarch butterfly.

Seventh grade included Physical Education, and Hygiene, which we knew was supposed to be Sex. But we didn't get much closer to Sex, only to diagrams of how flowers are fertilized, then chickens, then dogs—we don't get humans until next year, in high school Hygiene. The boys and girls were segregated for this, so I don't know what the boys learned. I see other naked girls now in Physical Education, where they line us up to check our bare spines; we stand there straight as a fleshy picket fence, splintering our wooden faces with tiny sideways glances at each other. Something about this is like Sex, but we know it isn't supposed to be. Then we gladly put on baggy clothes for calisthenics, and run around the gymnasium. We take the baggy clothes home once a week to be washed, but Monica brings a fresh suit every day, cleansed of sweat germs. I'm sure their maid does the laundry, with all of the other mother things; I can't picture Mrs. Thompson doing much besides standing off-center in a square salmon and charcoal room, idly brushing ash from her black skirt, both too nervous and too blasé to worry about any mother thing like laundry.

Someone steals next year's Hygiene textbook to pass around, which has the good chapters about Marriage and Our Maturing Bodies; I get a glimpse of a black-and-white drawing of a woman cut in half to illustrate her Reproductive System, like they did with the flower diagram. The uterus looks like a steer's head, one of those bleached bone skulls in pictures of the desert; sperm look like the strands of seaweed on the beach in Pacific Grove. We have schoolyard talks about Sex, in small groups at lunch and recess, referring to the stolen textbook to fill in the gaps. V.D., I finally learn, is a "venereal disease usually acquired through sexual relations," but it doesn't say if there is a vaccination for it, like for polio. The Hygiene words are unsatisfying:

intercourse, fertilization, mammary gland, erectile tissue—even when we look them up in the big dictionary, someone keeping an eye out for the librarian, who of course must know the dirty thing we are doing, the definitions don't sound human. The schoolyard words are the dirty ones, and mostly the boys say them: screw and dick and tits, they all sound harsh, but more real. The toughest of the boys sometimes says fuck, which we all know is the absolute worst thing. Unless you use the textbook word, intercourse, but that's boring to us—except for Monica, who prefers Hygiene to the gross and germy schoolyard talk of Sex. So the rest of us girls are trapped between Hygiene and being too dirty for words.

The first day here Grandma watched me, like she used to watch my mother. I didn't unravel, though; looking back I think my mother must have been very weak to give in so easily to Grandma's silent, searching inquiries. After a few days the litany started—Olivia, are you all right? Do you want to talk about it? Do you want to talk about your mother?—but I am hard and unsplit as the black beans she must soak for days in her big iron pot.

Grandpa comes down to the kitchen late at night, when I can't sleep and am there reading the encyclopedia, and makes us his root-beer floats in the golden glass mugs. We sit and spoon our floats and he asks me about what I'm reading; before I realize it he is talking about my mother, when she was my age, looking things up in these same books. I cannot stand it then, and I leave him to go back to bed, where I won't sleep anyway. At first I felt bad leaving him there but I knew Grandma would come down after I left; I watched them from the top of the stairs, in a pie wedge of light, holding hands across the table. I stayed upstairs; my grandmother, our little wizard, can't wave any of this away, and Grandpa can't sand it smooth, or oil away the scratches. They talked quietly about my mother, about why she did it, holding hands tighter and tighter.

My father hasn't let me visit her in the hospital the last few months; he says he doesn't want me to see her, she doesn't look quite right and it would only upset me. I don't point out that I *did* see her, lying on the floor of our cottage in a spill of pills and water and throw-up while he was off guarding other people. He was very busy around then—a few weeks earlier, late in September, there had been another escape; two cons on garbage duty had grabbed Officer Miller and tied him to a tree, the big eucalyptus tree right near our cottage. They threatened him with a knife, and told him a getaway launch was waiting for them offshore. Then they dove in the Bay; some other fathers found Officer Miller, and the siren went off again. The Coast Guard found one of the men a few hours later, clinging to a rock near the island's edge. The search for the other one was a big deal—Warden Madigan didn't know if he was still on the island, or had made it across the Bay. The FBI first searched all of the City, then California, then the whole country, and police bombed all of the island caves with tear gas that floated up to the parade ground and burned our eyes.

When the mothers found out what happened, that a con with a knife had been right outside our doors, could still be out there somewhere, everyone got very upset—some of us weren't even allowed to leave the house to go to school. But my father assured my mother the con must have drowned, of course he did, no man could swim that Bay; we just have to wait for the body to surface. The gas in the stomach balloons a dead body up after a while, we just have to wait. That's why, he explained, when they bury someone at sea they always slit the abdomen open, so the body disappears forever. Even if we don't find the drowned con it doesn't mean he escaped, it just means the crabs got him, ate through his stomach. He read to my mother from the *Chronicle*; a priest from the con's hometown was appealing to the con to turn himself in, and the con's father said all of his son's troubles started when he got mixed up with a no-account woman, that before he met her he was a mighty nice kid.

My mother didn't seem interested in any of the fuss, or concerned; her eyes were red, but I thought it was probably just from the tear gas. I found her the next day, after school. On the floor. I called my father up at the prison, and he hurried home. He folded her up inside a blanket like a big white fish to be gutted and cleaned, gills gaping for air, and carried her to the ferry because he didn't want the prison doctor to know, or to be bothered. He kept muttering Of all times, Vivian, of all times to pull something like this!

I didn't go to the hospital with him, because Jack LaLanne and some newspapermen were coming to the island that afternoon, and I wanted to see; he was going to swim from Alcatraz to San Francisco to show how easy it was, how the still-missing con could have made the escape. I watched with a bunch of kids from the cliff; he swam for more than an hour, his body constantly swept west by the currents toward the Golden Gate Bridge. He finally gave up, and crawled into an escort boat. Some of the boys booed. My father telephoned me that night from Saint Francis Memorial; my mother was fine, but she needed to stay in the hospital for a while. A few weeks later, right on schedule, a Tower guard spotted a pale lump floating offshore, and they dragged it in: a body swollen with salt, bloated with water, wearing a pair of crude wooden fins tied to its feet. His face was gone, my father said, washed away, and I thought of how Grandma soaks a label off a jelly jar. But they identified the con by his fingerprints. His name was Burgett.

My grandparents wanted to come up right after, but my father said my mother wasn't Up To It, didn't want to see anyone, even her parents, and that I would go stay with them for the holidays. Stell called home a few times, and Jerry sent a card from St. John's Military Academy, with a picture of himself sheared, in uniform, armed now to kill anyone who laughs at him. My father says she's getting better and asks how I am now, and that she sends her love. This is like getting a cheap card in the mail a day or two after Valentine's, when you know the person who sent it remembered you just a little too late, and you are an afterthought. I am glad I didn't go to see her.

I celebrate Hanukkah with my grandparents, which is simply lighting candles on the menorah for eight nights and talking about it. They asked me what I learned about the menorah in the M volume, and now every night they fill in the history to make it more real, so I understand about Jews and Christians and the Bible, and even World War II. They think that the different faiths have different stories, which are what makes them each special, but that all religions at some point boil down to the same few ideas we should live by. We don't say any prayers; Grandpa says whatever we think of on our own will be more real than words said so often they're sanded down to nothing and you can't feel them. Grandma says it's important to think about who we are and who the other people in our lives are; how we can give things to each other that aren't so obvious, like jewelry or a sweater, but the little things every day that make us need and love one another. I'm not even sure they believe in God; I think they just believe in themselves and each other, which to me shows much greater devotion and faith. It's harder; people who believe in God say he's always there and always listening, but you can't say that about the people in your life, not at all.

I'm allowed to go home on New Year's Day, 1959. My father comes to pick me up in the old Chrysler station wagon that says I LIKE IKE on the bumper and talks quietly out front with my grandparents, standing in the cold. Through the cracked front door I hear his voice—No, if she'd *really* wanted to do it, c'mon, there's a gun in the house, isn't there? Just her way of getting a little extra attention—but he sounds more scared than anything else. My grandparents argue with him—That's not *treatment,* what they're doing to her, Art, that's *barbaric*!—but they stop when I come out. My father starts putting my bags away in the wagon, and the boxes of books my grandparents gave me. I hug them goodbye, inhaling their cinnamon and wood dust; I'm not sure what I'm going back to, and I wish they could come with me. I remember them hugging my mother like this, easing her to relax, and I wonder why people bother to talk at all, or ever speak words, when it all blurs into noise and never feels as rich or redolent as this.

In the car my father informs me that my mother still isn't quite ready to come home yet; he wants to keep her at the hospital a while longer, because it is for her own good. He told my grandparents, but no one else has to know about it, because it is our family business, and private. So how's this, he says, you just go on back to school, and we'll get the cottage all cleaned up, ready for her. I hear myself saying Well *I* already cleaned up the vomit, didn't I? He is quiet a moment, then just says my name, Olivia . . . all drawn out and disappointed. We drive the rest of the way home without talking anymore.

There's a clown's nose of blood on my underpants. I hold onto the bathroom counter while bending way over to examine it, yes, it's blood, I'm bleeding. I know what this is, I've just read all about it, so I can't really be shocked; it's Menstruation, that's all, after Menorah and before Mental Illness. But the *World Book* only talked about eggs in my ovaries, and my uterus shedding—like the inside of an oyster shell, I'd thought—and there was nothing about what I do with bloody underwear and this red pulp, bright as pimento, still dripping out of me, I can feel it; a string of syrupy blood drops down into the toilet water and spins into a dissolving snake. That's all it is, Menstruation, I tell myself, a whole chapter coming up this fall in the high-school textbook, but I'm frightened anyway, now, and before I can stop myself I cry out, shrill and scared: "*Daddy*?! *DADDY*?!"

I hear him hurry down the hall from the living room, where I left him knifing open a box of books.

"Olivia?" I don't say anything, and he knocks. "Olivia? What is it? Are you all right?"

What do I say? I can't open the door, I cannot show him this, bring this to him, not my white underpants soaked with bleeding egg, not my *underpants*. It was wrong to call him, to lose my magnificent control. I'm ashamed. I say nothing and there is a long, silent pause.

"I'll be right back, Olivia." I hear him hurry down the hall, away from the bathroom door, and then more silence. I could yell for Mrs. Shotz, but they are in Florida. I can't call Stell, or my grandmother, the phone is way over in B Building. And my mother isn't here, she may never be here again. All I can think of is the Beautiful Queen, Snow White's real and dead mother, embroidering, stabbing her finger with her needle and bleeding onto snowy cloth, and her wish for a daughter coming out of that, wishing for flesh and blood. But I am wishing for my mother.

"Olivia?" It's a woman's voice, but not the Beautiful Queen's. "Olivia? Why don't you let me in, sugar? There's nothing to be scared of, hon, just let me show you how to fix yourself up, that's all."

I have to let her in, but I hate her, and I hate my father for bringing her to me. I unlock the door; she bustles in, a fake butterfly, with her sweet plastic smell and bubble of hair. She holds white elastic straps in her hand like a garter belt, and safety pins, and a box of thick white cotton rectangles. Stell used to keep such a box in the cabinet but never explained it to me. I have to let Mrs. Walker explain it to me now because only my father is left; my mother isn't here, she didn't get around to this, to teaching me, and I need her, I need a woman to show me.

# Drowning

## *Vivian*

> Science has done a great deal in certain fields, such as polio and other disease, but not much about the human mind. They've just got to dig out some cure for these people.
>
> And, until they do, Alcatraz, or some comparable prison will be a necessity in our penal system.
>
> Warden Edwin B. Swope,
> in the *San Francisco Chronicle*

It's a lovely party, really. They've hung those Japanese lanterns overhead, and, oh, the streamers are pretty. So festive. I've always wanted to come to the Saint Francis Hotel for cocktails. They needed those streamers, the ballroom would be too colorless otherwise. No one's here yet, though, except that woman on the chaise over there. She looks so pale; the eye makeup is a little much, too dramatic, even for an evening party. I'd love a cocktail, I hate that taste of metal in my mouth. I'm sure they're serving cocktails, I can smell the alcohol. Maybe when Arthur arrives he'll get me something from the bar—let him make me a martini! I don't quite feel like getting up; it's nice to lie here in the shade, relaxing. Haven't felt so relaxed in a while . . . what *have* I been doing? I must be very, very busy, for this to feel so nice . . . Stell must need me to, oh, no, that's right, she's gone. Funny, when I got married, the way I did, I thought, Well at least my daughter will have the real thing, orange blossoms and music and Mom's tatted lace. She used to show it to me when I was little, her wedding lace folded away in an old trunk. Like the paper snowflakes we used to cut out in grade school, trimming away little diamonds and hearts and curlicues and zigzags; if you cut too much, the snowflake just fell apart when you unfolded the paper, and that was a shame. Like the letters Arthur used to send me, when he was away at war. So much of what he wanted to say cut away by someone, and all I got were the little diamonds and hearts, still folded in half in my lap, not really saying anything. Maybe Stella didn't know I had that lace for her. Maybe I should have gotten it from Mom, shown it to her, then she would've known how much I loved her. She wouldn't have left. Maybe I can call and tell her I have it, that white lace, waiting for her. I have to remember to do that.

Why don't I remember so well . . . I think it's the currents, it must be, they flood in, they drown out my thoughts. It isn't like how *real* drowning must be though, thank God, like drowning in the Bay. No, it's the electrical currents here, they keep plugging me in to those, like I'm a giant appliance. A blender, a Broil Quick range, a television set. I'm scared they will do it one time too many, or turn the "light-dark" dial too high, and the generator will blow my mind out, with sparks, just like the toaster at home. That smell of burning wires. I can't seem to fix it myself, fix myself. The direct current is too strong, and Arthur keeps forgetting to bring home a converter. Or he should bring it here now, actually. Or maybe Dr. Gibbons can bring one; he's been invited, too, and I'm so glad. He comes in and asks how I am sometimes, but I'm too embarrassed to ask him to get me a cocktail. I don't seem to know anyone else here, although everyone knows me. They must've heard about me; I drove here myself, all the way across the country—see, I still have grease smeared on my temples, I must have rubbed my head after working on the engine. All the way, by myself. Like Amelia Earhart. Amelia, falling out of the sky, into the water. She must have drowned out there in the ocean. They never found her. Never found her bones, white as shells under the black, still water. So easy to drown if you're not careful, to let yourself slip under it all, just close your eyes. I'm sleepy so much of the time, and that's dangerous when you're swimming, or driving, not to keep your eyes open. Wake up, they keep saying, Wake up Mrs. Thornton, they keep calling me that, although it isn't really my name. You can borrow a sweater, but it is never, ever, truly yours, and you don't forget that. I saw it written down somewhere here, maybe on one of those old-fashioned dance cards: "Mrs. Arthur Thornton." It's so many layers away from who I am. I can't remember why I buried my own name inside of it, let it get lost in there, *my name,* all I have that's really me. The only thing that was ever mine.

Well, Olivia's mine. Jerry isn't mine, wasn't mine, I gave him back to Arthur, and Arthur gave him away. Military school. He'll be a soldier, he'll march and have discipline, which is important. What could I do with a boy? I couldn't teach him how to be a man. The only man I've ever known is Arthur, and I only know him as his wife, not as a person. My father is wonderful, but he's my father, I couldn't teach Jerry that. Although I can't teach the girls how to be women, either, because I haven't graduated yet. They say the best way to learn something is to teach it, but this is the one subject I fail, over and over and over again, and that keeps me from graduating. I learn the tricks of it, not the heart of it. They keep changing the rules, I think—they all need to get together and come up with a book, or a list of rules everyone will agree on, and then stick to it, finally. That, I could learn; I've always been good at memorizing what's in books, repeating them back. That's a student's trick, one I am good at, making them think I am smart, making them think I will be a doctor, an engineer. Something important.

But Olivia's mine. She must be at home, I must have left her with someone, but I don't remember who. Surely I did, I couldn't go off and leave my child, could I? What kind of mother leaves her child? I'm sure she's fine. Oh God, did I leave her alone? Maybe Arthur is with her. He must be. She's mostly grown-up now, isn't she? She'll be all right, won't she? I'm always afraid that Nurse is going to come get her, take her away like always because I'm doing something wrong, being a bad mother . . . There's no one to ask; the woman in the other bed doesn't care, she's just lying there, with her cut-off hands. No, that's right, they're not cut off, those are bandages, white bandages. I remember seeing them changed, by one of the cocktail waitresses, seeing the little barbed wire sticking out of her wrists. She shouldn't be at a party, not with those dark circles under her eyes. The Japanese lanterns are so pretty; they hang over my head on some kind of wire hook, full of clear liquid that sparkles in the light. The liquid drips down into the streamers wrapped around my arms; oh yes, I forgot it was a costume party. I must be dressed as one of those Greek girls, a pre-Raphaelite painting, with this flowing white gown and the streamers wrapped around my arms. Maybe the liquid in the streamers is some sort of cocktail, so I don't need to call the waitress. That's very clever, isn't it? It's a lovely party, it really is, but actually I feel like going home. But no, I can't, that's right, Arthur wants me to stay, says I have to stay. It's for my own good. And it would be rude to leave this soon. I should thank the hostess for inviting me, but I don't know whose party this is. Maybe I'm not really supposed to be here, though, maybe it's a mistake, or I'm crashing. What a terrible thing that must be, to crash. Even into the water, cool water feels soft but it's really so hard, so strong, airless, pressing down over you. Maybe I've taken a wrong turn somewhere, I might have, driving, I don't remember how I got here! What road did I take? I must have closed my eyes for a moment, just a moment. Oh God, my parents are going to be so disappointed that I got lost, I've let them all down, really, they'll all be so disappointed with me . . .

# Lady of the House

## *Olivia*

VACATION: Mrs. Arthur Thornton, back with us only a short while after her long convalescence with the Asian Flu, is going on an extended vacation for her health. We'll miss you, Vivian! Get better soon!

*The Pelican,* August 1959

The men in here keep their heads working every minute trying to think of something, of some way out.

WARDEN PAUL MADIGAN,
May 1957

A martini is an easy cocktail to make, because there are only two ingredients: six jiggers of gin to one jigger of vermouth, mixed up together. Then the olive, of course, but that's the garnish and comes after. I like to have a chilled shaker ready when he comes home; my mother let him mix his martinis himself, but the first time I surprised him with a cool, triangle glass, a green olive perfectly impaled on a toothpick, he seemed so pleased. We keep the gin and vermouth and cylindrical shaker in a locked cabinet I now have the key to; alcohol is technically not allowed on the island, but my father, famous for rules, is not always inflexible.

We quickly got sick of casseroles after she was gone this

time—I think casseroles are cheating, anyway—and I refuse to keep serving my father TV dinners; one more and I suspect he will never eat at home with me again, but have every dinner every night up at the prison, and that is no way for a family to behave. This was one of my mother's mistakes, and I will not repeat it. I will not be like her. Instead, I finally call my grandmother and ask her to send me recipes. Real ones, not ones from magazines that all use a can of Campbell's Cream of Mushroom Soup. At first she is reluctant—Olivia, that's not your job, honey!—but then sends easy things like baked chicken or meatloaf, things I can make in a few hours after I get home from school. I finally buy my own cookbook, to keep meals interesting. I set the table with the prisoner-made place mats and spotless flatware and the few dishes my mother didn't crack or chip, and we sit down to a perfect dinner, my father and I. He tells me everything is delicious, just wonderful, and I feel enormous pride at what I have served. He gives me a household allowance and I do all the shopping: I buy roasts, and pork chops to bread, and whole chickens I hack apart with a sharp knife. I always make a vegetable—he loves brussels sprouts—and a potato dish, but not merely baked: potatoes au gratin now, or scalloped or fried into little pancakes with onion and a parsley garnish. Once I buy a chuck steak, which I remember my mother making, but while I'm pounding it tender I start to feel a little queasy. I decide the meat must be bad—I am supposed to know how to tell that, now—and I throw it away, deciding to make lamb chops sprinkled with rosemary instead. Remembering my mother's soupy Jell-Os, I make real desserts, tart cherry pies and angel-food cakes and compotes with cinnamon and a dab of real whipped cream, nothing too sweet.

I also gather his soiled clothes up, to go to the prison laundry. It makes a smaller package now, just his things and mine. Except my underclothes; Mrs. Walker showed me how to rinse those out. You have to let the stained part soak in lukewarm water, and then rinse them well with plenty of bleach and hot water, and then a final cold water rinse. If they're too dirty I sometimes just throw them away, burying them deep in the trash that gets burned up in the island incinerator.

She bought me a bra, too, or a "brassiere" as she calls it, for the "support" I need now. I hate it. I used to put Stell's on, if I was home sick from school, stuff it with socks or handkerchiefs, then walk around in front of the mirror jiggling my chest and admiring myself. Stell's breasts were large and meaty, round as walnuts, but I'm smaller, hazelnut-size. And pointy, like almonds. But putting on Stell's bra was optional, and illicit; now I feel strapped in, buckled in, tied up. Mrs. Walker said It's part of being a woman, sugar, as she adjusted her dress over her own huge chest. I never saw my mother's breasts, without clothes, and when I realize I want to, that I wanted to see them, I am embarrassed with myself and change the subject in my head. But I probably never will see them now, so I just shouldn't think about it anymore.

After dinner my father helps me clear the table, then he turns on "Bonanza" or a news documentary. He narrates for me from the living room while I wash the dishes. I pull on my mother's bright yellow rubber gloves to protect my hands from the harsh dishwater; they are too big for me, but I wind rubber bands around my wrists to keep them on. My mother's wedding ring is still lying on the windowsill and I keep meaning to put it away, but I only think about this after I've put on the slippery yellow gloves, and then I forget. Later I sit with my father in the living room, to watch television and talk while we have our coffee.

My father talks to me more now, mostly about his work; I listen very carefully, to be sure I ask him intelligent questions. There are good cons and bad cons, but even the good ones you can't trust. You have to keep a certain distance, but stay cordial. Some of them he likes a lot, and he is a little extra friendly when no one else is watching. But there's been trouble before with officers sneaking in extra candy or little treats to favored inmates, who then take advantage. Instead, my father just gives them attention; he listens to stories about their lives, their families. He says listening respectfully to what they have to say makes them feel human; a lot of them are guys that got a rough break in life and were messed up. Warden Johnston used to say that, my father tells me; maybe we're doing the right thing at the wrong time, most of these guys got on the wrong road as kids, neglect, no guidance. But of course, that's no reason to become a criminal. It's not like the old days, anyway, when you had Karpis, Machine Gun Kelly, now those were criminals. The glory days. Even the Birdman's gone, and he wound up just some sick old man in a Seg cell at the hospital, still psycho, though.

There are bigger problems between the guards and administration; the guards feel underpaid, that the prison is understaffed. New guards coming in don't get the kind of training they used to, and many of them don't want to be here; getting sent to duty on Alcatraz is a threat to guards at other institutions, just like it used to be for prisoners. The older guards, one's who've been here ten, fifteen years, think the place is slipping. Madigan's getting ready to go, our Associate Warden's taking over, and he's a liberal, so it will be even worse. My father still likes it here, however, and still believes in the principle. When he tells me all of this I feel very important, because he is confiding in me, and I am the only one who really understands. It is a gift he cannot give to anyone else. He asks how my day went, but it's usually the same, Oh, fine. Galileo High is just like Marina Middle School, but bigger; everyone is tidier at the end of the day, now that we're all older, but sweatier. I have friends at school but I feel even still older than most of them; I have more responsibility, and it makes things like dances and gossiping over sodas seem childish.

I leave school at lunch period one day because I have to first go into Chinatown to find pomegranate juice, and then get home early to make my father a special dinner. Even Grandma is impressed when I describe my chicken with pomegranate sauce that I made up, but she makes me promise not to skip school again. I tell her I won't, if she won't tell my father. I do it a few times since then, anyway, because making things nice takes a little extra time, but it's worth it—he always notices when I do something special for him. There have been a few days I haven't left the island at all, I've been so busy here, but why should I? Almost anything I need is right here. This spring I'm going to plant a garden outside our cottage like Grandma's, so I can serve fresh vegetables instead of frozen. I read an article in *Ladies' Home Journal* that said fresh vegetables have more vitamins, and keep your family healthier. I also want Grandma to teach me how to knit; it gets very cold for my father when he is on Tower duty and I am going to make him a thick woolen scarf with matching socks, dark blue with little white diamonds.

We are invited to dinner at the Walkers', also; I don't want to go but my father insists, and it feels good that he wants me to be there, with him. I stay away from Mr. Walker as much as possible but he never comes near me now. Maybe when I was littler I seemed less attached to anything, like a guppy swimming around in a glass bowl that he could just scoop out with one oily hand, that no one would miss. But it's different now; the glass bowl is all mine and my father's, and Mr. Walker can't just stick his hands into that whenever he wants. He ignores me during dinner, but talks in a loud voice to my father about Fidel Castro taking over Cuba and the beatniks taking over the City, and President Eisenhower taking over the longshoremen's strike. He asks about Stell and her husband, and How's that boy of yours doing at boot camp? This annoys my father, because he's spending a lot of money for Jerry's school and insists on always referring to it by full name: St. John's Military Academy. Dessert is pecan pie, which I don't touch. Mr. Walker leaves after dinner for an 8:00 o'clock shift, and my father and I help Mrs. Walker take the dirty things into the kitchen. He invites her back to watch "Gunsmoke" with us but she says Thanks, another time. I am glad to have my father to myself—we sit on the sofa and watch shows together every night until late—but she's come over a few times since, and that's when I go to bed early. I'm still embarrassed with her, because she's seen me bleed.

My mother did come home after the hospital last year, but she was Vacant, a shell with its insides, the living animal part, scooped out and eaten by a bigger animal. My father didn't know what to do with her, for her. He brought her glasses of water and told her how beautiful she looked, and when he went to work I sat with her to watch whatever was on television. She smiled at me a lot, and ran her fingers through my hair, or spun her pinkish gold wedding band around and around on her finger. I knew she was thinking about things, plotting something, that her mind wasn't as empty as it seemed she wanted my father to think. You know when water is boiling hot, even if it's not bubbling. It was impossible to say anything to my father—Look, Daddy, Mom's *thinking* about something!—because no one ever came out and said there was anything wrong with her in the first place. So I kept her secret and let her think to herself, and helped her take TV dinners out of the oven for dinner and make sandwiches for lunch, and went to school trying not to think about anything too much myself. I came in the cottage late one afternoon and knew she was gone because the house smelled empty. There was nothing to clean up, this time. Her suitcase was gone, and some of her clothes, and the feel of her fingers in my hair. Her pink gold wedding band was on the kitchen windowsill, where she always left it to wash dishes. I waited for my father to come home from his shift; there was no point in alerting him up at the prison, and no point in searching, calling the Marines or the Coast Guard, I knew. When I told him he got, I think, hysterical, swearing, and ran down to talk to the ferry pilot on duty; yes, Mrs. Thornton had gone into the City. Sure he was sure, why, it was the same trip that took Robert Stroud, the Birdman, off the island. He was transferring to the Medical Prison for Federal Prisoners at Springfield, Missouri, that crazy old man, ending his forty years of isolation. He remembered telling all that to Mrs. Thornton during the crossing, and they talked about it a while. No, she seemed fine, smiled and waved a little when she stepped off the boat at Fort Mason. Oh, yeah, she had a suitcase. Figured she was off on a visit somewhere, ladies sure enjoy that.

My father went into the City and found the Chrysler Windsor station wagon gone from its garage near Fisherman's Wharf. He called my grandparents; he called Stella in San Diego and Jerry off at school; he told me he'd find her, or she'd be back on her own, probably turn up in a few weeks. I thought about my mother's body floating up in the sea, crabs still chewing through her stomach. Or maybe her long mermaid hair was snagged on a coral rock, holding her down, far beneath the water. But I knew she was Vanished. That night I found an envelope she left me on my pillow, just where Stell had left me the charm bracelet with its dangling, hollow hearts. I put the envelope away in my nightstand without opening it; if I don't open it, it means I always can.

Mrs. Walker has come over the last three nights of the Nixon–Kennedy debates to watch with us, and I am tired of hearing how good-looking John Kennedy is. His teeth are too big. She has also started wearing those little hats, a pillbox, that the Senator's wife wears. They look ridiculous on her big bubble of hair. My father gave me one for my fifteenth birthday—pearly pink with a little bow—and I'm sure she talked him into it. It's too old for me, anyway, and I have no interest in wearing a pillbox on my head. I told him it was pretty, and just put it away with other things I'll never use. Mrs. Walker is very pro-Kennedy and applauds everything he says, but then my father points out what is better about what Mr. Nixon is saying and Mrs. Walker says Well, that's true, Arthur, that's very true, silly me, I didn't see that at all, now, did I? We're supposed to be watching the debates for school, but I already had my turn as a mock debater after the third night and I don't feel like sitting there with them anymore, so I go to bed. Mrs. Walker says So soon, sugar? Well, sweet dreams! I kiss my father good night and go to my room, thinking her smell is filling up our house now and taking up far too much space.

I go to get a glass of water, it must be almost midnight, and just when I enter the living room I see them on the sofa. Mrs. Walker is on her back making little panting moans, but my father is very quiet, except for his breathing, which comes out in throaty puffs like he's struggling with something heavy. Her skirt is pushed up way over her hips so I can see the straps of her garter belt, and her blouse is unbuttoned and pushed down to her waist. Her empty brassiere sags up around her neck and her breasts make two enormous mounds on the sides of her chest, like Grandma's rising bread dough. She is a tangled and fleshy blur, but all I see of my father is his fully clothed back, lying mostly on top of her. His belt is on the floor. There is a lot more movement than I thought there would be, in intercourse; the books only talk about the husband inserting his penis into the wife's vagina, like closing a box of cereal, and then how sperm swims to meet the egg, but this looks nothing like swimming. It isn't flowers or chickens or dogs, either. It looks nothing like how I pictured it, but the sounds are dully familiar; I have heard them before, but a long, far time ago.

She is all spread around and taking up too much space here, but it hits me that there is space to be had—I am still too small to fill it up. It is a failure of some kind, not being able to fill the house up for him, be everything, like I've left an important thing undone. There is nothing I can do about it, though, because it takes a complete, real woman; these are sounds my father has to make, and he cannot make them with me.

# Mermaids

U.S. Expert Declares Organized Crime Threatens Existence of America.

*San Francisco Chronicle*, July 1933

Upon Attorney General Homer Cummings's announcement in 1933 of Alcatraz's imminent transformation into a federal penitentiary—his highly visible, solidly symbolic threat to the "nation's incorrigibles"—San Francisco reporters began filling their copy with the coming threat of those "arch criminals," "desperadoes," and "killer gangsters and others of like ilk." Al Capone's absolutely "top secret" transfer to Alcatraz from Atlanta was serialized in August 1934 newspapers nationwide, while Cummings ingenuously told the *Chronicle* that "Capone is not headed for Alcatraz. That's all I can say at this time, since we never discuss such matters." The next day the early-morning papers announced Capone's arrival in the Bay area—on the government's top-secret train—at 8:30 A.M. The train was mobbed by a crowd of "spectators and newspapermen" gathered to watch this secret, surprise transfer. Symbols must be seen, not secret, to carry weight.

But Cummings had severely underestimated the opposition of Bay area citizens; the junior and senior Chambers of Commerce, the women's clubs, the District Attorney of San Francisco, and police chiefs from Marin and the East Bay opposed bringing "all those undesirables here," opposed the dangers, the detriment, the unwholesome element about to be unleashed. Keep them in Chicago, Atlanta, Kansas, Washington, but not here, not a mere mile and a half from our peaceful, safe shores, our families.

Officials rallied. We have been misunderstood, they said, pledging "to take every precaution structurally and administratively to prevent escapes and protect surrounding cities from marauding outlaws . . . all scientific devices will be employed to insure the restraint of inmates." In appealing for civic cooperation, they fell back on the flag: "In short, it seems to the Department there is presented a splendid opportunity for the citizens of San Francisco to cooperate in a patriotic and public-spirited manner in the government's campaign against the criminal."

The steel bars on cellfronts grew thicker overnight in newsprint; the cement walls expanded and hardened, becoming impervious to man, machine, or monsoon . . . but always, always, there was talk of the choppy, chilly Bay—the world's ultimate moat, the water dropping by degrees to Alaskan frigidity, almost cold enough to deep freeze the man-eating sharks breeding by hundreds in the sea around the island, those circling sharks hungry for the blood of any man foolish enough to attempt escape. The Bay will help Uncle Sam protect his citizens.

A seventeen-year-old girl named Anastasia Scott was living with her family on Alcatraz in 1933, her father being George Scott, Staff Sergeant of the U.S. Army Disciplinary Barracks. On the morning of Tuesday, October 17, Anastasia—a trained, medal-winning swimmer—slipped into the water off the island and swam to the San Francisco mainland in forty-three minutes. The papers reported it the following day; this "San Francisco mermaid," this "curly-haired miss," "slender, red-haired, and full of vivacity," "without batting a dusky eyelash" was "showing her contempt" for the officials' claims—and in the same article was quoted as denying her feat was in any way connected to the recent announcement of Alcatraz' imminent new function, that she'd been thinking about making the swim for a year, and "yesterday turned out to be a nice day, so I tried it."

But if, as reported, she dove in with no more thought than a shrug of her slender shoulders, why did she arrive at the dock of the Dolphin Swimming Club, at the foot of Larkin Street, accompanied by "her pilot" in a rowboat, Herbert Derham, and two other members of the Dolphin Club? And how did the press arrive in time to snap her picture as she crawled onto the dock, "not the least bit fatigued," announcing "it's an easy swim!"? No, let it be *our* protest, our statement, not yours, Miss Scott; a girlish whim is more attractive than political propaganda, more feminine. Impulsive is fine; calculating is not. We want her to look good.

A nice story, but not enough. A quarter column on a back page. The *Examiner* sees a good thing. They contact Phil Patterson, manager of the Fairmont Hotel Plunge; Patterson recruits two local girls who frequent the Fairmont swimming pool, and an event is arranged. Gloria Scigliano, twenty, is a national junior swimming champion. Doris McLeod, eighteen, is a "Fairmont Plunge Mermaid." On Thursday, October 19, with full press and cheering crowds, they dive off Pier 45 for a swim to Alcatraz, in order to prove the viability of the water's temperature, the absence of sharks, and the meager minimum of physical strength required for the feat—After all, if a *girl* can do it! . . .—the desired end result being, of course, the abandonment of the penitentiary plan on the basis of public safety, and, to boot, a vaguely salacious news story; two civic mermaids being sacrificed to the sea gods.

Phil Patterson is to follow them in a launch provided by the *Examiner.*

Doris and Gloria dive in prettily, losing their marcelled curls, white legs disappearing into the green sea like Icarus, and surface, foamy and slick, to wave to the crowds. Cameras click; people cheer them on. They begin their mile-and-a-half swim "like a pair of seals and set off at a brisk pace." They "laughed and wisecracked all the way across." Boyishly athletic is fine, but don't work up a sweat. Gloria Scigliano lands on Alcatraz in fifty-seven minutes. Doris McLeod arrives at the island, where she "flashed white teeth in a smile," swims around it, and returns back to the South End Rowing Club in two hours, cramping, her lungs sodden, but victorious.

They have proven a point, but not for themselves. Every newspaper story emphasizes the "ease" of the swim; their photo in the *Chronicle,* unlike the shot of Anastasia Scott half submerged in mid-stroke, her eyes bleary with salt, shows both of them on land, earlier or after, Doris in a kittenish, Betty Boop posture, under the caption "Who's Afraid of the Big Bad Bay?" Their success is attributed not to skill or training or determination, but to the welcoming flow of the Bay itself; theirs is a negative triumph, an anti-feat, a below-standard scale against which other swimmers, those potential fleeing men, can be measured. If those *girls* could do it . . . why, then the men, any men, can, will.

That same year commercial airlines were using Amelia Earhart to promote air travel; fellow pilot Louise Thaden remarked that "nothing impresses the safety of aviation on the public quite so much as to see a woman flying an airplane . . . the public thinks it must be duck soup for men." Of course, females interested in aviation were hired as stewardesses, not pilots, but Amelia made their point for them.

After winning a medal for swimming in the 1932 Olympics, Eleanor Holm told *Women's Sports* that it was, yes, a great thrill but "the moment I find swimming is making me athletic looking, giving me big, bulky muscles, making me look like an Amazon rather than a woman, I'll toss it to one side." The Amazons were women, just not decorative, or as delicate, as the Mermaids with their lacy, floating hair and naked frolics in the sea.

Alcatraz to San Francisco is not an easy swim, by any means. At that time of year, the water is anywhere from fifty to sixty degrees; the currents can run at nine miles an hour; there are undertows. Between 1934 and 1963, of all the escape attempts by highly motivated mermen, only one man, once at the water, is known for sure to have swum successfully to the mainland, aided by inflated surgical gloves; he arrived half-dead from exhaustion and hypothermia. Other men who made it out of the cellhouse gave up at the shoreline; the water was too damn cold, the currents too violent to take on—No, take us back in the violence of capture, instead, toss us in Isolation. Jack LaLanne, the Amazon of men, couldn't do it in 1958. After Doris and Gloria succeeded in 1933 an editorial in the *Chronicle* stated: "It is now plain that there are any number of girls who can swim rings around Alcatraz any time they wish to do so . . . girl swimmers have made the island theory ridiculous." Another one referred to Alcatraz as the "Isle Where the Mermaids Sport."

Officials were undeterred; in February of 1934 the *Chronicle* reported "Swim Scoffed At" by Attorney General Cummings, who declared that "the fact that some young lady swam out there and back is of no consequence one way or the other," again stressing that adequate precautions would be taken *inside* the prison to prevent escapes, and that the "whole country applauds" the plan. In June 1934, almost a year after the plan was announced, the first federal penitentiary guards moved onto the island with their families. An article in the August 19 *Chronicle* has pictures of Cummings inspecting the new and improved prison with Warden James A. Johnston. A photo at the bottom of the page shows a guard in silhouette against the San Francisco skyline, on the catwalk between a Gun Tower and the cellhouse. The caption reads "Death Steps Out on Patrol." I don't know which guard it was, whose father it is. Capone came a few days later. My parents arrived in 1945, right before I was born.

I don't know what happened to Anastasia, or Doris and Gloria. I suppose they were feted for a while; did they go on to win more medals at Aquatic Park? Gertrude Ederle had already swum the English Channel, and the 1932 Olympics were a memory, so perhaps girl swimmers were passé. They did not become Babe Didrikson, or turn to movies like Esther Williams—we would have heard from them, of them. So they had a story for their grandchildren; what more do I want them to have? Isn't the victory, the story, the clippings, the footnote, enough? I myself am ambivalent about them—am *I* devaluing their feat, by feeling the pure act of their achieving it is somehow not enough? *I* couldn't make that swim. They don't owe anyone more medals, more fame.

I have those clippings, the photos; I found them in my mother's things. I don't know how she got them, or why she kept them. In 1933 she was a college coed, back in Wisconsin, inland, far from mermaids and the islands where they sport. Who gave them to her? They are a mystery to me. Were they heroines to her? Maybe Anastasia; she swam away from the island, not to it. What about Doris and Gloria? Did my mother later stand on the dock at Alcatraz, watching in her mind the two of them swimming toward her, watching their dolphin arcs through the waves, headed not to open sea, but to the prison, the human fishing net? Was she yelling in her mind, or wanting to, aloud, No, stop! Go back! Don't swim this way!?

# New Frontier

## *Olivia*

> OFFICER AND MRS. STANLEY WALKER are leaving us! After years of distinguished service, Officer Walker is transferring back to Atlanta. We'll miss you, Stan and Martha!
>
> OFFICER ARTHUR THORNTON tells us his daughter Olivia has gone to stay with her grandparents in beautiful Pacific Grove; have fun, Olivia!
>
> *The Pelican,* October 1960

Daniel is a prophylactic salesman, like part of a dirty joke. He moved here from Los Angeles six months, or a year ago, I'm not sure; he has an uncle, or maybe an older cousin, who owns a small chain of drugstores there and gave Daniel this job. He has small suitcases full of samples that he carries around to drugstores, showing rolled-up and unrolled rubbers, taking orders. So far he hasn't sold a single one, but he doesn't care; he isn't on commission and his uncle, or cousin, gives him a small salary. His parents also send money; his father is some kind of doctor in Beverly Hills, a dermatologist, or podiatrist, I think. I don't listen to him very carefully, I don't bother underlining anything he says. I do remember that his mother is a chemist, because this is amazing to me. There are lots of famous women by now, of course, but other than actresses they are usually a famous man's wife, or if they've contributed, are mostly dead, like Madame Curie or

Joan of Arc. Famous women who have contributed never seem to be alive, or someone's mother. I have a flash of seeing her carved overhead at Marina Middle School, DANIEL'S MOTHER, or MRS. EDELMAN, because I don't know her first name. His mother is the one thing I ask him questions about, until Daniel points out he tells me everything about his family, so why will I tell him nothing about mine? So I don't ask about her anymore. Daniel says his parents are willing to support him until he's twenty-one, or even after, as long as he has a direction. He isn't sure what he wants to do, but he's only nineteen, so there's still plenty of time. Maybe photography school.

We have a two-room apartment off Grant, near the base of Telegraph Hill. The last tenant painted our hardwood floors with layers of whitish lacquer, so at night we seem to be ice skating. There is a king-size mattress on the floor of the second room, and orange crates turned upside-down for furniture, and a red bulb in the bathroom. Our apartment smells like cooking garlic and parmesan and hardening sticks of salami, but that is the illusion created by restaurant air wafting up from the streets. The only thing I've ever cooked here is water for tea. Daniel thinks I don't know how to cook and doesn't seem to mind—we go out, or bring in sandwiches, pizza, Chinese. I don't clean up, either; even our used and limp rubbers lie on the icy floor like a woman's soiled stockings until Daniel picks them up and throws them away. My lack of laundry skill is genuine; when Daniel and I go to the laundromat I sit on top of a vibrating washer and read while he sorts our clothes, stuffs them in, and feeds nickels to the machine.

We do what everyone else does here: go to movies on Market Street, sit in coffeehouses until very late at night with thimbles of espresso, listen to jazz, play chess, drink gallons of Chianti with spaghetti, even for breakfast, but Daniel takes none of it seriously—he knows it is just the form of all of this that is left, that we are two or three years past when it really functioned as something. Now high-school girls from Pacific Heights come to the Subterranean or the Sooty Fox, wearing black cashmere turtlenecks from Saks and think they are on the edge. We are nowhere near the edge but in between, and are unsure what follows, where the next edge is; we will just see what happens. Everyone here also smokes cigarettes, but we don't; Daniel thinks it is gross, too, and we always take a shower when we come home, and hang our clothes out the window to breathe.

After Kennedy won, many of Daniel's friends were very upset; it is not that they voted for Nixon—they didn't vote at all—but it is difficult to remain darkly fatalistic when the nation has suddenly turned cheery. They want to remain subterranean, waiting for bombs; they don't like dawn, or the idea of our country as a big happy family, everyone chipping in for each other; they are as private and shelled in as turtles. They fill up the basement coffeehouses but mostly ignore one another, wearing dark glasses that make them look like human insects. They especially ignore the girls with them; each girl is tucked away tight as a rib at her guy's side, or hangs over his shoulder like the long wooden bows the Indians used, gracefully curved but strung taut. These girls all have very black hair that reminds me of Monica and Mrs. Thompson—I wonder sometimes if they've wandered down here, in black sheaths, smoking cigarettes, looking blasé and nervous. They belong here, not me. But I've never run into any old friends from school. The girls without black hair are dyeing it black to look stark; as a result they mostly look the same and I wind up looking stark when we're around them. I keep my hair pulled back in a braid, partly because it makes me look older but also because I kept seeing my mother from the corner of my eye, a blond flash, if I turned my head suddenly. The same thing happens when I see a Chrysler station wagon, but there's nothing I can do about that.

Some of the guys still write poetry, wanting to howl, hoping to be banned, but no one seems to care how many times they say fuck. They say it more than they do it, Daniel says; he thinks the only time the word counts for anything anyway is during sex, because that is when it is fleshed out, sibilants and not just consonants. I tell him he means fucking is onomatopoeic, and he laughs and says Yes, that's exactly what he means. He thinks I understand him, but mostly I'm just guessing. He doesn't tuck me away; we usually talk to each other, face to face, because no one else is very interested, or interesting to us.

A few people here are tired of being private and are slowly becoming public; they are sleeping eight or ten to a basement room and sharing their wine and toilet paper, eating spaghetti out of one big pot. To the boys it means also sharing their girls, and so they are passed around. It is free love; it is no cost to the boys. Most of the girls, to me, look spent; they seem to think they are contributing to something important and edgy by doing this, by backing up the boys like a footnote. I feel hungry for these girls sometimes, but they still scare me a little, and I just stay close to Daniel. A few of these people-groups are drifting west, heading toward Golden Gate Park or the Haight, to start being public there. They like poetry, too, but they like it to music; there is always someone in these groups with a guitar, singing, warbling.

Daniel and I like it here, waiting for something without caring how long it takes. I wear his clothes, his jeans and denim shirts, and dark sweaters, although he is much bigger than I am and everything has to be rolled up from where it ends—it is sort of the opposite of Daniel putting on a rubber, rolling it down and onto himself. It made me laugh, the first time, this little balloon between us—between us and venereal disease and babies. He does it with one hand, which I find impressive; I can't put on a sock with one hand, even Daniel's roomy ones. Piece by piece my old clothes, the girl things from the fifties, have rotated to the bottom of a pile in our second room. I don't even wear the two bras I own anymore, which no one would notice to look at me, anyway; it took Daniel by surprise, after I stopped, the first time he came up behind me and slid his hands under my shirt. Shoes, black boots, I have to buy, because his don't fit. He is very tall, with huge feet and hands but his body is slender, almost delicate, and he smells like soap, not that stronger smell of men, their hair and oil and sweating skin. There is a long scar down his back from when he broke his spine as a little boy, as if someone laid him down flat and he cracked open, like how a book breaks its spine. At first I was careful handling him, as I am handling books, but I realized soon that he is very strong and not going to break again no matter what I do. He has dark curly hair that comes out a slightly different shape every time he washes it. Once a month or so he lets a tuft of hair on his chin grow, before deciding it looks like he's trying to be something he's not. He says that's what drew him to me—that I seemed not to be trying to be anything I'm not. I am still unsure what I am, however, so this isn't too difficult.

He asked if he could take a picture of me and I first thought he must be a detective, working for my father. Then I knew my father wouldn't hire anybody like this, only a few years older than me and too beat-looking to be trusted. Washington Square was full of people and I didn't know why he wanted me, but I thought about Stell and being a magazine girl and said Yeah, okay. I began to comb my hair but he said

No, just like you are. He wanted me sitting as I was, on a bench with my feet propped on my suitcase. My hand started bleeding again at the base of my thumb, from a broken plate, and I put it in my mouth to suck on it and stop the flow. He said Yeah, stay like that, and took the picture. Then he sat down next to me and took my hand to see if I was badly hurt, but I took it back.

I'd stayed in my room until my father left for an 8:00 A.M. shift, then wandered into the living room, which was tidy and empty, the sofa the same as always. No evidence of the night before, the spread-out bodies, the tangled clothes. The kitchen, too, was clean, as sterile as I'd left it. On the counter was the envelope my father always left me, with that week's household allowance. But whatever food I bought, whatever I made, whatever I did, wouldn't be enough. I'd still be too little. I opened every cabinet and swept all the glasses and dishes onto the floor, what was left of them, so they crashed and splintered, a riot of jagged china and glass and porcelain for my father to clean up. My hand got cut on a broken plate, bleeding a little; I picked up part of a martini glass and tried pressing the shard harder across the tissuey wrist skin over a vein. I drew out a thin line of blood, with a small bead of it at the end, and stopped; I didn't want to bleed anymore. I thought about the gun in my father's nightstand, his Colt; it would hurt less than this hurt, and I wouldn't even see the blood. I'd only touched it the one time, but how hard could it be to fire a gun? And then my father could clean it up, would have to clean it all up, the pieces of glass and the pieces of me. I liked this idea a lot and left the kitchen, heading down the hallway. I stopped outside his bedroom door. I stopped with my hand on the knob. I just didn't want to go into his bedroom, even if there was a gun in there. Finally I went back in my room and took down the suitcase I used to go visit my grandparents. I filled it with a few of my things but not the pillbox hat, then added a few things of my mother's, in a bloodhound way, but not her wedding ring still lying on the windowsill. I reached into my nightstand for the envelope she left me, still sealed, and took that. Outside our cottage the air was like wet gauze, and I couldn't even see the cellhouse when I left on the ferry, the week's household allowance in my pocket, playing ostrich by not looking back, expecting any second to hear the escape siren scream. I told the ferry pilot I was going visiting and waved goodbye to him when I stepped off the boat and onto the dock at Fort Mason. He waved goodbye back.

Daniel asked if I needed a place to stay, because he had room. I said Yes, but only if I could sleep with him, and not on a sofa. He said Sure, but then asked how old I was, but then said never mind. I let him take my hand again, then, and he wrapped a paper napkin around it. We went back to his apartment on Grant and I kissed and then fucked a person for the first time, on his king-size mattress on the floor, and thought it was a bizarre thing, but All right, this is what a woman is supposed to do, it is the last thing I have to do. I thought for some reason of my mother making Jell-O, stirring in ice cubes to hurry up the chill and finish it, harden it, because she'd waited too long to start dessert.

I call my grandparents from a pay phone; they both cry at the sound of my voice and beg me to tell them where I am, which I won't do. Am I all right, at least, and what am I doing and do I need money; if I don't want to live with my father, I can go live with them, don't I know that? I tell them I'm fine, and ask them please to call my father and tell him I'm fine. I don't want to talk to him. I tell them I love them and will call them soon. That night I surprise Daniel by making us root-beer floats; we don't have any golden glass mugs, but they're still good.

Daniel thinks I'm running away from a family in Oregon, or Arizona; it seems I don't know San Francisco very well, and in fact, other than routes from Fort Mason to school and my mother's doctor, I don't. Daniel likes to take long walks, and I'm still surprised that almost wherever we go you can see Alcatraz if you look north, like it's a point on the compass. It shows up in many of the pictures he takes, hovering over my head. At first San Francisco felt so far away I thought I would never see anything left behind, but it is like those space satellites to the moon; they all look back at what they've left, and take pictures of Earth. Everywhere, too, are bars with neon martinis out in front, the olive garnish a lime green glow.

When Daniel develops his pictures in our red-bulbed bathroom he makes copies of the ones where I'm smiling and fully dressed and you can't see any city landmarks or spectral island behind me, and gives them to me in an envelope; he wants me to send these back to my family in Oregon or Arizona so they know I'm OK. I put them in my suitcase, with my mother's sealed envelope. I like the other ones he takes better, where I don't look like a magazine girl: pictures of me naked, braiding my hair, or caught in the rain, glowering at Daniel because he won't hand over the umbrella, or when I'm lost in one of his dark sweaters, big as a dress on me. My favorite ones are where you can't see my face. I take pictures of him, too, often naked, when I catch him off guard. Sometimes he sets up the camera to shoot both of us. I tease him that they are evidence; I am underage, after all, and he says Sure, I'd go to prison for you. I tell him that's a riot. He's concerned that I don't go to school, that I will have a deficiency, like not getting enough vitamins. I tell him I'm waiting to see what I'm going to do, just like he is. Something is going to give, or dawn, some time soon.

Each time we do something new that is Sex it embarrasses me, because I think *this* thing we're doing now must be bad, dirty. Then we do it and I'm struck by how it is nothing in itself, not good or evil; it has a name, but not a label. Daniel likes doing things most when I'm bleeding; he says he likes the salt, it makes him feel elemental. The first morning I woke up to find I had bled through my underwear and onto the sheet I was mortified, but he ran his fingers over the spot and shrugged, said it was just a dying flower. It reminded me of Hygiene, then, of stamens and pistils, and I felt cleaner. He doesn't add bleach to the sheets when he does the laundry, so now there are lots of dead brownish flowers in our bed. The first time he gathered our laundry together, mostly things that reeked of cigarettes, he picked up all my dirty underwear to wash and I had to stop myself from fishing them out of the pile to scrub by myself in private. It seems babyish to hold that kind of thing back now, underwear; Daniel has bleached out the shame.

So I can finally use the schoolyard words because I've earned them, I've made them real; Daniel and I fuck all the time, and I can call it what it is. I want mostly to do this one thing, be this one thing, for him—somehow that, and all the other things I've already done, will add up together and add up to me. A woman me. I am waiting for this to happen, while he pushes into me and I listen to the sounds he makes in his throat; they are sounds I can't imagine him making with anybody else. At the most frenetic moment he tells me

I'm beautiful and I tell him to fuck me harder. I want the being-pounded feeling of it, like my fibers inside are being softened. He likes squirming his fingers and hands into my mouth, my ears, my nose, both holes between my legs; he says he likes the salt, but sometimes I think he is just trying to worm inside me. Now and then I get annoyed and push him away. He is salty, too, his mushroom cap and creamy juice—it spurts out in long bitter strings I catch with my tongue—but it doesn't get me inside of him at all, he doesn't have the same entrance. I only theoretically think this is unfair, that Sex is mostly him wedging into my insides, because I don't really care about getting inside him, anyway. He licks and chews and swallows me when I'm very wet or bloody and says it's delicious; I forget where I am, for just a second, and wonder what it is I have just served him.

He holds onto me at night like a buoy; I usually try to turn it into Sex, but sometimes he wants to just hold on and talk. What he wants with me and what I want with him are two different things—Let me be a body, just a body, I think—but he is waiting for me to forget this and really hold onto him too. Meanwhile, we use up his sample rubbers. He tells his uncle, or cousin, he has been handing them out as free samples, hoping to increase business. We got a big new package of them in the mail, but he was told to stop giving them away. They smell like the rubber life preservers from the ferry, or like tiny rubber rafts kept rolled up and away, to catch all that sperm trying to swim away and get somewhere.

After he falls asleep I sometimes still use my bed stories, but they don't work as well anymore; my head gets like the hamster wheel too often, my thoughts spinning around without going anywhere. I get up and drink tea, or read, or just lie in bed until morning. It's also hard to sleep without the foghorns in my ears, like when I was little, during a fogless, too-quiet night. I curl away from Daniel so there is a moat of empty sheet all around me. I don't hold onto anything. I am not going to slip into loving him just because he is here.

I'm not looking for her, really. Maybe she is in Oregon, or Arizona, or maybe she is one block away, eating cold spaghetti from a big pot, her blond hair dyed black in disguise. Maybe she is in Mexico, shaded from the sun by fluttering Monarch butterflies. I know she is alive, that she made it across the water, somewhere, and that one day I will be walking down the street and smell her like a hug, because she has finally come looking for me. I will give her the envelope full of pictures of me smiling, so she will know what about me she missed. I don't open her envelope, still, because I know one day I will hear everything there is to know, from her.

# Corrosion

## *The Prison*

> What did in Alcatraz was the very thing it imposed so punishingly for 29 years on its 1576 of the nation's worst felons—the ravages of time.
>
> *Newsweek,* April 1963

Salt is a cheap and paradoxical thing: abundant in nature, yet once highly valued as currency; powerfully corrosive to matter, yet esteemed as a preservative. It veins the earth, and flavors the human body; it is a dependable seasoning, a kitchen staple, and a biblical punishment for disobedient wives. When alien fluids are introduced into us, the eyedrops, the IVs, they are often salinized to familiarize them to our own brackish chemistry, but too much salt to the system is a shock and produces anxiety in our blood. Salty is ribald, pungent, faintly distasteful, while the salt of the earth is virtuous and worthy. There is the old tale of a poor sailor given a miraculous machine capable of producing for him anything on earth; he chooses, of all things, salt, and the machine pours forth such piles of it the sailor is ecstatic, knowing he will be rich. However, the piles turn into drifts, and the sailor, panicked, cannot shut off the miraculous machine. He is in danger of drowning in the briny dunes, and so throws the forever-churning miracle overboard, into the ocean, giving us a salted sea. We are meant to see a parable of greed in this, but it is also a tale of ambivalence: what it is we choose to value, and how we fear the results of the choice. We love flavor, but too much is terrifying, sickening; it is best kept under control, in a tiny glass cellar, in safe view on the kitchen table.

CONVICTS TUNNEL OUT OF ALCATRAZ WITH A SPOON—faintly quaint, a tea party gone awry—ran the headlines in June of 1962. Frank Morris, and brothers Clarence and John Anglin, over eighteen months' time, chipped away at the ventilation grills at the backs of their cells, squeezed into the utility corridor between cellblocks, climbed the laddered maze of pipes and conduits leading to the cellhouse roof, slipped into the water and disappeared on the night of June 11. They'd left dummies in their beds to dupe the night guards; their disappearance was not discovered until early morning, some eight hours later. Officials insisted the men had drowned; telescope operators on Pier 43 made a small fortune as tourists with handfuls of change gathered to scan the water and the island's silhouette. Everyone waited out the ghoulish two weeks, but no gassy bodies surfaced in the sea. A June 14 editorial in the *Chronicle* said:

> If Morris and the brothers Anglin have in fact gotten away with it and stultified all the art, science and penological abracadabra that went into making Alcatraz "escape proof," we offer them a silent cheer for having at last destroyed the myth of its inviolability.

The only officially acceptable excuse for the destruction of that myth was time. A few journalists were invited onto the island, although not allowed in the cellhouse ("too much unrest" in there) to hear about the scooped-out cells, and a denial of any custodial lapse or willful negligence; simply, Alcatraz was falling apart. *Newsweek* reported on its natural, elemental decay, pointing out that "conspiring with the Pacific's corrosive salt air, time corroded the watch towers until guards had to be called down in a high wind." If there was any human error, it was only due to a lack of training, which was directly the fault of insufficient funding. Later, the two guards on cellhouse duty the night of June 11 were quietly suspended.

Madigan's last years as Warden had been beleaguered by a flood of writs prepared by convicts using the library to educate themselves to articulate protest; inmates were suing Madigan, the Bureau of Prisons, and the United States government, saying they deserved compensation for good behavior time arbitrarily taken away, health ruined by confinement on the island, and abusive, brutal treatment by the guards. Incidents of inmates slashing their Achilles tendons—a more desperate and mute form of protest—peaked in 1960; the rash of cuttings was explained, and dismissed, as inmates simply frustrated with official indifference to their pseudo-complaints. Associate Warden Olin Blackwell described them as "attention getters."

Blackwell took over for Madigan in 1961; he lessened censorship of inmate mail, again increased their recreation hours, and allowed them to knit and crochet doilies to kill time. His relaxed style would later be blamed as a factor in the death of Alcatraz—he was acting Warden at the time of the Morris escape—but by then the prison was in its death throes anyway, a corroded relic of penal philosophy. All Blackwell could do, really, was take its pulse now and then, and watch it die.

Finally, the argument everyone could agree on, with no burden of failed responsibility to anyone, was the well-worn issue of cost. The price of an inmate's stay on Alcatraz was almost $14 a day, as opposed to the $5 or so at other federal prisons. Millions would be needed to overhaul the deteriorating buildings—meanwhile, the new maximum-security prison at Marion, Illinois, was ready and waiting. Philosophy is debatable, but money is ultimately decisive; on June 24, 1962, Attorney General Robert Kennedy announced Alcatraz would close, creating great savings for taxpayers. By November the "phasing out" of inmates was in full swing, transferring them off the island at a rate of twenty a month. Officers and their families living on the island began collecting boxes, and deciding where else they might like to live.

One final inmate beat the families off the Rock. In December of 1962 John P. Scott and Darl Parker cut through a barred kitchen window with a piece of notched spatula, sneaked out, and entered the water off the northern tip of the island. The prison launch found Parker about half an hour later, freezing and in despair, clinging to the rock that is Little Alcatraz. A few hours later two teenagers found a body near Fort Point, at the southern end of the Golden Gate Bridge—before San Francisco police had even been notified. It was Scott, almost dead, with inflated surgical gloves still stuffed into his jacket and trousers. He spent some time in a mainland hospital, accessible to overjoyed reporters; Scott told them he and Parker had cut through the bars with string covered in ordinary kitchen cleanser, which was believed and printed. His success gave rise again to the idea that Morris and the Anglins—maybe even Roe and Cole, who'd disappeared in 1937—had actually made it, had vanquished the dangerous Bay.

Scott went back to an isolation cell at Alcatraz, but only for a few months; he left the Rock again in March 1963, when the last of the prisoners were transferred off—some of them to finish out their sentences at mere medium-security prisons. The families finished phasing themselves out, too, leaving a few stragglers behind to oversee the last official business, the last Golden Gate sunsets screened through salty fog. It was over.

# Alcatraz, 1963

## *Olivia*

I finally find somebody to take me over to the island: an eager guy a few years older than me, who has sunk his college tuition into a rickety old dinghy with an outboard that couldn't power a blender. He's going to rake it in, he says, by cashing in on Bobby Kennedy's announcement and taking tourists on a forty-minute spin around the Rock, complete with a verbal history and limited-supply-only, overpriced T-shirt. Technically only "authorized personnel" on "official business" are allowed to dock at the island, but for an extra twenty bucks Gary agrees to take me out and drop me off. The last convicts were transferred months ago, back to McNeil and Leavenworth, or the new prison at Marion that's meant to replace Alcatraz, and I know the families are mostly long gone, resettling on the mainland in or around San Francisco, or heading south to LA, or back to the Midwest—anywhere federal penitentiaries offer jobs and the familiar rhythm of a prison community. The papers say only a few prison employees are left on the island to wrap things up, and the official ferry is down to two trips a day: early morning, and late afternoon. All the old ferry pilots, our Charons, would also be gone, and I was unsure of my ability to convince the new federal ferryman that I was on official business. Gary seemed easier. Once we docked, I'd be fine. I haven't been on the island in almost three years; I haven't seen it for two, even in a photo.

I finally gave in to Daniel and my grandparents; we live with them now, in Pacific Grove. I gave in, too, to letting my father know where I was, and he made no protest about my staying with my grandparents. I have my high-school equivalence degree; this fall I start applying to colleges. My grandparents think I should go back east and be Ivy League, but I'd rather go to Berkeley. Grandpa bought me a car, a shiny Chevy Camaro, so that I can be independent. I was not allowed to drive it all summer, until I proved to him I could practically take the engine apart and put it back together; he says independence without responsibility is dangerous. I have to show my grandmother, too, and Daniel when they get back from Washington; they went to the civil rights march and heard Dr. King's speech. Grandpa and I watched it on TV, eating root-beer floats and trying to spot them in the crowd. Daniel only comes back for a month before leaving for Central America. He made a deal with his parents; he gets to do one year in the Peace Corps—I picture him handing out sample rubbers to Honduran teenagers—and then he will go back to school, which they will help pay for. They don't realize he is going to study photography at the San Francisco Art Institute. He wanted me to travel with him this last summer, but I said no and we had a fight; he told me I'm a cold and hard person, that it's like trying to love a chilled brick, an icy marble stump. I said Well, *you* made the mistake, then, in loving me, didn't you? He just grabbed my old suitcase packed full of his jeans and dark sweaters, and left with Grandma. She's called to talk to Grandpa a few times, but Daniel won't get on the phone. I sleep better alone, anyway, when there isn't something there wanting me to hold back on.

I've never crossed over in such a little boat, where you sit so far down near the water, shawled in the fog. Gary seems inspired, maybe due to the extra twenty, to launch into his rehearsed tour-guide speech with what must be extra gusto. I hear all about how evil spirits haunting the island kept the Indians away; it was "Hellcatraz," the "Rock," the "U.S. Devil's Island"; about Capone and Machine Gun Kelly. Nobody ever successfully escaped, he says; anyone trying was ultimately shot, drowned, executed, or surrendered on his own. I hear how inmates were beaten and tortured and mutilated, in the early days for merely speaking aloud; strung up in dungeons; attacked by drooling mastiffs kept on starvation rations to whet their appetite for convict flesh; how sadistic guards were trained in judo and weaponry, and selected specially for their honed discipline and icy blood. We're lucky, we've got a boat to get us across this water, he says with enthusiasm, imagine trying to swim it! You'd *really* have to be crazy! Even those latest guys, who dug out with a spoon, Morris and the Anglins, they for sure drowned, maybe; I am instructed to keep my eyes on the water, to look for bloated bodies. But the Bay is smooth and innocent as a pond today, like it's never heard of it's duty to be dangerous or seem threatening, to spit up drowned men. As we head around the curve of the island, I know the sign becomes visible behind me. Gary reads it aloud with theatrical flourish:

"'Warning: persons procuring or concealing escape of prisoners—'"

"'—are subject to prosecution and imprisonment,' yeah," I finish for him. He looks at me curiously, disappointed.

"You from around San Francisco?"

"No, Oregon. Or Arizona." He looks confused, and shrugs.

The boat scrapes the deserted dock. No boat linesman; no inmates loading trucks; no snitchbox. Gary glances up toward the looming cellhouse, suddenly ill at ease about letting me go.

"You know, maybe I should come with you . . . or wait for you. There's still people here, they might think you're an ex-con or something, shoot you on sight . . ." He laughs nervously. "I mean, seriously, you're a girl . . . I can't just *leave* you here. I oughta look after you . . ."

I climb up on the edge of the boat and leap onto the dock, surefooted. Like riding a bicycle. I have nothing to drop in the sea, anyway.

"Don't worry," I tell him. "They don't shoot the girls."

I smell the familiar salt, and reek of fish; it doesn't come from the ocean itself, it comes from the seagulls who gorge on so much fresh herring the fish comes out in their shit, the creamy shit that covers the island like spilled paint. The parade ground is smeared with it, as always. I expect the door to our cottage to be unlocked, as always, but it isn't; both the knob lock and the deadbolt are in place. I fumble for my key, the key I still carry on its thin chain, and hear:

"Yeah? Who's there?"

"It's me, Daddy." I pause. "Olivia."

The bolt is thrown back, the door opens with its old groan, and my father is standing there in his uniform pants and shirt but no tie, sleeves rolled up, holding an empty water tumbler in one hand, a section of the *Chronicle* in the other.

"Hey!"

We don't embrace, merely smile brightly.

"Well! Well, come on in, honey . . ." He waves the newspaper at me in greeting. I enter like a crab scuttling sideways onto a rock. Boxes and piles of newspaper are everywhere. The walls are bare, and most of the furniture is gone. On the floor near a stack of chipped dishes is the glass and chrome martini shaker, half full of clear liquid, and a jar of green olives. Another water tumbler, this one almost full and olive garnished, rests on a cardboard box serving as a table. There is a hole in his left sock, a white toe peeping through.

"Just packing up what's left . . . wasn't really expecting . . ." He sits on the floor next to a box full of newspaper-rolled tumblers. He rolls the empty one he's holding up in newspaper, and packs it away. "So . . . hey, how'd you get here?"

"Paid somebody off." I shrug, to emphasize how casually I break rules, my indifference to authority.

"How're your grandparents?"

"They're fine. They send their love," I say, although they hadn't.

He nods, and drinks from his glass. "You OK? You need anything?"

"No, Dad, I'm doing fine. Everything's good."

"It's good to see you, honey."

I bend to kiss his cheek, fragrant of juniper berries, and notice the tumbler he holds—one with big purple grapes painted on it. I guess it survived, although there is a thin crack down the side.

"I got a letter from Stell," he says. "Maryland. Looks like her and the jerk turned out OK. She sent me a picture of the kids. It's around here somewhere . . ."

"Oh, yeah . . . how many does she have now?" He looks at me, and I feel shamed. "Grandma and Grandpa get letters, but I don't really listen."

"I guess you girls were never real close."

"No, I guess not."

"Jerry's doing good. Stationed in, uh, Asia, I guess, yeah, military training in Vietnam. Says he's bored. But, it's good discipline. The service is doing him good. Thought it would. Good kid. Following in his old man's footsteps."

"Yeah." He finishes his drink and plucks the olive out of the cracked glass. "Well . . . I'll be heading up to San Q tomorrow. You oughta come up sometime, if you want, they got a nice place for me. Maybe sleep over."

"Sure, Dad."

"I saw that movie they did, *Birdman of Alcatraz*? About a year ago. You see it?

"Uh-uh."

My father chuckles. "Burt Lancaster. I bet Stroud loved that. Guy's still trying to get out." He shakes his head. There is a long pause. He looks at his drained glass, then wraps it in newspaper and packs it with the others. He seems about to ask something, and I wait . . . but he then lets go of it, and looks absently around the cottage.

"So, is there anything around here you want? Take anything you want . . . what's left."

"No, thanks. I don't need anything."

He looks at his watch. "Hey, I gotta go make the rounds. You, uh, you want to take a walk with me?"

"To the cellhouse?"

"Sure. No one's there. Takes about fifteen minutes for a walk-through these days. You've never been inside, huh?"

He gets to his feet with a slight groan like our door, his hip hurts him, I think. Why does he seem so much older, so old? He is not an old man; he is fifty. He puts on his uniform jacket. The brass buttons glint at me, shiny as ever. If I look close enough, I'd see a lot of little me's looking back.

"Geez, look at you," he says, buttoning up. "My big girl."

Suddenly I want out of that house—I want to close the front door behind me and lock it with bolts and chains, and a big, heavy medieval padlock, too thick for the fog to rust through.

"Come on, Dad, let's go, let's get out of here."

We step out the front door and he turns away from me a moment, fumbling with keys, not meeting my eyes, and says, "Hey, you hear anything from your mother?" Too casually, as if it has just occurred to him.

I watch him lock the front door—a man on a deserted island, guarding against imagined threats—and I wonder why he never locked it before, when it mattered, to protect us.

The little dangers slip in. Maybe he only saw the big ones, the ones that weren't there and never came, and didn't mind about the little ones just walking in our front door.

"No," I say, moving past him to the parade ground. "Not a thing."

There is a sculpted eagle over the entrance to the cellhouse, its wings spread in frozen flight. My father shows me the Armory, the Warden's office, and then we enter the cellhouse.

It is a concrete honeycomb. The floor shines like a thick slab of ice, like my old apartment, but it is cement, not wood. I peer down into it, expecting to see fish, or a lost bicycle, or a small child frozen somewhere in a bottomless lake below. The cellblocks rise up on either side of an aisle, three tiers high, just like cake tiers, and I think of wedding cakes, and then weddings, as my father and I head down the aisle.

"Now, this is called Broadway, sort of the main street, and up there at the end, that's Times Square, right by that door, see? Past that's the dining hall, used to be a snitchbox there for cons to go through." Our steps echo on Broadway. "That's A Block on the right, we never really used that, maybe for storage, and D Block's on the other side of that wall. Then this is B and C here, facing each other. Sort of a trade-off, being celled on Broadway. Warmer than the other rows, but less privacy, you know, always facing someone else. We had room for about six hundred cons here, but you know, we only ever had about half that. Morris's cell's over there, see the grill? You hear about that, last year?" I nod. A skylight overhead lets in weak sunbeams, showing particles of dust floating down on us like confetti. "See those big windows? Some of 'em still broken from forty-six. The big Battle, you were just a baby then. Lets in a lot of light, but a lot of cold air. Or cons would throw stuff at the window sometimes, sort of acting up, and break the glass. No hurry to fix them. Wasn't meant to be a stay at the Mark, right?"

The power has been shut down and the cell doors, automated by a key punch at the end of each block, are left open. Each cell is five feet wide by nine feet long, with a metal cot, a small steel wash basin and a lidless toilet, two flip-up shelves at staggered heights, and a naked light bulb hanging dead center. It is like a small closet to store a life away for winter. I touch the round steel bars; they are cold.

"Sometimes it got so cold in here, almost like doing Tower duty. Your mother . . ." A brief pause, a brief laugh. "Yeah, your mother always used to remind me to put on a woolen undershirt when I pulled a night shift in here. Now, the bars, we went around tapping them with a mallet, see?" Tap, tap, tap, with his key chain. "Sounds different if they've been tampered with. Cons'd try cutting through, then rub soap or maybe ashes, or dirt over the cut."

"Why do you still do a walk-through?"

He shrugs sheepishly, like I've asked a too-personal question. "Just . . . I like doing it. Habit. Don't really need to, anymore."

"What happens when you leave?"

"Oh, they have a full-time caretaker. Mr. Ludwig, remember him? He and his wife are staying on, I think. Kennedy doesn't want a prison, fine, but he oughta figure out something else to do with it, or give it to someone who will. What a waste."

We round the end of C Block at Times Square, and enter the dining hall.

"Now, we call this the Gas Chamber, see those canisters up there? A guard could trigger them during a riot and tear gas'd come spraying out. 'Course, we'd get gassed, too, but . . . Never had to use them, though, 'cause the threat was enough, the threat's all it took. Johnston's idea. Back in there is the kitchen, that's not very interesting. I'll show you the hospital."

We climb a small staircase at the entrance to the dining hall. "Cons would line up here every morning on sick call, if they wanted to go to the hospital. Usually just looking for attention, you know . . ." There are examining rooms with tables and overhead lights, an X-ray, a pharmacy, a small room with a dentist's chair and equipment, another with several strange-looking bathtubs with extra pipes and spigots. At the end of the general ward is a section with heavily barred windows.

"Here's for the psychos, we call this the Bug Cage." He points out two spaces that look like bathrooms, or showers, really, with floor-to-ceiling tile. "We'd lock 'em in these till they calmed down. A couple of cons really flipped out, they got sent over to Springfield. But most of 'em weren't really psycho, just faking it. Thought slashing a tendon would get 'em out. Madigan's last couple of months, we had fourteen heel cutters in about two weeks. A few days in here, a couple of stitches, and they get back to normal pretty quick, I tell you."

"Uh-huh."

" 'Course, there were always the nutcases who really tried to knock themselves off. They'd cut a wrist, or get a hold of some pills. We'd find 'em half dead, and . . . well, you know . . ." His voice winds down like a clock. "C'mon, I'll show you D Block."

We leave, but then he stops, suddenly, on the stairs. "Hey, you know what . . ." He looks at me with an unsure smile, figuring. "It's your birthday today, huh? Right?"

"Yeah."

"Eighteen." He is proud of knowing this. "Well, happy birthday, honey. All grown up."

I nod.

"Wish I had something to give you . . . hey, how's this, we'll go through your mother's stuff, maybe find—"

"No, that's OK, Daddy." I wonder if her wedding ring is still on the kitchen windowsill, shining pink and hard in the sun. "I really don't want anything."

"Oh . . . OK . . . well, come on then, Olivia, I'll show you the Recreation Yard."

"No, that's all right, I've seen that."

"You have?" He looks at me, puzzled.

"Well, no, I mean . . . it's sort of cold out, you know?"

"Yeah . . . well, come on, I'll show you Isolation." We go downstairs.

D Block, on the other side of a wall and heavy door, has larger but otherwise similar cells, and an evocative view of the Golden Gate from the upper tiers.

"Now, this block's Solitary Confinement, for cons that're special trouble. Not allowed out for meals, movies, anything." We walk to the south end of the block. "Here's real isolation. The Hole. Treatment Unit."

These six dark cells are different; they are empty of toilet or cot or shelving. Outside of each barred door is a heavy, solid one that opens and shuts manually, cutting off light, sound, the flow of air. My father demonstrates.

"Yeah, these're for when a con really acted up. We'd lock 'em in for anywhere from a couple of days to a few weeks, depending. They'd pretty much stay in line for a while after that. I never liked it. Wouldn't want to put a dog in there. Sometimes you'd leave the solid door open a crack, for a little light. Still, good to have, for the troublemakers."

I look in the closest cell; a box of chilled space with a drainage hole in the floor.

"Can I go inside one?"

"Yeah, sure . . . if you want to." He chuckles. "Never had anyone *ask* me to go in there." He opens the solid door a little wider.

I step inside the cell, and he closes the barred door. A bleak light comes through the ten-foot windows of the cell-house wall, facing out to sea.

"Dad, close the other door. The solid one."

"You sure, honey?"

"Yeah, go ahead. I want to see what it's like."

"It'll be pretty dark."

"That's OK. Go ahead."

"I don't know . . ."

"The door's not going to lock, is it?"

"No . . ."

"Go ahead. It's OK. I want to see what it's like."

My father slowly closes the massive door; it clangs shut with a solid metallic crash. I take a deep breath.

The black air seems to weigh more than lighted air; it sinks into my skin, but I can't absorb anything past that, into my brain. I hum a little, to feel sound, then stop. I can't see my own body; I wave a hand in front of my face and feel it flutter like a bat. I stretch out a hand till my fingers brush concrete wall, but I can't reach the ceiling. Instead, I drop to the ground, before I fall. I suddenly realize I could be sitting *on* the ceiling, or I could be sitting *on* a wall; who is to say the ordinary laws of physics apply in here? Maybe nothing applies. I could spin around endlessly, or float, and there would be no one to see it, or set me right, nothing to orient myself by or find a balance against. I could dissolve in here, spread my molecules out like fog and there is nothing to prevent it, or hold me together. This is isolation, then, and it is familiar, strangely warm and comforting. A cocoon. No one, no thing can find me, see me, hear me. Touch me. I knew it would be like this, this extreme of how it's always been, if I could only, ever, get deep enough away, find this isolation, womblike, fluid around me, surrounding me like sea around an island. I am lulled here, a floating fetus, I'm ready to go, drown in it. They say drowning's a peaceful way to die, once you give up and stop fighting. Breathe in the water. People are always drowning in something. Just give up and stop fighting, be blotted up, breathe in this black air like the black Bay water at night, into my lungs.

And I start to scream, then, making waves in the fluid, as if sound waves bouncing off the concrete walls would hold me up, support me. I scream louder and louder, finally hysterical, hoping my throat will bleed and warm me, and rinse something out. I scream to force myself against something and leave a mark, to wedge myself into time, to force my being heard like a slash in the silence, to drag me back onshore. I am still screaming after my father has flung open the door and slapped me, wrapped his coat around me, and dragged me out into the thin afternoon light. And I keep screaming until I've screamed out all of it, all the empty soundless black air I'd breathed in and held trapped, until it is gone and I am clinging to the dock, breathing light air, clinging to my father because he is here and no one else is, and I must cling to someone, to anyone, anything I can find. I must hold onto something, because I cannot live like this anymore, alone.

*Dear Olivia,*

*There is no excuse for what I'm doing, and I know that you're big enough to know that. Maybe that means, though, that you're big enough to understand it, to see it clearly. By the time you were a little girl I'd already driven myself somewhere I couldn't get back from, and I was too lost to get back to take good care of you. So I want to believe that in some way this is best for you, too, but you're also big enough to know how desperate, how wrong, that is.*

*I can't stay with you now, because there isn't anything left to stay, there aren't any pieces left. All the inside pieces have slipped away from me, one by one, and now the outside pieces are being cut off, my hands, my ears, my eyes, so I can't touch anything anymore, or hear or see anything. I can't even see you.*

*There's something maybe buried deep inside that is* <u>*you*</u>*, Olivia, that has nothing to do with anyone or anything else, that you have to hold on to. Sometimes it's so tempting to give it away, to let someone else keep it for you, or even let someone else tell you what it is, because it seems safer. But if you do,* <u>*that's*</u> *when you're* *really alone, because you can't get it back, and then you will never be yours. I lost that, the most important piece, and that's what I have to look for now.*

*Please let Grandma and Grandpa take care of you a little. They know how almost everything works, and when they don't, they'll tell you. And they love you so much. Just because you're almost grown-up doesn't mean you always have to act that way. You don't have to act any way, or always be a good girl.*

*I will come back and find you, and until then I will miss you every moment of every day. You've been the brightest thing in my life, my sweet pearl, but it's like being blind now, seeing only darkness. I love you and I know you'll hate me, but I can't see the love or the hate anymore. When I find my way I will come back, even if you still hate me. Because even the hate will be a lovely thing to see.*

*I love you.*

*Your mother*

## *Acknowledgments*

Thank you to the staffs of the San Francisco Public Libraries, the National Maritime Library, and the Bancroft Library, UC Berkeley; Donna Middlemist and the guides of the National Park Service, Golden Gate National Recreation Area, Alcatraz; and Dana Hursey.

In addition to excerpts quoted and attributed in the text, many thanks to these authors for sharing their knowledge and experiences in the following works: Wallace Stegner, essay, and Susan Lamb, foreword, *Alcatraz: the Rock*; Robert Burger, text, *Robert Cameron's Alcatraz*; Frank Heaney and Gay Machado, *Inside the Walls of Alcatraz*; James P. Delgado, *Alcatraz, Island of Change*, John A. Martini, *Fortress Alcatraz*; Donald J. Hurley, *Alcatraz Island Memories* and *Alcatraz Island Maximum Security*; Jolene Babyak, *Eyewitness on Alcatraz*; F. J. Clauss, *Alcatraz, Island of Many Mistakes*; Pierre Odier, *The Rock; A History of Alcatraz, The Fort/The Prison*; Bruce J. Campbell, *Escape from Alcatraz*; Leon "Whitey" Thompson, *Rock Hard*; Howard Clark, *Six Against the Rock*; Don deNevi and Phillip Bergen, *Alcatraz '46, The Anatomy of a Classic Prison Tragedy*; Thomas E. Gaddis, *Birdman of Alcatraz; The Story of Robert Stroud*; James Quillen, *Alcatraz from Inside: The Hard Years*, and E.N. Thompson, *The Rock; A History of Alcatraz Island 1847–1972*.

One last acknowledgment . . . to a gentleman I met during the course of my research, who himself grew up on Alcatraz as a correctional officer's son. I told him about the book I was working on; he graciously shared several memories before suggesting we collaborate, and write the story of his own boyhood on the island. I thanked him for his interest and offer, but reiterated that my novel was, specifically, about a little girl. To my surprise he grew hostile, and said:

> But you can't do that! There's no story there—only the *boys* had any fun on the island. The girls couldn't do anything. The girls *have* no stories!

And so I owe him thanks—for the inspiring reminder why the girls' stories still need so desperately to be told.

ISO
Ison, Tara.
A child out of
Alcatraz
WITHDRAWN
'97